RED
TIDE

*For Scarlett,
Daughter. Sister. Warrior.*

x

Red Tide is a Fox & Ink Books book

First published in Great Britain in 2026 by
Fox & Ink Books
Part of the University of Lancashire
Preston, PR1 2HE, UK

Text copyright © Curtis Jobling, 2026
Cover illustration copyright © Gavin Reece, 2026

978-1-917894-05-0

1 3 5 7 9 10 8 6 4 2

Curtis Jobling and Gavin Reece to be identified
as the author and illustrator of this work has been asserted
in accordance with the Copyright, Designs and Patents Act, 1988.

All rights reserved. No part of this publication may be reproduced, stored in
a retrieval system, or transmitted in any form or by any means, electronic, mechanical,
photocopying, recording or otherwise; or be used to train any AI technologies without
the prior permission of the publishers. Fox & Ink Books expressly reserves this
work from the text and data mining exception subject to EU law.

Set in 10/16pt Kingfisher by Amy Cooper.

A CIP catalogue record for this book is available from the British Library.
Printed and bound in Great Britain by Clays Ltd, Elcograf S.p.A.

THE VAMPIRE EMPIRE

RED TIDE

Fox & Ink Books

CHAPTER ONE
HILDE

The horse tossed its head, eyes rolling as the breeze whipped its mane. Hilde had to wonder whether it was aware of its imminent fate. A dozen Norse men and women were gathered on the clifftop, including Hilde's mother, Jarl Frida. The fur of the chieftain's wolfskin cloak rippled as the wind raced across it, the raised hood shrouding her face in shadow. She might have been carved from granite, so motionless was she beside her daughter. Mikko the Silent, Jarl Frida's huscarl, stood to one side of the stallion, reins clenched tight in the bodyguard's fist, while the mysterious *gothi* waited on the horse's other flank. The peculiar holy man held his sacrificial sword in one hand, a wooden bowl in the other, his chalk-daubed face grim and emotionless. Gripping the cliff edge behind them loomed the God Tree, a rowan over twenty feet tall, defying gravity and the elements. The collective gaze of the Norsemen was fixed upon the eastern horizon, the first sliver of dawn's autumn light threatening to rise from the sea.

Hilde's eyes returned to the ceremonial blade in the gothi's bone-white hand, flitting from the weapon to the horse's throat. Torch flames were reflected across the surface of the polished metal, their dance mesmeric to Hilde. She knew what was coming, was prepared for the horse's final moment. There was no greater *blót* offering to the gods than the life of such a powerful beast. Well, not these days, anyway. It wasn't so long ago that men and women would give their lives – often willingly – for the blessing of their village. That tradition had all but died out, certainly on Unst, as the Norsemen and the islanders found a way to live in harmony (or something approaching it). Not all those who called the Hjaltland Isles home enjoyed such kinship. Like the Orkneyar archipelago to the south, the Hjaltlands formed part of the Kingdom of Norðvegr, right on the edge of King Harald Fairhair's realm. The Hjaltlands, once home to the dwindling race of Picts, had been colonised; these islands belonged to the Vikings now. On Unst, however, Jarl Frida had proved a more benign chieftain, allowing her remaining Pictish subjects to worship the deity of their own choosing, and there was none so popular as the Christian god.

With that thought in mind, Hilde glanced back to the village far below. Torches lined the shore and jetties, burning away the chill touch of sea mist that had encircled the island. Unst, of all the Hjaltland Isles, was embracing its shared festivities as Norsemen and Christians jointly prepared for the equinox. Visitors had arrived in the last few days, traders come to market, neighbouring islanders seeking a moment of Jarl Frida's time. Those Norse men and women who had once been Vikings had turned their backs on their warring past, swapping sword and shield for fishing net and plough. And so, the island of Unst enjoyed a relative peace.

Hilde felt a pair of small, taloned feet grip her shoulder, firm but gentle.

"Eyes front," croaked Siv into her ear, the old raven urging her charge to pay attention.

Hilde turned in time to witness the sun break the waves and the gothi's silver seax pass across the horse's throat. Mikko's muscles bunched as he held the struggling stallion, blood erupting from the fatal wound, to be gathered in the bowl by the holy man. Hilde watched on as the horse's struggles slowed, its legs buckling as Mikko eased the beast to the stony ground of the clifftop. Then the gothi proceeded around the small group of Norsemen, bowl in the crook of his arm. He dipped a spindly twig into the bloody soup, flicking the steaming contents into the faces of the participants, prayers accompanying each blessing.

In truth, Hilde barely listened to the gothi. Her attention kept wandering to the village below, where other young'uns had gathered on the beach. A monk from the mainland had arrived on Unst the previous day and was delivering dawn blessings of his own to the locals. She could see him now, his robes hitched up to his knees as he stood in the sluicing tide, anointing child and adult alike with sea water. He couldn't have been much older than Hilde, but that hadn't stopped him from becoming an elder in the eyes of his Christian god. *Baptism*, the Picts were calling it, and to Hilde it was fascinating. And decidedly less bloody.

Another squeeze upon her shoulder from Siv, and Hilde's head swivelled back to the front. Warm blood spattered her face as the gothi administered his blessing upon her with a flick of the wrist. The holy man looked her up and down, gaze lingering on her tummy, the chalk mask cracking along his brow. Feeling suddenly vulnerable, Hilde drew her cloak about herself, obscuring her torso from the gothi. She looked to her mother, only to find Jarl Frida staring back with a vacant expression. Blood streaked down the chieftain's spattered face, gathering around her mouth. Her lips parted, tongue flicking out to taste the coppery ichor.

Hilde shivered.

Jarl Frida strode up to the God Tree. With the wolfskin hood still shielding her face from the elements, she dipped her forehead and rested it against the rough surface. The fingertips of her right hand traced over the various likenesses of the gods that were carved into the rowan's surface. Her palm eventually settled upon the chest of Odin, the All-father's mouth fixed in a perpetual roar from within his gnarled beard of bark. This was the most holy of sites to the Norsemen on Unst, where they could be closest to the gods.

Hilde saw her mother's lips move, her voice a whisper.

"Forgive me."

A stiff wind raced over the clifftop and through the rowan's groaning branches, the God Tree appearing to respond to Jarl Frida's prayer.

"She is no longer a child," said the gothi ruefully.

It wasn't a question: more like a statement, and a weird one at that. *Not a child?* Hilde had seen fifteen winters. She hadn't felt like a child in a long time.

"She became a woman twelve moons ago," replied Siv, the black bird answering on Jarl Frida's behalf as if Hilde weren't even there.

What on earth are they talking about? wondered Hilde. Once more, she felt the reassuring touch of the raven's feet, as the bird beat her wings in the breeze.

"I wonder how much of her mother is in her," said the gothi.

Only now did Jarl Frida briefly look Hilde's way, daughter catching mother's fleeting glance within her wolfskin cowl.

"That's yet to be seen," boomed Mikko, loud as ever, as he beckoned other participants in the *blót* ceremony to join him. "Have the horse brought down to the village. Erskine will butcher it. The entire village should enjoy the meat at tonight's feast." A considered pause. "Even the Christians."

"*Especially* the Christians," added the gothi, glowering disapprovingly at the beach below and the monk in the water. "Every year, more of our people turn to this foreign god."

"It's not so simple as that," said Mikko. "Our people are Pictish, as well as Norse. And the handful of souls you see gathered on this cliff are all that remains of those who accompanied Jarl Frida and me to Unst. We are outnumbered."

The gothi sucked his teeth and shook his head. "Whatever happened to that fierce shieldmaiden?"

Mikko the Silent looked at Hilde and gave her a friendly wink. Of all the Norsemen who had helped her mother settle on the island, he was Hilde's favourite. A hammer blow to his helm as a young man had apparently left his hearing in ruins and earnt him the ironic nickname, but there were none so loyal to Jarl Frida as Mikko.

"She had a child," said the old warrior, his voice that rare thing: quiet.

The gothi watched the chieftain as she remained transfixed by the rowan tree.

"A shame, huscarl," said the wise man. "Such sagas they

might have written about her."

As his companions began binding the legs of the slaughtered horse to carry poles, Mikko turned on the gothi, so quickly Hilde flinched. A coldness clouded the old warrior's eyes, come out of nowhere, darkening his already hard expression. There was an implied threat of violence there, and it caused a shiver – *of excitement?* – to race down Hilde's spine. He was aged and frail, but a strength remained.

"You want to meet the shieldmaiden?" shouted Mikko, his seemingly oblivious chieftain still as one with the God Tree. "Perhaps we can rouse her from her slumber, eh?"

The gothi shook his head, respect making his voice crack. "No, my friend. Best to let sleeping dogs lie."

As quick as that, the threat had passed, and the calm Mikko returned.

Siv let out a guttural cry, her midnight feathers batting the side of Hilde's face. "Let us away."

Girl and raven set off down the steep cliff path back to the village, leaving Jarl Frida behind. Though treacherous, it was the quickest route back to the settlement, switching this way and that as it hugged the jagged granite of the cliffs. Some thirty paces down the trail they passed by the wattle and daub hut that was the gothi's home, its makeshift door a deerskin curtain that clapped in the stiff breeze. Spattered with gull guano and lichen, the shelter was wedged into the rockface, a wholly unwelcoming abode. As they rounded another bend in the path, Hilde glanced back. The God Tree and the gothi came back into view, and she caught the wise man watching them depart.

"Did you ever see her fight, Siv? My mother?"

"No, child," said the old bird, a note of sadness in her voice. "But I'm told she was fierce. A force of nature, they say."

"He might be a wise man, but the gothi would be a fool to get on the wrong side of my mother."

"Let's not be badmouthing the gothi, child," said Siv, tapping Hilde's head with her shiny, black beak. "Lest he put a curse upon you."

Hilde grunted. "He's welcome to curse me. My life couldn't be much worse. I'm already stuck on this rock when there's a world out there waiting to be explored."

"Your mother explored plenty yet turned her back on that life to settle here. That should tell you something."

That didn't cut it for Hilde.

"You heard what Mikko the Silent said: *she had a child*. That 'force of nature' would probably still be out there sailing the seas and forging a saga and a great name if I hadn't come along."

Siv flapped her midnight-black wings, batting her young charge's head in the process.

"Your mother's deeds as a shieldmaiden are legendary, never forget that. That blood runs through your veins too, that lineage reaching back to the golden age of gods and monsters. Jarl Frida is touched by the Old Ways, Hilde, and so are you. Her name was known, and feared, from here to Uppsala."

Hilde's imagination was instantly fired: *gods and monsters*. It had a ring to it, undoubtedly, and Siv was well-versed in all those old tales. A gifted storyteller like many of her kin, there was little the raven didn't know about the sagas. The notion of a bird that could speak left the Picts on Unst both fearful and suspicious; here was a living, breathing, crowing remnant of that time of gods and monsters, as alien to the islanders as the gods of Asgard themselves. And Siv was painfully aware of those prejudices, keeping her chatter reserved for Norse ears as much as possible. Many was the time she would nestle beside her young charge before the fireside, filling Hilde's head with wonder.

As they reached the village edge, the raven regarded the cliff top where Jarl Frida was now in conversation with the gothi.

"That woman did more in her youth than many achieve in their entire lifetimes. And then she'd had enough. Your mother chose to leave that life – and that name – behind. Just you remember that."

"All because of me," grumbled Hilde, which earnt her a nipped ear.

"There was a little more to it than that, child."

Hilde frowned. "Did you know my father?"

The bird cackled. "No, that was before my time. You were already born by the time I was blown onto Unst by an ill wind. All I know is he used to sail with her, back when she was still a Viking. Quit dawdling, now."

Hilde made her way down the mud-churned path towards the heart of the village, passing stalls set up ahead of the day's market. She craned her neck, spying several unfamiliar boats moored to the jetties. More strangers were destined to materialise from the churning veil of sea mist throughout the day. Directly ahead, the jarl's longhouse dominated the surrounding buildings, twice the height and length of any of its neighbours. Unlike the other homes in Unst, which were stone structures with turf rooftops, the *jarlshof* was wattle and daub with a thick thatched roof. A ribbon of dark smoke curled from the tall central chimney, as preparations for the evening feast were already well underway.

The chatter of cheery voices grew as the freshly baptised emerged along the shoreline, cutting across the path of Hilde and Siv. Many were children, soaked to the skin but grinning and embracing one another, the freezing tide having failed to dampen their spirits. Aidan Erskine, the butcher's boy, was already staring open-mouthed at Hilde as she approached, no doubt contemplating some witless insult. Cormac Tulloch was amongst them, shaking the sea from his shaggy matted hair as his bare feet squelched through the sucking mud. Spying her through the throng, her friend gave her an enthusiastic wave.

"You here for a baptism, Hilde?" he asked, his teeth chattering through his grin as he held a small wooden cross in his hand. "C-c-come on in, the water's lovely!"

"You stick to your god, Cormac, and I'll stick to mine," she replied, as Siv took flight from her shoulder.

"It's not as c-cold as it looks, I promise," said Cormac.

"I suppose this Christian god can't be all bad," said Hilde with a sly look. "He got you to take a bath, and that's nothing short of a miracle."

Cormac gestured at Hilde's face with an awkward nod. "You've got something on you."

"Huh?"

She raised a hand and wiped her face, the palm coming

away bloody. With the sleeve of her woollen smock, she gave it an embarrassed scrub. Then the monk was stood before her.

His brown habit was wet and heavy with seawater from the waist down while his face was flushed red. So young for a holy man. Hilde always expected them to be old and gnarly like the gothi, as if a stiff fart might break their backs. Annoyingly, the monk shared a similar joyous smile to those he had anointed moments earlier.

"So, you're Hilde?" He placed a pale hand on his chest. "I'm Brother Benedict."

His accent was peculiar to Hilde. He was no Pict, that was for sure. A Saxon, perhaps? She eyed him suspiciously, choosing not to reply.

"Cormac has told me all about you," said the monk cheerily, fishing about in a deep pocket of his habit. His hand emerged clutching something, which he instantly handed over to Hilde.

"For you, jarl's daughter," said Benedict, placing the small, crudely carved crucifix into her open palm. "A gift from our Lord, the One True God, to you."

Hilde was unsure of how to respond. The gathered villagers looked at her with surprise, delight, and no small amount of hope. All except for Aidan. The gift drew a sneer of disapproval from the butcher's boy. But Cormac's expression was more gormless than ever. He gave her a nod.

Take it.

CHAPTER TWO
FRIDA

"Has she begun to change?"

Jarl Frida didn't answer the gothi's question immediately. Staring down upon the beach from on high, she observed her daughter interacting with the monk. Jarl Frida and the holy man were alone now, Mikko and the other Norsemen having already departed with the slaughtered horse, taking a circuitous route back to the village, the dead animal carried between them on their litter of poles.

"She has a rage," said the shieldmaiden, "much like I had when I was her age. But whether that becomes *something else* is yet to be seen. With Odin's blessing, perhaps it will pass her by."

The gothi glanced at the God Tree where it clung to the clifftop, the stiff sea breeze bending its branches.

"You believe you enjoy the All-father's favour?"

"I pray so. The good I have done in the world surely outweighs the bad, doesn't it?"

No reply to that question, as the gothi clumsily swerved it.

"Perhaps the child yet figures in Odin's plans," said the gothi ruefully. "You'd be wise to not look upon it as a curse. It could be the making of her."

"Or the ruin," said Jarl Frida bitterly. "I came to Unst to escape my old life, wanted Hilde to be born far away from that world."

"Everyone's running from one thing or another," said the gothi, pushing past her and descending the crooked path.

Jarl Frida followed, drawing her cloak tight about her. The wind was chill, biting her bones. The aches were constant, dogging her day and night. *When was the last time my muscles didn't cry out in pain?* The legendary warrior seemed a distant memory, another's tale, not Jarl Frida's. She felt old beyond her years, like she'd lived a life three times over. *How am I a woman of only thirty-some winters?* Her past continued to take from her in spades, eating away at who she was, punishing her for dark deeds long done. Worse still, Jarl Frida knew her torment was far from over.

She reached a hand up to her face, dragging a thumb across the now congealing blood that covered her jaw. It came away with a glob of dark goo upon it. Jarl Frida's belly rumbled in response, the sight and taste of the blood pricking something grim within her, half-forgot memories stirring. The shieldmaiden had been covered in so much of the damned stuff back then – if not that of her enemies, then her own. Jarl Frida placed her thumb in her mouth, sucking the blood clean from the skin. It tasted good. A convulsion, within her guts and chest, her insides reacting to the sensation as a buried hunger was suddenly, briefly, sated. Something called back to her, from Jarl Frida's past, a disembodied voice returning from the depths of a cave, the echo changing it. Distorting it.

The holy man arrived at his shack, which had somehow withstood the ravages of the *Nordsær* storms. He unhitched the deerskin door and pushed his way in, Jarl Frida stooping after him. A pall of smoke greeted them, thick with the aroma of intoxicating herbs, belched into the cramped chamber from a stone firepit. An iron pot sat upon the coals, the stew within simmering, bubbles of fat popping. A host of animal skulls leered at Jarl Frida from where they adorned the walls, judging her through hollow eyes. With great reverence, the gothi placed his ceremonial sword onto a small slate plinth, before taking a seat before the fire. Jarl Frida regarded the weapon, the silver seam that ran through its steel acting like a mirror by the flickering light. Her pale face stared back. She was suddenly aware that her hand was rising, fingers shaking, reaching for the decorative golden handle of the seax.

"You want it back?" asked the gothi. "Such a precious blade. Take it, Jarl Frida. I am only its custodian."

As quick as that, the jarl snapped her hand away.

"Do not tempt me, gothi. That seax has tasted enough blood by way of my sword arm. I said when I came here that I no longer had need of it. Nothing has changed. Better it remains in your keeping than mine."

"You and I never knew one another before we arrived on this island, Jarl Frida. We both had our lives, our *secrets*. All we ask as Norsemen is that when the reckoning comes, the scales balance. You're a warrior—"

"*Was* a warrior," she corrected him, pulling her gaze away from the silver seax.

"Valhalla is your reward in death, earnt by your deeds in life."

Her face was a stoic mask. Emotionless.

"Tell me, Jarl Frida, do you believe your fallen brothers and sisters await you in Odin's hall?"

Jarl Frida shuddered, and it wasn't missed by the gothi. He knew her well enough, had no doubt heard stories of her deeds in her youth. Was he playing with her? Teasing her? The gothi nodded ruefully and glanced back at the open door of the hut. The tufts of gorse and heather that peppered the path beyond were buffeted by the wind, rattling like runestones in a soothsayer's palm. Storm clouds gathered on the horizon, churning in the distant heavens.

"An ill wind approaches, Jarl Frida, carrying with it a host of unknowns. If the Gods are good, they will have witnessed the *blót* ceremony and heard our prayers. The storm may pass us by."

"And if it doesn't?"

The gothi sucked his teeth. "If it doesn't, a great harvest comes, the likes of which Unst has never known."

Jarl Frida frowned. "But harvests are good."

He turned away. "Not all of them."

When she spoke, it was a low growl. "Just once, it would be good if you could speak straight, gothi. The people of this island – farmers, fishermen, simple souls – those who look to me as their chieftain and guardian: are they in danger?"

The gothi picked up a bone and struck the rim of the iron pot, sending a feeble wave on its way towards the centre of the steaming stew.

"We sit here on the edge of a wider world, far removed from the All-father's plans. It's hard to imagine how our actions might impact upon those at its heart, upon the realms of the Gods, and the feats of monsters and men."

The gothi reached into a bag on his hip and removed a

wobbling lump of offal, scavenged a short time earlier from the sacrificed horse. He weighed it in his hand for a moment, blood pooling between his fingers.

"Perversely, events that happen at the heart of that world have a far greater and graver effect upon those who cling to its edge. Even those events that occurred in the not-too-distant past . . . like a pebble in a pond, those ripples have a way of reaching all of us."

Jarl Frida watched as the holy man dropped the glistening innards into the soupy pot with a resounding *plop*. Larger ripples rolled out from the centre, sloshing against the edge, the liquid spilling over the iron rim and hissing upon the coals.

"There are consequences to all our actions, Jarl Frida."

The shieldmaiden stepped towards the door, confounded by the gothi's words. It wasn't unusual for the holy man to speak in half-truths. Hell, it was likely the only way he could protect his reputation if his portents failed to materialise. But this one irked her like no other. She felt it too, looking at the gathering storm over the sea, and the mists that hung over the harbour like a death shroud. *What approaches?*

She glanced over her shoulder at the gothi, who sat cross-legged before the fire, staring into the glowing coals.

"Will my daughter be safe?"

"From what's to come?" The gothi arched an eyebrow, the white paint of his face cracking. "I suppose it's down to a mother to protect her child."

Jarl Frida didn't stop to close the door, the gothi's riddles having got under her skin. In truth, he was only voicing what she feared deep down: that her past had caught up with her, that whatever was to come was the result of her own indiscretions.

She stumbled as she traversed the scree path, reaching out a hand to support herself against the rockface. Her bones and muscles ached, as ever. The dizziness was returning, a dull hum at the back of her head, throbbing behind her eyes. For a heartbeat, Jarl Frida imagined she might keel over and tumble from the path onto the rocks. She fixed her gaze upon the beach, took a steadying breath, drew her hood about her face and set off once more. With each step, she told herself the same familiar lies.

Eat. Drink. Rest. Just get back to the longhouse. You'll be well.

She found Hilde on the beach path, surrounded by the locals who'd just been baptised by the visiting monk. As Jarl Frida drew closer, she spied her daughter was holding something, and caught the preacher gesticulating some bewildering Christian blessing.

And there it was: a wooden cross in her daughter's palm.

Before Hilde could thank the monk for the gift, her mother gently plucked it from her grasp and handed back to the holy man, who was little more than a boy himself. Hilde looked up, her cheeks flushing red as if she'd been discovered doing something terrible, which in the eyes of the gothi she no doubt was.

"Thank you for your kind gift, Brother Benedict, but we cannot accept it," said Jarl Frida, her voice warm and pleasant from inside the heavy wolfskin hood.

As the villagers nodded respectfully, the monk joined them, bowing deeply.

"I meant no disrespect, Jarl Frida."

"None was taken," said the jarl. "Please, enjoy our hospitality this night. Know that whenever you visit Unst, you're always welcome at my hearth."

With that, Jarl Frida took Hilde's hand in her own and went on her way to the longhouse. Hilde glanced back, the crowd's celebrations continuing behind them. As they strode on, Jarl Frida spoke low but loud enough that Hilde heard her words, which somehow cut through the hubbub.

"Always remember this, my child: you are a wolf."

"Yes, Mother," Hilde replied, her voice a scratchy whisper.

"And a wolf does not run with the sheep."

CHAPTER THREE
CORMAC

The sound of laughter speeding by the smithy door was enough to lure Cormac away from his chore. In truth, it didn't take much: it felt to him like he and Pa were the only fools working on Unst this day, while every other soul was having fun. Broom in hand and following the noise, Cormac stepped into the lane, keen to see what he was missing out on. Aidan near bowled him off his feet, the butcher's boy snorting as he spun out of the collision.

"Steady there, Cormac Tulloch," said Aidan breathlessly. "If I twist my ankle, how am I ever going to catch them lassies?"

Cormac looked past his friend, saw Eithne and Erin halfway up the street, the giggling twins waiting for Aidan to return to the chase. The sisters waved at Cormac, who returned the greeting sheepishly.

"Your pa got you working hard, then?" said Aidan, clapping his pal on the shoulder. "Take a day off. Come have some fun."

Cormac so badly wanted to say yes, was jealous as all hell that Aidan was enjoying the company of two of the prettiest girls on the island, but work came first. Work *always* came first. Cormac's broom made a playful *thunk* sound as it connected with the top of Aidan's head.

"You keep chasing your tail, soft lad. When the twins are

bored of you, I'll sweep in and charm them."

Aidan brayed like a donkey as he set off again. "The only sweeping you'll be doing is in that smithy, ya wee neep!" Cormac's smile disappeared the moment Aidan's back was turned. With a slump of the shoulders, he stepped back into the heat of the smithy.

Hamish Tulloch was still toiling over the forge, hammer clanging as it struck and shaped the horseshoe. One meaty fist clenched a heavy pair of tongs as Pa turned the metal over the curved head of the forge, the iron glowing volcanic orange before he plunged it into the slack tub. Steam billowed and water hissed before the finished shoe emerged, clattering to the slate floor alongside half a dozen others.

Cormac headed over to the workbench where a pair of tankards stood beside a pitcher of water. He filled one and handed it to his father, who set about sinking it in quick fashion. A leather apron covered his body, though his arms were bare, glistening with sweat from his labour. Hamish held the tankard out once again for a refill, Cormac obliging as his father dragged a forearm over his dripping mouth and beard.

"Who were you jawing with?" asked Hamish.

"Just Aidan," said Cormac, feigning disinterest unconvincingly. "He's mucking about in the market with the other young'uns."

Pa's frown made Cormac instantly feel guilty.

"You're wanting to join them?"

Cormac scratched his head. Of course, he wanted to be with his friends, but equally he knew his father depended upon him. He was the extra pair of hands that Pa needed, the fetch that made his back-breaking work that bit easier. Equally, Cormac needed time away from the smithy, where he could enjoy the company of those his own age. He loved Pa dearly, but Hamish was a dour soul at the best of times. Spoke more to his forge than he did his son.

"I wondered—" Cormac began to say, only for his father to cut him off.

"You spend too much time with that one."

Cormac was taken aback.

"Aidan? Since when?"

Hamish grunted and wiped a leather cloth over his sweaty, soot-stained brow.

"Ain't talking about the Erskine boy. I'm on about *her*. The jarl's daughter."

"But I wasn't—"

"This morning, after your baptism on the beach. Saw you call out to her. Hell, I heard you from the smithy. Not exactly subtle with your mooning, lad."

Cormac felt the colour flush his cheeks, and a sudden churning in his belly.

"I wasn't mooning, Pa. She's a pal."

Hamish stared his son down.

"She is the jarl's daughter, Cormac, and the likes of you shouldn't be in her company."

"Likes o' me?" That irked. It was typical of Pa to put his own kind down.

"Why are you always so quick to draw lines in the sand between us and them?" Cormac went on. "The Norsemen have lived here for years. Unst is their home, Pa. When will you get used to that? And you make it sound like Hilde's my better, but I don't believe that. She's a young'un, just like me. She and I are no different to one another."

"Give your head a shake, lad. She's Viking!"

"They're only Vikings when they raid. Besides, she was born here on Unst, just like me!"

Hamish's eyes went wide, bright white within his dirty face, and for a moment Cormac thought he might explode. Whatever he was about to say, Pa decided against it, biting his lip as his whiskers twitched with annoyance.

"A dog gets born in a stable, that don't make it a horse, Cormac. It's still got teeth, and if you rile it, it'll bite. The Norsemen just ain't like us, and we ain't like them."

Cormac simmered. "I still say they ain't as bad as you make out."

Hamish clenched and unclenched his jaw. "They may be farmers and fishermen now, but they were raiders before that. Don't be lulled by their performance. It's an act. And that's why I want you to keep your distance."

"Sounds like you hate our neighbours," grunted Cormac, setting back to sweeping.

"It's not hate," said Hamish wearily. "It's a wary respect. Their kind have killed our kin once. They could do it again."

"Well, I think you're wrong," Cormac muttered under his breath, only not quiet enough. His father heard him.

"Maybe I've got them all wrong, eh?" said Hamish, slapping his hands against the scorched leather of his apron. "Perhaps we should be more like the Norsemen, son? Is that it?"

When he strode across the room to Cormac's cot, the boy felt a sinking sensation in the pit of his stomach. Hamish dragged the bed aside, calloused fingers finding the loose floorboard which he prised up. Cormac was already regretting his choice of words, as his father retrieved the small hand-axe from the secret cavity. He tossed the crude axe in his hand, head over haft, catching it. A sniff and a nod.

"A good weight. Probably throws well, too. Your first effort?"

Before Cormac could answer, his father had launched it across the room, the axe-head splintering the side of the slack tub. Cormac watched the water gurgle from the fractured timber as the wooden handle of the weapon came loose, clattering to the slate floor. When he turned back to his father, Hamish had already crossed the smithy and was looming over him, scowling.

"We don't forge weapons or armour, lad. We craft pots and tools, fishhooks and horseshoes. Should wicked men ever visit our home again, let the Norsemen face them. They have their axes, swords and seaxes. They have their history of violence. Ours is one of peace, and that's where honest coin is to be made. Put all thoughts of battle from your mind, Cormac. Leave them in the sagas, where they belong."

With that, Hamish took a step back from his son, letting the lad recover some composure. He grabbed a small wooden box from a workbench.

"Here. Nails for Blair, the shipwright. He was expecting them yesterday." Hamish held the box out to Cormac, rattling it. "Be a good lad and take them to him."

Cormac looked at the box long and hard, and then at his father.

"Can't you take them? That old drunk gives me the chills. He ain't right."

Hamish dismissed his son's objections with a wave of the hand, and thrust the box towards him again, the contents rattling.

"Don't start that again. Blair's had a hard life – harder than you could imagine."

"But he scares me, Pa—"

"Quit your whining!"

Hamish's shout was loud enough to make Cormac jump, his father's patience worn thin. The blacksmith closed his eyes, tried to compose himself, but Cormac could see he was struggling.

"What you don't understand, about Blair . . ." Hamish shook his head, changed tack. "He's an elder, and he's harmless. Show some respect."

He was done debating. He slapped the box into Cormac's palm and propelled him towards the door. Cormac looked back before departing and saw Hamish on one knee beside the busted slack tub. The blacksmith tugged the axe-head loose from the splintered wood and brought it up to his face for closer inspection, turning it this way and that. Cormac was surprised to see his father nodding. *Was he appreciating the craftsmanship?*

When Hamish turned back towards the door, he seemed surprised to see Cormac still standing there. He gave the boy a hard but fair stare, the implication clear: *you still here?*

Cormac stepped out into the lane, into the chill air of midday, box of nails in hand. Thanks to the morning sun, the mist had all but burnt away on the island, but the fog still hung over the water in the bay, an impenetrable soup. Straight ahead of Cormac was the village heart, laughter and shouts of good cheer sounded, peeling out from the growing market. Yet more folk were arriving, the jetties and pier bustling with rowboats and sailboats, livestock and merchants. These travellers would bring stories to Unst, news of the world beyond.

Cormac turned on his heel and looked in the opposite direction, away from the source of all that was interesting. Way out on the edge of the village, as far removed as one could be, perched the shipwright's boathouse, set into the shadows of the cliff.

With a resigned sigh, Cormac set off, each step wearier and more joyless than the last.

CHAPTER FOUR
HILDE

"Can we use swords yet?"

Hilde's shield met Mikko the Silent's quarterstaff with a resounding clatter, the girl putting her shoulder behind the block and pushing the old warrior's weapon aside. Mikko swept the staff back, fast low and at the girl's ankles, only for Hilde to drop into a crouch and push the strike away. The huscarl wasted no time, letting the staff ride off the practice shield's cloth-swaddled rim before descending upon his apprentice in a double-handed blow. Again, Hilde's shield was up, the impact jangling her bones as the old man seemed to hold nothing back.

"You won't always have a sword to hand," shouted Mikko, as he struck out with his boot. Leather connected with wood as he kicked the shield, sending the crouched Hilde tumbling back into a roll. She came up, still crouched, panting as she peered over the shield's rim.

Mikko grinned. "Besides, you don't always need a sword to win a fight."

"If I don't have a weapon, how the hell do I hurt you?"

Hilde stretched and cracked her neck, the old man prowling across the paddock towards her, quarterstaff poised for attack. A nearby pony whinnied its appreciation of the spectacle, while maintaining a healthy distance from the sparring humans.

"You're forgetting the fact your *shield* is a weapon," said Mikko loudly, edging ever closer. "Your enemy gets in close, you can bash 'em with it. If you're low, hit their jaw or throat with the rim. Crack 'em in the sweetmeats. If they're in the dirt, bring it down on 'em like a hammer. There's plenty o' ways you can hurt someone with what you have in your hands, child."

Inspired by Mikko's words, Hilde lunged up and forward from her crouch. The old huscarl was already bringing his staff around towards her now-exposed legs. Only Hilde's attack wasn't aimed at Mikko's torso. She brought the practice shield down hard, like a cleaver onto a chopping block, striking it across the warrior's closest booted foot. The shield might have been wrapped in padded cloths, but it still hit with some force. A howl of surprise and pain erupted from Mikko.

He hopped back, casting his quarterstaff aside as he landed on his rump, but there was no hiding the smile on his face.

"That's what I'm talking about," he roared. "We'll make a shieldmaiden of you yet."

Hilde shrugged. "What's the point of being a shieldmaiden when I'm stuck on this rock?"

Mikko the Silent got back to his feet gingerly, shaking life back into his bruised foot. He tapped his nose conspiratorially.

"Better to know how to defend yourself and not need it, than the other way around, child."

Hilde inspected her shield. It might have been swaddled, but it was full size, Jarl Frida having insisted her daughter familiarise herself with the real thing.

"Did you ever fight in the shield wall alongside my mother?"

"Can't say I ever did," said Mikko. "I sailed with a warband out of Hedeby. Thirty strong, we were. Mostly raided and skirmished with our neighbours."

"In that case, did you ever fight *against* her?"

Mikko's laughter was infectious. "I'm standing here, living and breathing – that should answer your question! Jarl Frida arrived on Unst on the same ship as me, looking to make a new life for herself and the bairn in her belly. We knew she had a past, though she never spoke of it. Seemed keen to leave it behind. We all came here to farm, not fight."

It wasn't the first time Hilde had scavenged whispers of her mother's past. She'd asked all the Norsemen on Unst what they knew of her exploits, but the stories were always hazy at best. Hearsay and rumour. And it wasn't like she could ask her mother. Jarl Frida remained a difficult woman for anyone to get close to, and that included her daughter. It was hard for Hilde to imagine her mother's glorious past. If she had indeed been a great warrior, Jarl Frida was a pale shadow of that now, sleeping most days and roaming her hall at night, haunted by the ghosts of deeds long gone.

"I'm fetching a drink," said Mikko, making for the back of the jarlshof. "You want one?"

"Pint of mead, please," said Hilde hopefully.

"Pint of water, coming right up," said her teacher as he entered the building.

Hilde walked up to the paddock fence, hopping onto the lowest rail and leaning out into the lane. She could see the market beyond the longhouse, and past that the harbour. Siv wheeled in the sky over the water, bickering with the local gulls, whilst small boats bumped against one another below. *So many unfamiliar faces, here for the autumn market,* thought Hilde. Siv had mentioned that a sealskin trader from the Føroyar Isles had landed that morning, with the finest cloaks and gloves the bird had ever seen. That news had left Hilde looking forward to the evening feast, when all the visitors sought audience with Jarl Frida, bestowing gifts upon her. In turn, it wasn't unusual for these presents to be passed on to Hilde.

She jumped down from the fence with renewed vigour. *There are some perks to being the chieftain's daughter after all,* reasoned Hilde, *although training in a pony paddock isn't one of them.* She kicked a dried-up husk of horse dung away, sending it spinning across the field. Such was life on Unst. In the Norse homelands, there was huge importance placed upon the training of young men and women in the ways of the warrior. Not so much on the island, and in a tiny settlement. One had to compromise. If that meant sharing your training paddock with a knackered old hill pony, then so be it.

"Look at that shaggy-arsed beast in the paddock!"

Hilde turned in the direction of the voice. It was Aidan, with a handful of young'uns around him, the whole gang of them leaning on the fence on the far side of the paddock.

"And there's a pony too," he added, which prompted braying laughter from his companions.

Hilde turned her back, concentrating on the rear door of the longhouse, expecting Mikko the Silent to return at any moment.

"Looks like I've upset her. Maybe she'll do the coward's

trick and go running to her mammy!"

She and the butcher's boy had enjoyed their fair share of encounters in recent times, much of it stemming from their mutual dislike of one another. Hilde had made a promise to her mother to stay out of trouble, but it was proving damned tricky. Aidan clearly resented the fact that Hilde was better than him in every conceivable way, while Hilde ... well, Aidan was just a bully. Figured just because he was bigger than everyone else his age that gave him the right to punch down. That kind of arrogance curdled Hilde's blood, and she never knew when to bite her lip. She wasn't sure why Cormac still hung around with the fool.

"Nothing to say, Hilde?" shouted Aidan, growing ever cockier. "Not so mouthy without your Norse friends at your back, eh?"

Hilde picked her practice shield up and picked the dirt and straw off the cloth wrappings with her free hand. Better to prepare for Mikko's return and push the boy's taunts from her mind. Or at least pretend to, anyway.

"Aww, look," brayed Aidan. "They've even given the princess a toy shield so she can play at being a warrior."

Hilde exhaled slowly, let the shield drop to the floor and looked back over her shoulder at the smiling Aidan and his friends. Her ice-chip blue eyes narrowed. He was a head taller than her, and brawny with it. All neck and thick shoulders.

"A shield doesn't make me a warrior, and I sure as hell don't need one to beat that stupid grin off your face. You and me, butcher's boy. Right here, right now."

"Big words for a jarl's spoilt daughter," said Aidan. "I'm not daft."

"You *look* daft."

"I step into that paddock, and you'll call the Silent one out to fight your battle for you."

Hilde slowly walked across the pony field towards the gang, raising her hands at either side in a show that she was unarmed, ready for a fair fight. She came to a halt a few yards from the young'uns, got a good look at their faces. They weren't all bad, just easily led. *Sheep*, just as Mother would say. A few looked away, but as many sneered and gave Aidan a dig in the ribs, urging him to vault the fence. He hesitated, as Hilde stood waiting.

"Who's craven now?" she said.

That was all the goading it took. Aidan hurdled the fence, and in a few strides was into Hilde. He didn't come out swinging: he made to grab at her, looking to wrestle rather than punch. Perhaps he saw that as somehow more acceptable with the crowd of onlookers? He was, after all, brawling with a girl, and one who was smaller than him at that. He was the biggest lad on Unst, almost a full-grown man already. *There's no way he comes out of this with any glory*, thought Hilde.

She batted his grasping hands aside, ducking away and slipping out of reach. She got one good kick in, cracking him on the shin, and that was enough to ditch his previous mode of attack. Aidan hoofed back, catching Hilde on the side of the thigh and staggering her. The butcher's boy had some power and kicked like a donkey, and it was enough to put

Hilde in the straw and mud. Before she was able to get back to her feet, he was on top of her, straddling her waist, pinning Hilde to the ground. She felt his hands about her shoulders, trapping her in place.

"Yield!" shouted Aidan, teeth bared as the muscles in his arms bunched.

Hilde's hands came up, raking at him, only reaching his shoulders as he strained to keep his face out of reach. She squirmed from the waist down, trying to get her legs up and around him, but after all the insults, Aidan was no fool. He sat high on her chest, keeping his torso out of reach. She could feel the air getting crushed from her lungs, heard the shouting of the other young'uns, their allegiances varied.

"Yield, Hilde!"

"Let her go!"

"You've got her, Aidan!"

Her hands scrabbled either side of her, looking for something, anything, that she might use against her larger opponent. Fingertips connected with an object, her nails digging in for better purchase as she dragged it into her palm, making a fist around it. Her hand came up, swinging the makeshift weapon directly into the jaw of the butcher's boy.

The husk of horse dung exploded in his face, hard enough to crack his chin and send him toppling off Hilde. She rolled and followed, her turn now to sit astride her foe. As he spluttered to spit crap out of his mouth, nose and eyes, Hilde wasted no time in raining blows down upon him. Her hands came down, clasped together, striking him in the chest.

Aidan tried to cry out, only for one of Hilde's hands to

seize his throat. The other rose as a fist and fell, finding its target, planted straight onto the boy's nose. She heard – *felt* – the cartilage crunch, as blood streamed from both nostrils.

"Blood! You've drawn blood!"

"Get off him!"

She heard the shouts of the others, but they were somehow muffled, as if pushed away from her. Distant. And besides, she rather liked the sight of the blood. Her fist went up, came down again. And again. And again. The hands of the other young'uns reached for her, tried to pull her away, but they couldn't get near. Wouldn't dare get too close. The world blurred around Hilde, until all she saw was the red mist.

It took a well-placed crack from Mikko's quarterstaff to put an end to the brutal barrage and bring a curtain of cold and all-consuming darkness down upon the girl.

CHAPTER FIVE
CORMAC

It wasn't entirely clear to Cormac what was holding Blair the shipwright's home together. Lichen, mould and barnacles was his best guess, by the looks of things. The boathouse stood over the water on a set of crooked stilts, one end open to the elements and facing out to sea. The half-finished and never-completed remains of various small boats littered the stony ground around it, while a collection of rotten timbers and twisted planks struck and clattered against the boathouse's wooden legs, caught on a tide of weeds and detritus.

Cormac looked back at the village, the closest building a few hundred yards away. He could hear music playing now, the thump of a bodhrán drum accompanied by strings and song. The market wasn't the only thing in full swing: seemed the ale was already flowing too. Still more boats were arriving in the harbour, having braved the fog to get there. Cormac squinted: some bigger ships, beyond the cove, further out to sea? The thick mist obscured much, but one thing was for sure: Unst's population had bloomed in the last day or so.

Cormac returned his attention to the shipwright's house. It appeared abandoned, forgot, the only sound the groaning of stilts and the clacking of flotsam as the waves sloshed against its timber legs. The carcass of a small dog flopped back and forth in the spume below it, half-eaten by the crabs, and ignored by the house's occupant. A carrion crow, partially hidden by the building's shadows, hopped in and out of the water beside it, beak stabbing at the corpse and gulping down morsels of rotting flesh. All in all, a welcoming sight.

Guess he's a real people person.

"Anyone home?" Cormac called out, hoping this was as close as he had to get to the ramshackle shed.

With no reply, he edged closer, clutching the box of nails. Cormac reached out and rapped his knuckles on the moss-covered door, the rotten timbers creaking open on rusted hinges.

"Hello?"

Cormac gulped, his throat full of thistles, then stepped into the boathouse.

The first thing that assailed him was the smell, the combination of odours hitting him like a wave in a squall. The stench of stale sweat and spilt ale wasn't the worst of it: there was the stink of rot in the boathouse, as if something had crawled beneath the floorboards to die.

If the building looked neglected from outside, that went doubly so for indoors. The floor was littered with wood shavings, busted tools and splintered debris, like a couple of carpenters had gone at one another in a duel. A pair of gulls took flight from the eaves, swooping past Cormac and sending his fringe a-flutter as they flew, squawking, out to sea. A single small boat hung suspended from ropes in the middle of the room, a large section of floor beneath it missing, exposing the tide below.

Cormac edged around the hanging vessel, mindful of the opening and keen to avoid a misstep and a dunk. He gingerly made his way through the rubbish towards a crude-looking stove, a scrawny rat darting from its surface, kipper scraps in its teeth. A couple of smoked fish still hung over the stove, looking far from enticing, while a pot of tar sat upon the cold iron hot plate. Cormac had seen other shipwrights use tar, especially when repairing large boats in the harbour that had sprung leaks or needed protection against the elements. A good coating on the hull of any ship would better its chances against the cruel *Nordsær*. He picked up a piece of wood and jabbed at the black sludge in the pot, only to find it long hardened.

Not the busiest of boatmakers then, Mister Blair?

He continued on his way around the deserted boathouse, pulling out drawers beneath benches, kicking empty ale kegs aside and standing on his toes to nosy around shelves. If there was a method to how Blair kept his workshop, it was a mystery to Cormac. It was the exact opposite to his Pa's workshop, in every regard. Everything was in disarray, at least to the boy's eyes. There wasn't a clear area to work, the best bit of bench coated in a host of useless and knackered odds and ends, including scraps of leather, a cup of animal fat, empty ale mugs, twisted lengths of iron and a badly bloodied rag. A bracket on the wall would ideally be the home to the shipwright's tools, although only one sad looking, well-rusted and toothless saw hung there.

Place is a death-trap – how does he get anything done in here?

The creaking of ropes startled Cormac, his heart skipping a beat. He turned quickly, looked about the boathouse, attention returning to the hanging vessel in the rafters. The sea breeze from the exposed end of the building had caught the hemp harnesses, making the boat groan where it hung. He went up on his toes once again, peeked through the stained and uneven glass of the window to the yard beyond: still no sign of Blair. Perhaps he'd gone hunting or fishing, or whatever an old hermit did when he wasn't making ships. Or *failing* to make ships, as the case appeared to Cormac. *Where is the old coot?* A tall cupboard loomed in the shadows, its warped timbers held together by bent nails, animal-gut twine and oaken pegs. It was perhaps seven feet tall, from the floorboards up to the beams above. *Maybe I'll find him in here, roosting like some fiend, awaiting the moonrise!*

Cormac unhitched the twine, hooked his fingers between wood and frame, and prised the cupboard open. To his surprise, he had discovered the one area of the boathouse that wasn't cluttered with rubbish. A heavy boot-length black cloak hung from a peg, the hood draped off the shoulder and trimmed with fur. Cormac reached out to touch the thick material – it was quality, far too fine for the hermit, which instantly got the boy to thinking it was stolen. That quickened the heart once again.

Pulling it to one side, he found more prize pieces of booty stowed within the locker. A small round shield with a bronze boss at its centre was wedged into the bottom of the cupboard. Cormac's fingers brushed against the shield's surface, the weathered leather depicting animals and fantastic beasts. It had seen better days, the material frayed and torn – whether through age or use in battle it was hard to tell.

Shoving the box of nails into his armpit, Cormac twisted the shield free, bringing it out into the half-light of the boathouse. It was well made, no doubt, and he desperately wanted to show it to his Pa. Cormac's eyes went wide. Behind where the shield had been stowed, he spied a sword in a leather scabbard, a bronze chafe at the base that matched the boss of the shield. The sword handle was fashioned from what looked like bone, while its pommel and crossguard were forged from the same bronze as the shield boss.

A tremulous hand reached out towards the sword, Cormac struggling to remain calm. He'd never made any secret of his fascination with weaponry. Hell, he'd tormented his father for as long as he could remember, trying to persuade Pa to make swords for warriors and not shoes for horses. But this was the closest he'd ever come to a genuine weapon of war, and a sword at that.

A box sat in the base of the cupboard, also previously hidden by the shield. It was a fine piece of carpentry, better than anything Cormac had seen on Unst. Its intricately carved lid was adorned with a Celtic cross, inlaid with pearl. He flicked the latch, and when the lid flipped open his breath was stolen from his chest.

It looked to Cormac like a king's ransom in the box, the unmistakable glitter of gold making his head spin. Cords of the stuff, twisted into rope torcs, rings and necklaces, some studded with gems that dazzled the eye. And on top of the pile of jewellery, silver, and lots of it, coins of all sizes featuring strange and unfamiliar faces.

What in the world is the hermit doing with such a hoard?

Most alarmingly, Cormac had to wonder who the treasures belonged to. They sure as hell didn't belong to the shipwright.

As he pondered these and further thoughts, he heard more creaking from the ropes at his back, this time louder as the boat strained and bumped against the rafters. He peered over his shoulder as a shadow rolled down over him, looming at his back.

Turned out he wasn't alone in the boathouse after all. A figure was slowly descending from the boat, where moments earlier he had been stowed away, hidden within the dank darkness of the rafters. He wore a pair of filthy britches and nothing more, his skin lean and weathered, covered in old scars and new sores. A wild grey beard erupted from the old man's face, only his nose and eyes visible, poking out of this nest of whiskers. A similar mass of scraggly hair hung matted and dirty around his head, the top of which was bald and caught the faint light of day as he dangled there. The stench of stale ale came off him in waves, causing Cormac to gag. The hermit stretched, lowering himself further, long toenails catching the wooden boards around the exposed section of floor as he strained to avoid falling into the waters below.

Cormac had seen enough.

He dropped the box of nails, its contents scattering across the boathouse floor, some of them skittering off the launch and into the briny below. As he dashed for the door, Blair landed clumsily, reaching a skeletal arm out towards him, dirty yellow fingernails catching thin air as Cormac shot by. The door was left banging on its hinges as the smith's lad crashed out of the building into the daylight.

He didn't look back.

CHAPTER SIX
HILDE

From her seat at the foot of the jarl's dais, Hilde scowled. The jarlshof was full to bursting, every bench and trestle occupied by villagers and visitors alike. Those who couldn't find a seat stood around the edge of the feast hall, leaning against pillars or sitting cross-legged on the floor, backs to the wattle and daub walls. Servants carried platters of food and drink around the chamber, guests quick to lighten their loads. Torchlight made the mead sparkle like liquid gold as it sloshed from overflowing tankards.

Folk took turns approaching Jarl Frida's throne, presenting Hilde's mother with all manner of gifts, from livestock to finely crafted goods. In one hand she held a golden goblet, which she would take occasional sips from, her lips coming away dark with what appeared to be wine. Rumour had it the cup was a spoil of victory, stolen during a raid on a Christian monastery, but Jarl Frida never spoke to her daughter of her past. Her old war shield, which hung off the back of her wooden throne, remained cloaked in shadow and mystery. Hilde had always loved the shield, would often linger behind the heavy chair to admire it, letting her fingers trace over the various chips and nicks that scored the wood. If shields could speak, this one had some tales to tell.

Of course, it wasn't Jarl Frida who Hilde was scowling at.

Mikko the Silent was the object of her ire, the half-deaf huscarl greeting his jarl's guests with a cheery smile as he presented them before the throne.

"Trying to put a hex on Mikko?" asked Siv, stabbing at gobbets of meat that bobbed about in a bowl of stew. "You got the evil eye now, child?"

The raven was stood on the table beside Hilde, all too aware of the girl's foul mood. Not for the first time, Hilde raised her fingers to the back of her head, wincing as they brushed the pronounced lump that had appeared since the fracas in the paddock.

"Still say the old coot didn't need to hit me so hard. He might have left me a witless idiot."

Siv cackled. "Quit your mewling. He was saving you."

"By cracking my skull?"

"Saving you from *yourself*."

Hilde hid her bruised fists beneath the tabletop. "For a moment there, it was like I stepped out of myself, and someone else stepped in. Does that make sense? Felt like a red mist fell over me. All I saw was an enemy. All I felt was rage." She shrugged.

"I don't know what came over me."

"I do," muttered Siv.

"What's that?"

"Ignore me," replied the raven before gesturing to the dais with the blink of a beady black eye. "Look, your mother calls you."

Hilde sat suddenly to attention. Sure enough, Jarl Frida was staring her way, gently beckoning. If Hilde expected a hint of warmth from her mother, nothing was forthcoming, the jarl's expression hard as ever. Hilde weaved between the tables and stepped up onto the dais, careful not to stumble over the various pelts and rugs that carpeted the platform. Jarl Frida took her daughter's hand and presented her to the guests who stood before them.

Hilde's heart sank instantly.

Aidan glowered at her through his one good eye, the other closed-up like a purple fist, the skin split across his cheek right down to his busted lips. His nose was a swollen lump of battered flesh, a tuft of wool crammed inside each nostril, keeping the blood at bay. Most alarming of all were the marks around Aidan's throat, violet blue outlines where Hilde's fingers had closed about his neck, gripping him tight as she'd whaled on him. Rab Erskine stood behind him, meaty hands on each of his son's shoulders, holding the lad upright, adding strength to weak legs. Hilde avoided the butcher's gaze, felt his eyes burning holes into her, sensed the anger rolling off him.

"Hilde," said Jarl Frida calmly, her voice barely audible over the sounds of merrymaking that filled the feast hall. "Is there something you'd like to say to Erskine's lad?"

"Like what?" said Hilde, looking to her mother with astonishment.

It was Rab Erskine who answered, his voice a low rumble. "Sorry would be a start."

"You want an apology?"

"You damned near almost killed my boy," growled Erskine. "Be thankful I'm not asking for one of your eyes for his – he may never see again through this one."

Erskine held Aidan's jaw with one hand, roughly twisting it about and presenting the ruined side of the boy's face to jarl and daughter. It did look a mess, all of it Hilde's handiwork. She spied the curl of Aidan's lip as he sneered her way, smarting from the fight and the subsequent fallout. He was a rotten piece of work, and he'd got what was coming to him. Hilde tried in vain to keep the smile from twitching upon her face.

That was enough for Aidan. He spoke at last, tears making his one good eye wet as he pointed an accusing finger at Hilde.

"She's an animal. Thinks she can do anything, lording it over the rest of us just because she's the jarl's daughter. She needs teaching a lesson."

Hilde chuckled. "Like the one I dealt you this afternoon? If you didn't want a beating, you shouldn't have come up to the paddock, shooting your mouth off."

"Listen to her," said Erskine with a shake of the head. "Not a shred of remorse."

"I didn't start it," said Hilde defiantly.

"You sure as hell finished it, girl," said Erskine, before returning his attention to the chieftain. "This doesn't look much like an apology, Jarl Frida."

Again, Hilde turned back to her mother. "This is madness!"

"Mind your tone, child," said Mikko the Silent, chiming in from beside her. "Remember who you're speaking to. That's your jarl."

"She was my ma first," Hilde snapped back at the huscarl, having still not forgiven him for his earlier intervention.

"Haven't you got some young'uns to strike with that staff o' yours?"

Mikko grimaced. "I was protecting you."

Hilde looked at her split knuckles. "I didn't need protecting. I was *winning* that fight."

Jarl Frida raised a hand slowly, enough to put an end to the bickering. The stern look she gave Hilde was enough to make the girl shrink where she stood, withering under her mother's gaze.

"The fight was *won*, Hilde," said Jarl Frida, the disappointment all too evident in her voice. "The lad was beaten. If Mikko had left you for a few moments longer, we would have had a dead boy on our hands. How would that have looked for you, for me? A village child, killed by the jarl's daughter?"

Hilde ground her teeth. She thought back to that red mist that had descended as she pummelled Aidan's face, realisation dawning on her. She'd *enjoyed* the sensation, and the knowledge of that brought a wave of sudden shame. *What's wrong with me?*

She looked back at Erskine and his son, managed to hold the man's gaze. Aidan she ignored – the lad was a fool and a stone-cold bully – but did his father really deserve to hear her apology? Yes, the butcher was respected throughout the village, regardless of the idiocy of his offspring. Yet rumour had it Rab Erskine had arrived on the island years ago, having fled some terrible crime on Alba. He wouldn't have been the first man who had run to the Hjaltland Isles, escaping their dark past. He was certainly feared by Aidan and was known to knock the boy about. Quick tempered and just as quick with his fists; that's what they said about Erskine. Hell, he was *worse* than Aidan! Those about Hilde, certainly those sat closest to the throne, were all watching now. Seemed she'd earnt herself an audience.

Hilde took a breath. *Just when I thought this couldn't get any more humiliating.*

"I'm sorry, Master Erskine," she said to the man, her voice cracking. "I didn't mean to cause such upset and hurt. I lost my head for a moment back there. I hope you can forgive me."

Hilde dropped her head, heard a grunted acknowledgement from Erskine. She was about to leave the dais, when she caught her mother clearing her throat.

"The boy deserves a word also," said Jarl Frida.

Hilde slowly swivelled her head around to face her mother, whose expression remained cold and impassive. Hilde took a few steps towards her, drawing close so only Jarl Frida could hear.

"Are you serious? I gave Erskine his apology, and that was for you. It certainly gave me no joy. But that's not enough? You need me to say sorry to that rat?"

Jarl Frida's jaw clenched; the closest thing Hilde saw of any emotion upon her mother's face. The chieftain looked down at the goblet in her hand, sloshing its dark contents about, seemingly unable to look Hilde in the eye.

"Such is the price we pay, daughter. Those of us who sit highest must be held as accountable for our actions as the lowliest of our number."

Hilde felt the anger boil inside once more, only this time

it was different, fuelled by the despair she felt towards her mother. She opened her mouth to speak, found the words catching in her throat like a fishbone. Her heart was racing, vision clouding around its edge. She could feel her self-control slipping away, and it took every fibre of her being to control her emotions as she forced the painful words from her lips.

"Just once, I wish you could act like a mother to me."

Hilde turned and stormed away from the dais. She heard Mikko the Silent shout after her, only to be silenced by Jarl Frida. She caught a smug smile breaking across Aidan's ruined face as she passed him, pushing her way through the crowd as she made for the exit. Her vision was blurring, tears building in her straining eyes, her mother's lack of love and loyalty overwhelming. Over the hubbub, Hilde heard a familiar voice call out her name – Cormac. She spied him waving frantically at her through the crowd, trying to catch her eye. Perhaps her friend had witnessed what had just played out and sought to provide her with a shoulder to cry on. She wasn't for stopping, though.

Hilde was so caught up in her misery and desire to escape the longhouse that she didn't see the man standing before her, blocking her path. She walked straight into him, bouncing off his midriff and staggering back to regard him.

"Steady, my young friend."

The stranger was lean in both chest and face, his cheekbones sharp, bruised shadows around his eyes. Unruly black hair was held back by a braid about his brow, while he wore his pitch-black beard drawn tight beneath his chin, encircled by a ring of gold. Hilde suspected the grin he gave her was his best attempt at disarming, but it came across as menacing. The smile of a shark. He was accompanied by two equally haggard-looking Norsemen.

"You don't know me, and you sure as hell ain't my friend!" snapped Hilde.

"You hear the mouth on this one?" chuckled Blackbeard to his friends.

Of his two companions, one was heavy-set, his belly hanging over his belt, a collection of suspect stains displayed across his tunic. Missing his left hand, the fat fingers of his remaining right drummed over his gut with a nervous energy, like he was waiting for something to happen. A dark tattoo coiled around his fat throat like a noose, giving him the look of a hanged man walking. His mate was perhaps as old as Blair the shipwright, although in much better condition. Weatherworn skin clung tight to his bare head, but it was the man's eyes Hilde was drawn to. His left socket was a dark, hollow pit while his right eyeball scanned eyeball scanned the room, unblinking. The three of them weren't here for the market, that much Hilde was sure of.

"This one's got more nerve than them sheep in Scatness, eh?" said the fat Norseman, winking at Blackbeard.

"You ain't wrong, Einar," added the bald one, his solitary eye lighting up. "Got ourselves a little wolf cub here."

Hilde wasn't about to stay and talk to the strangers. She barged past Blackbeard and his friends, not bothering to look back, balling her fists and screwing them into her eyes as she burst out of the hall. The crisp night air was fresh and bracing, chasing away the smells of the feast in an instant.

Fog still shrouded the water, the waves invisible but for the crashing sound of breakers that struck the shore. Hilde let the tears flow freely, the brackish spray hiding them as the sea air lashed her face.

She glanced back at the jarlshof, heard the festivities from within. Cheers and laughter, singing and shouting. *Fools, the lot of them.* Hilde tossed a curse over her shoulder, aimed squarely at her mother, then made for the solitude of the cliffs. The gulls were the only company she needed this night.

CHAPTER SEVEN
FRIDA

Jarl Frida gave her goblet a swill, the sloshing contents catching the torchlight. It was clearly Hilde's gift, to get under her mother's skin as much as she did. Was there ever a child who caused such consternation in a parent? She tried thinking back to her own mother, and whatever had passed for a relationship between them, but like so much it was lost in the mists of time. Jarl Frida took a sip from her cup and grimaced. She couldn't remember the woman's face, but she remembered her fists. Had she not been doomed to follow in her mother's footsteps? Perhaps it was as she'd always feared: there was too much of Jarl Frida in Hilde. Too much fire in the girl's belly to ever back down from a fight. It was in their blood.

"Got another visitor here to see you, chief," said Mikko the Silent, pulling Jarl Frida's attention away from her goblet. "Says he's one of your old friends."

Jarl Frida winced. "I don't have any *old* friends."

"You hear that?" Mikko called over his shoulder towards the visitor. "My jarl says she has no old friends."

"Then I'll settle for old acquaintance," replied the man, stepping out from behind Mikko's shadow, and into the light of the dais torches.

Many years had passed since Jarl Frida had last seen

him, but unlike her mother's, his was a face she would never forget. Her weary slouch was gone in an instant, her back straightening so she sat tall upon her humble throne. She lifted her chin, all the better for looking down her nose upon the man before her. He flashed a wolfish smile within the black whiskers of his beard, his fingers playing with the golden ring beneath his chin. The man bowed at the hip, raising a fist to his breast by way of a greeting.

"It's been too long, Frida Blackheart," said the man. "Feared I'd never see you again."

"*That* was what you feared?" said Jarl Frida, a hint of incredulity in her reply.

Mikko the Silent grunted, hand resting on the handle of his axe, which remained tucked in his belt. "So, you do know one another, then?"

"Hydyr the Hungry knew me once," said Jarl Frida, "though he does not know the woman who sits before you now."

Hydyr grinned, looking up at the chieftain with an air of serious mischief. Everything about his poise, how he presented himself, was like a cat about to pounce: he hadn't changed. Didn't look like he'd aged a day, in fact. Jarl Frida let her own gaze flicker around the room. Who had seen him arrive on the island? So many folk had come and gone this day, and none of her carls, those guards who kept Jarl Frida and her guests safe, were keeping any kind of score. *Is he here alone? Who else is with him?*

Hydyr took a step forwards, black leather boot alighting on the lowest step of the dais.

"Surely there's a bit of the old Frida in there still, lurking beneath that icy exterior?"

"It's *Jarl* Frida," said Mikko, turning himself full-on to the raven-haired warrior, blocking his path.

"Well, well," said Hydyr, sucking his teeth. "I've had warmer welcomes on other islands."

"What other islands have you visited, Norseman, where you could speak to a jarl in such a way?" sneered Mikko. "Remember where you are, Hydyr the Hungry."

"Apologies. I meant no offence. It's just that *Jarl* Frida and I were very . . . familiar, once upon a time."

"'Once' being the key word," said Jarl Frida, her eyes narrowing as she smiled, though they projected all the warmth of a blizzard. "So, Hydyr the Hungry, what brings you to Unst?"

Hydyr retreated a step. Mikko remained tensed.

"Truth be told, it was the tale of a woman named Frida being the jarl of this rock. Thought to myself, that can't be the same Frida who I sailed with back in the day, can it? Who I laughed with, fought with . . . had so much fun with. My only option was to sail here and discover for myself if the stories were true."

"And did you sail here alone?" asked Jarl Frida. "Are you still part of a crew?"

"I've shared a bench with many men and women over the years," said Hydyr, rubbing the small of his back as if it ached from a long voyage. "Not too proud to pull an oar, even at my age."

"Your age?" snorted Mikko. "You don't look a day over thirty summers."

"Guess I've been blessed with a youthful complexion, eh, old timer?"

Jarl Frida was no fool, though Hydyr clearly took her for one. She hadn't missed his inelegant attempt to dodge her question. *Whose crew did Hydyr sail with these days?* She felt her stomach sink, as if she'd just downed a jug of soured milk. *It couldn't be the* old *crew, after all these years, could it? Surely the* Sea Wolf *hadn't sailed into her harbour?* Once again, she glanced around the feast hall, saw plenty of faces she recognised but equally as many strangers.

"So, what brought you here?" asked Hydyr, taking a moment to turn leisurely on his heel and take in the hall. He waved at a huddle of villagers who were already in their cups.

"A desire to start anew," said Jarl Frida. "Leave the past where it belongs."

Hydyr nodded slowly, approvingly. "Rumour had it you came here with a bairn in your belly."

His head snapped around to check her reaction.

"Rumour is the refuge of the wicked and witless," replied Jarl Frida coolly.

Hydyr placed a hand on his chest, dirty fingers splayed wide. There was that damned grin again, all mirth and menace.

"I'm far from witless."

Jarl Frida breathed in and out. Slow.

Hydyr's gaze settled on Mikko. The huscarl's bushy eyebrows met on the bridge of his nose like a pair of plunging arrowheads, his hand returning to his hip and the handle of his axe.

"Does your huscarl wish to proposition me?" Hydyr asked Jarl Frida. "You should tell your man that, flattered though I am, I don't lie with Picts."

"I'm no Pict," said Mikko the Silent, his voice loud enough to quieten the nearby chatter. "And I take special interest in all who come before my jarl, especially those who claim to have known her in days gone by."

Hydyr made a show of being surprised, holding his arms out wide before him.

"If I've done something to offend, I apologise," said Hydyr, tossing his cloak back to reveal a simple leather belt, devoid of axe, sword or seax. "I fear you've mistaken me for a Viking, old man," continued the black-bearded visitor. "No weapons. I'm but a simple traveller from Norðvegr. My raiding days are a dim and distant memory. Like you, Frida, I'm a changed soul. It's not gold I seek these days. It's knowledge, wonder and wisdom."

"*Jarl* Frida," said Mikko, never taking his eyes off Hydyr the Hungry. "If you're happy with this Norseman's presence at your hearth, just say so, and I shall step down. I only seek to serve and protect."

By way of a reply, Jarl Frida spoke directly, and carefully, to the unarmed man.

"And this is the peril of following rumours, Hydyr the Hungry. There's rarely a shred of truth in them, and so often they lead to crossed words, or worse. You shouldn't believe everything you hear."

Hydyr looked back through the feast hall in the direction Hilde had earlier departed. "Thought for a moment the girl who bumped into me might've been—"

"No relation," Jarl Frida said with a shake of the head, cutting him off dead. "A fisherman's daughter."

"Can't blame a man for thinking otherwise," said Hydyr. "She's your double, Blackheart. Blue eyes, blonde hair, a snarl that would curdle a goblin's guts."

Jarl Frida shrugged. "What can I say? There's plenty of Norse blood mixed with that of the Picts on Unst, which is all for the better, at least in this community. Old enmities are now in the past. If only all mistakes could remain there."

Hydyr wagged a finger and laughed. "I hear you, Frida. Fret not, my visit to your kingdom was only ever going to be fleeting. I just wanted to see with my own eyes if the tale was true. And here you are, sat upon your throne, queen of all before you."

"I never proclaimed to be queen," said the chieftain. "The title of jarl sits awkward enough upon my brow. You'll be leaving, then?"

Hydyr glanced at the roast pig that turned on a spit over the firepit and smacked his lips.

"If it's all the same with you, I may just stay for a bite to eat first, Jarl Frida." He winked. "You know me: always hungry."

"You may eat and drink in my hall this night, for the sake of old kinship. I expect you shall be leaving Unst in the morning."

It wasn't a question, rather a statement. Hydyr struck his chest with his fist once more and bowed.

"I'd have settled for a corner of a pig sty, my lady," said

Hydyr. "A night in your hall is a most unexpected and welcome gift."

He paused, as if remembering one more thing. His smile was bright white and set a shiver racing up Jarl Frida's spine.

"Naturally, I'll be gone before dawn. Enjoy your drink."

He nodded at her goblet.

Does he know what I'm drinking?

And with that, he backed away from the dais, turning and retreating into the depths of the hall.

Jarl Frida watched him go, Hydyr pausing to snatch food and drink from passing platters, glancing back to the throne just once as he went. Jarl Frida grabbed Mikko the Silent by the wrist, fierce enough to startle him. She drew him close, so she had his ear.

"Have your carls keep an eye on our guest," said Jarl Frida.

"He is without a weapon," said Mikko, struggling to keep his voice low yet audible over the sounds of merrymaking. "If he starts anything, they'll finish it. Quick, like."

Jarl Frida gave Mikko a withering look. "He may be unarmed, but even a toothless wolf can draw blood. Watch him."

Mikko nodded, his expression grave. "My carls won't let you down. Anything else, chief?"

Jarl Frida scanned the room, taking in the folk who filled her hall this special night. Some were clearly merchants and traders, farmers and fishermen, still haggling and closing the last of their deals after a busy market. She spied a huddle of Christians from the neighbouring Hjaltland Isles who'd sought Brother Benedict and his baptisms.

Then there were the harder faces, craggy and scarred, beaten and battered, nubbins for ears and noses broken. All unarmed, of course: weapons were left outside the jarl's longhouse as a matter of course, though some of these newcomers looked like they'd bloodied steel in their time. Brooding eyes gleamed like polished jet from beneath heavy brows and bearded faces. Men of violence once, perhaps, hopefully no more. Very few were familiar to her.

"Find Hilde, Mikko. Keep her safe."

For the first time ever, Jarl Frida felt outnumbered in her own home, and she didn't like the sensation one bit.

CHAPTER EIGHT
CORMAC

"How does Blair make a living, that's what I want to know," said Cormac as he smeared the pork fat from his lips with the back of his hand. "Man lives like an animal, is a stone cold drunk, and his workshop looks like where boats go to die."

The feast hall was bouncing, everyone in the village and those visiting Unst for the market having descended upon the huge jarlshof to enjoy Jarl Frida's hospitality. Hamish Tulloch was certainly making the most of the jarl's generosity, as he allowed a servant to refill his mug for the umpteenth time. He took a slurp of ale and glared ruefully at his son.

"Learn when to quit bumping your gums, lad," said Hamish. "Leave folk to live their own life. So, Blair may not be the best shipwright in the world."

"I'm not sure he's even the best shipwright in the village—"

"—but he's a good man. He's just . . . different."

Cormac licked grease from his fingers, thinking carefully on his next words. "I heard he's a thief, Pa. Rumour is he's got a stash of stolen treasure hidden in that boathouse."

Of course, Cormac knew fine well there was loot in Blair's hovel, but there was no way he could admit to his father that he'd been rooting through the shipwright's belongings. When he said he'd delivered the box of nails, Cormac had omitted the part where he'd scattered half of them into the sea as he fled the waking hermit. He'd also avoided any mention of the armoury and treasure trove Blair kept in his cupboard. Better to make up a small white lie than throw a noose about one's neck.

But where in all the far-flung isles had *Blair got that hoard from?*

Hamish stared at his son – did he know what Cormac had been up to? The blacksmith thought on his words for a moment, pausing between sups of his cup. Cormac could read his old man like a fisherman reads the tides; something was bothering him. He always got a little loose-lipped after a few ales, and it seemed he wanted to spill something to Cormac. Hamish was clearly on the verge of some momentous decision.

"You and I shall talk about Blair later, Cormac. But for the time being, don't judge a man for how he looks. Judge him for his deeds."

"Yes, Pa."

Cormac returned to the rib, worrying the last bits of gristle from it. Through the smoke from the firepit, he caught a flash of familiar golden braids as his friend pushed through the crowd of revellers. He rose from his bench, shouting and waving.

"Hilde! Over here!"

Cormac saw her face, half turned, flushed red, cheeks wet with tears. That was never good. He threw a leg over the bench and made to depart, Hamish grabbing the sleeve of his shirt and halting his progress.

"Where you going?"

"After Hilde."

"And there he goes!" said Hamish to the others who shared their table. "A bat of the lashes and my lad's up and running."

"Eh?' said Cormac, genuinely confused.

Hamish frowned. "She's the jarl's daughter. Leave the girl be, Cormac. Stop running after her like some love-sick pup whenever she calls your name."

Cormac felt the colour in his own face now, as his father's companions clapped and snorted at the remark. Typical of his old man to embarrass him like this, the ale playing its part. He tugged his sleeve free from Hamish's grip.

"It ain't like that, Pa," he said sulkily, stepping away from the laughing men. "I'll see you later."

Hamish waved him on his way. Cormac loved him dearly, but the man could be an ass. Displays of emotion, large or small, weren't in his toolkit. He was all hammer and tong, smoke and fire.

Cormac pushed his way through the bodies, edging ever nearer the doors. There must have been close to a hundred people in the longhouse, filling every bench and trestle, crowding every corner. He passed by a couple of carls who stood at the entrance, the pair agitated and on their toes. He stepped between them without so much as a nod, the guards looking in as opposed to out of the hall, scouring the crowd for someone.

Cormac cleared his throat, catching the ear of the closest carl. "I'm looking for Hilde."

The guard gestured to the exit with a hooked thumb,

his attention returning to the feast hall. Cormac followed the carl's gaze. Unless he was mistaken, the object of scrutiny was a Norseman with a soot-black beard. While all around the man feasted, tearing into haunches of bloody meat or downing tankards of mead and ale, he simply sat, patient, as if waiting for something or someone. The bearded Norseman was looking directly back at the carls, an amused smile flickering upon his thin lips. Cormac shivered. There was something unsettling about the stranger, and he didn't blame the carls for watching him like hawks.

Then Cormac was out of the hall and into the market square beyond. The muddy lanes were now devoid of human activity, replaced by wandering chickens, the odd crow and seabird, and a solitary dog, turning in circles as it tried to sniff its own back-end. *Who needs the mainland, when one has the majesty of Unst?*

"Hilde!"

Cormac's shout carried a short distance, only to be drowned out by the crashing of waves. Footsteps squelching in mud followed him from the longhouse. Cormac turned, found Aidan stood beside him. His friend's face was an ugly mess, bust lip, broken nose and an eye so swollen and purple that it put Cormac in mind of a ripe turnip.

"What do you want with the witch?" asked Aidan, spitting into the wind and wincing with discomfort.

Cormac didn't bother replying. What was the point? His two friends couldn't stand one another, and he found it best not to take sides whenever altercations arose.

"You been to see the gothi yet?" Cormac recoiled as he

inspected Aidan's face. "He's probably got something that will hasten your healing. Perhaps even get your nose back on the front of your head."

"I'll pass on that," said Aidan with a pained snarl. "Don't want anything from those Norse dogs. They cause nothing but trouble for those of us who truly belong here on Unst."

"Careful. You're beginning to sound like your pa."

The apple hadn't fall far from the tree when it came to Aidan and his father. Rab Erskine was well known for his opinions on the Norsemen, though he kept his thoughts amongst his own kind. The butcher may have disliked the jarl and her people, but he wasn't such a fool that he could do without them, and at the end of the day, she was his chieftain. The island, and those around it, belonged to the Norsemen, and all on Unst had sworn fealty to Jarl Frida. Erskine had benefitted from the woman's patronage down the years and had to keep the chieftain sweet. It couldn't have been easy for Erskine when the jarl's daughter and his own son had come to blows.

"I'll stick to honest Pictish remedies, if it's all the same. Maybe even get Brother Benedict to bless me, just to be sure."

Aidan made the sign of the cross clumsily; like so many on Unst, he was still new to the piety game. He was unsteady on his feet.

Just how hard did Hilde hit you? Cormac got a whiff of his friend's breath, and it wasn't great.

"You been drinking?"

"Pa's let me have a few," said Aidan, puffing his chest out like a prize cockerel. "I'll say this for the Norsemen; they know how to brew a good mead."

Aidan frowned as he cast his one good eye over the bay. "I know I'm half blind, but is that fog getting worse?"

"Looks that way," said Cormac. "Thick as broth."

Through the gloom, he could just make out a figure stood on the main pier in the harbour, a big man, silhouetted by what moonbeams had managed to pierce the strange mist. By the looks of it, he appeared to be missing a hand. Struck Cormac as odd what a soul might be doing out here on such a grim evening, when the food and drink was flowing in the feast hall.

Cormac was about to mention this when he heard a steady gushing sound. He half-turned and found Aidan stood in the shadows to the side of the jarlshof, urinating against the wall.

"Bloody Vikings," said the boy, chuckling to himself as his work steamed against the timbers.

"You've lived alongside the Norsemen your entire life," said Cormac. "How is it you haven't learnt that these people are no longer Vikings. That's a name from their past, when they raided and pillaged. Jarl Frida and the rest of them ain't like that. They're peaceful folk, like you, me and our kin."

"Ain't nothing like us," grumbled the other, still emptying his bladder.

"You do realise there's a perfectly good latrine out beyond the stables?"

"What? And miss my chance to decorate the jarl's palace?" scoffed Aidan.

"And that's my signal to get gone," said Cormac, heading away from the longhouse. "Hilde!"

"I saw her head towards the cliffs!" shouted Aidan after him, staggering clear of the building before falling through the open door of the stable block. His voice echoed from within. "With a bit of luck, she'll fall off 'em!"

That was enough to send Cormac up the cliff path, stepping carefully. He clutched at a clump of heather as a loose stone was dislodged underfoot, the slate discus cartwheeling down the hillside into the night.

He knew where to find her. Hilde's favourite spot: the God Tree. Said it made her feel close to Odin. If there was anywhere the All-father might hear her prayers (or complaints, for that matter), it was the old rowan tree that clung to the highest clifftop. Cormac wasn't fond of the tree. He'd never had a head for heights, and there was no loftier point on the whole of Unst. The God Tree might have made Hilde feel closer to her gods, but it made Cormac feel he was about to meet his real soon.

He passed by the gothi's hut, the door to the holy man's ramshackle home flapping, lazily slapping the door frame, a dim light glowing within. Though less afraid than others, Cormac quickened his step; the gothi's reputation as a bogeyman amongst the young'uns of Unst ensured that few if any Picts would linger alone in the dark with him. Not unless they really had to.

Cresting the hill, Cormac strolled across the summit, the wind whipping over the cliffs and flattening the grass before him. Sure enough, there was Hilde, sat beyond the gnarled and carved trunk of the God Tree, perched upon the cliff edge, feet trailing into the night. He walked slowly over.

"I can hear you breathing," said Hilde as Cormac approached. She didn't even turn around, knew it was him.

"You've the ears of a bat," said the blacksmith's boy as he joined her, plonking himself down onto the cliff edge. "That was me being stealthy, by the way."

"I've encountered stealthier cattle."

"As it happens, I was *trying* not to scare you."

Hilde's laugh was humourless. "Worried you might scare me? In your dreams, Tulloch."

"Hey, a sudden noise from me and I could've startled you right off the cliff. Last thing I need is having to explain to Jarl Frida how I killed her daughter."

"Trust me, there's no sudden noises when it comes to you. You provide a steady cacophony night and day."

Cormac grunted. "You ain't never heard me at night."

Hilde nodded. "Nor do I ever want to."

She turned to him at last, her face as dark and troubled as the night sky.

"Why are you here, Cormac? I wanted to be alone."

Cormac felt the wind tug at his ankles, reminding him that he was perched atop a hellish high cliff. He drew his legs back up to where he sat and folded his arms around them, hugging his knees to his chin. The boy was terrified by the drop but refused to show it to his friend. He had to appear effortlessly cool, even though his insides were coiling and squirming like a nest of serpents.

"Suits me fine," he replied. "We can both be alone. Together."

They sat in silence a while longer, each content with their

own thoughts. God only knew what preoccupied Hilde: no doubt the repercussions of her scrap with Aidan. The butcher's boy had seemed awfully pleased with himself moments ago. Hilde wasn't some quick-to-cry bairn; if she was hiding it was because she was genuinely upset. Something had got under her skin, and it was a splinter Cormac wasn't prepared to pick at.

He was about to ask Hilde what her plans were for the following day, when there was a harsh shattering sound at their back accompanied by an explosive roar. The jagged remains of an oil flask flew in all directions from around the trunk of the God Tree, causing the two youths to throw their arms around one another, shielding themselves from the shower of shrapnel, as fire engulfed the ancient rowan. They turned back towards the blinding light, felt its instant heat upon their faces as the flames raced up the trunk and into the branches.

Beyond the blazing tree, blocking their path away from the clifftop, stood a bald, one-eyed stranger. He threw his head back and howled triumphantly at the night. Cormac watched the sparks from the burning God Tree flutter into the night sky. They were a swarm of fireflies, headed to the heavens, carried on clouds of boiling black smoke. And far below, in the heart of the fog-choked bay, Cormac saw lights appear. The hoods were removed from a host of lanterns on the deck of a dreadful vessel that materialised through the mist.

A longship.

"He's one of them," whispered Hilde to Cormac, clutching

his forearm as the two rose unsteadily to their feet, supporting one another, death before them and at their backs.

"One of who?" asked Cormac.

He was overwhelmed, and scared beyond the telling of it, the fire roaring and the turf loose beneath his heel where it barely clung to the cliff edge. Far below, the white foam crashed against the jagged rocks.

It was only now that the warrior saw the pair of them through the inferno. He smiled as Hilde found her words once more.

"He's one of the Vikings."

CHAPTER NINE
HILDE

As the God Tree burnt directly between the youths and the Viking, Hilde squinted through the fire. Her gaze alighted upon the weapon in the warrior's hands: the gothi's ceremonial blade, dripping with gore. The raider grinned, his one good eye sparkling with demented glee. She winced as Cormac gripped her elbow fearfully, the pair wilting before the inferno.

"He's a Norseman," said Cormac. "You can reason with him, right?"

"Does he look like he's ready to reason?" Hilde shook her head. "He's a Viking. We ain't alike at all."

The heat from the burning tree was overwhelming, and Hilde could already feel her cheeks threatening to blister. Stay on the precipice any longer, and they would be likely forced off the cliff or be burnt alive. The bald warrior threw his head back and hollered. By the firelight beyond the rowan tree, Hilde could see the man's face and chest was spattered with fresh blood. Did it belong to the gothi? Had the killing already begun?

The Viking pointed the tip of the ceremonial blade at the two youths.

"You want to die on this miserable peak?" the raider called out over the cackle and crackle of the flames.

"Seems as good a place as any," Hilde shouted as she

and Cormac peered over the cliff edge at the rocks and waves far below.

"Come now, child," said the one-eyed man, his ruined face now serious. "You shouldn't be in such a hurry to meet your maker. I can keep you safe, keep you breathing, least for a while. There's plenty of dying to be done this night, but don't be making a bairn-killer out of Finn Frostmark."

Hilde spat. "I'd sooner die than go anywhere with you."

Frostmark shrugged. "Big words for a wee lass," he said in a resigned fashion as the sickly grin returned. "Bairn-killer it is."

Hilde tugged Cormac close. Her friend couldn't take his eyes off the Viking, sweat and tears mingling upon his face.

"We could always jump," he whispered. "It'll be quick, won't it?"

She managed a smile. "If the Gods are kind, it will."

Before they could take that final, fatal leap, and as if in answer to Hilde's words, a splintering roar startled the pair of them, as the God Tree suddenly toppled towards Frostmark. The rowan had clung to this barren clifftop for countless years, its roots gripping the unforgiving rock through all the sea and sky could throw at it, but no more. Engulfed in the hungry fire, it crashed down directly onto the spot where the Viking stood, sparks exploding into the air with the impact, allowing Hilde and Cormac their chance to run.

Boy and girl leapt through the churning, burning storm, hurdling the exposed roots of the ruined tree as they made a break for the cliff path. They could barely see where they were stepping, the air thick with black smoke and dancing embers.

Hilde was a yard ahead of Cormac, leading the way, when she heard a cry from behind. She stumbled to a halt, turning back just in time to see the gothi's silver sword spinning towards her, thrown with precision by the Viking.

The hilt of the weapon hit her hard and square in the chest, its polished blade bouncing up to strike her face. Hilde didn't have time to think about the pain, as the air was punched from her lungs, sending her toppling onto the turf of the clifftop. She rolled about like a beached fish, gasping for air as Frostmark swaggered nonchalantly out of the smoke towards her. Blood streamed into her eyes, from Odin knew where, and through her blurred vision she spied Cormac lying motionless on the ground behind the Viking. Alive or dead, Hilde had no idea, but he had clearly fallen foul of the raider.

Frostmark stopped above her, tilted his head, sizing the girl up like a piece of meat. A deep, sucking hole was all that was left of one of his eyes, the socket as black as the killer's heart. He smacked his lips.

"Maybe I do let you live," said the Viking. "For a while, at least."

He may have wanted to say more but never got the chance. A spear whistled through the night, striking him in the back, the weapon's iron head bursting from his chest. Frostmark burbled where he stood, fingers fondling the crude spearpoint, before stumbling in the direction of the burning tree. From the scree path another figure emerged, scrambling towards Hilde, relief writ upon his face as he found her alive.

"Thank Odin ... you're still ... with us."

Mikko the Silent knelt, bending double beside her. The old

huscarl was panting hard, hands on hips, desperately trying to recover his breath. Behind him, lying face down in the gnarled roots of the flaming rowan tree, lay the one-eyed Viking, Mikko's spear stuck through his middle. Hilde tried to blink away the blood, her fingers clumsily searching her face for the wound.

"You saved my life," said Hilde, fighting back nausea. "Did you run all the way up here?"

"Well, I didn't fly," Mikko managed to say, lovingly placing his hand over her face to try and wipe the blood clear. "Your mother... said I was to watch over you... and I always shall."

In spite of her head wound and her crushed ribs, Hilde's thoughts returned to her friend. She batted Mikko's hand aside and pointed a trembling finger at the toppled tree which continued to blaze.

"Cormac," she managed to say.

"Right you are," said the old timer, struggling to get to his feet once more.

But as Mikko rose and turned, he stepped straight into the embrace of Frostmark.

"No!" screamed Hilde, as she watched the Viking swiftly draw the Norseman onto the head of the spear, which still stood proud from the centre of his chest. Frostmark pulled Mikko in like a lover, the spear sinking into the huscarl. The raider held the old man there for a long, awful moment, chuckling and patting Mikko affectionately on his back, before sliding him from the spearhead and tossing him aside.

The jarl's daughter and dying huscarl looked up as the Viking loomed over them, the spear now dripping with the blood of both men. The weapon must have splintered Frostmark's ribs and torn through his innards. By rights, he should have been lying dead on the ground, his soul halfway to Valhalla. And yet here the swine stood, seemingly unfazed by the mortal wound he'd suffered.

Frostmark gave Mikko a kick with the toe of his boot, the old warrior defenceless and desperately close to death's door. Lying a little further away was Cormac, and Hilde spied her friend beginning to stir. However, Frostmark wasn't done with his fun. By the light of the burning God Tree, Hilde saw the Viking's peg teeth glistening crimson as he stood over Mikko. The hungry look on his ruined face was that of a predator, as if deciding what part of its prey it might devour first.

"You're a gamey old bird, but there's still some meat on your bones. You'll do. You *and* the girl."

Mikko turned his face towards the blazing remains of the God Tree. His threadbare voice cracked when he spoke, a whisper in Old Norse to the All-Father, praying for safe passage to Valhalla.

"Pray to them all you like, old man," said the Viking, the bones in his broken torso grating as he spoke. "They're not listening. The gods are dead. Just like the rest of us."

The raider brought his attention back round to Hilde. He carefully put a foot on her chest, pinning her to the cold, hard ground. She squirmed, tore at his legs, balled her fists and punched him, but it was like striking iron. He pressed down harder, driving his heel into her breastbone, grinning all the while.

This was her end. No saga song for the shieldmaiden's daughter. Hilde flailed, gasped, knew something was about to give.

"Leave her be!"

Half-stunned and staggering, Cormac collided with the Viking from behind, seizing hold of the spear shaft that was buried in Frostmark's back. Say that for her friend, he was tough, both of his arms strong and seasoned from toiling in his father's smithy. Cormac twisted his body, crying out. The raider staggered away, reaching behind his back in a futile attempt to grab the blacksmith's boy. In that moment, the pressure lifted from Hilde's chest, and she kicked out at the flailing Frostmark.

Boy and Viking turned on the clifftop, as Cormac steered his foe away from his friend. Hilde caught sight of Cormac's fleeting smile, a self-indulgent moment of triumph as he propelled Frostmark past the burning rowan towards the cliff edge. It was premature.

As they passed the God Tree bonfire, Frostmark stumbled directly into it, dropping to one knee as he plunged his hand into the flames. Cormac continued pushing, directing, grunting as he hefted the Viking back on his journey over the cliff edge.

Then it all happened so fast.

Frostmark threw his clenched fist back, unleashing a handful of flaming embers and sparks directly into Cormac's face. The boy let go of the spear shaft, blind and bewildered as he stumbled forwards. As for the Viking, there was nothing beneath the bald raider's feet as he stepped off the precipice, already turning as he began his death-fall to the rocks and breakers far below.

Only he wasn't alone.

Frostmark's flailing hand caught tight about Cormac's wrist, and, with a last, despairing cry, the blacksmith's boy followed the raider over the edge.

Hilde's scream near broke her bruised and battered breast, the horror of her friend's fate too much to bear.

She collapsed to her knees beside Mikko, the old huscarl's last breaths too escaping his bloodied body. Hilde dragged the gothi's weapon through the grass and gave it to Mikko, an end befitting any Norseman, to die with a blade in his sword hand. His other, so rough and calloused, was gentle against her cheek, and it was all Hilde could do to read his lips as he mouthed his final words.

"Run. Hide. Live."

And then he was gone.

CHAPTER TEN
CORMAC

That the Viking had decided to take hold of Cormac and not relinquish his grip might well have been the reason the boy survived his fall. Half-blinded by hot ash, he was at the mercy of Finn Frostmark, tied inexorably to the raider's fate. As the cliff face flashed by and the world turned, Cormac sensed the wall of rock whip past, ever closer. One more rotation and it was the Viking who struck the jagged cliff face with a sickening crunch. Cormac collided with Frostmark's body, the Viking's corpse absorbing the initial impact and cushioning the blow for the boy. In the next breath, the pair struck the freezing water of the sea, plunged into a swirling maelstrom of darkness.

Cormac thought he was already dead, so sudden and absolute was the chill weight that crushed him, driving him down to the depths. But in the next heartbeat, he was dragged across the seabed, razor-sharp rocks tearing and raking. He was helpless, caught in the grip of the undercurrent as it shook him like a hound with its prey. The last of the air was leaking from his lungs, his last breath streaming from his lips as the life faded from his battered body.

A lull in the surging storm. Cormac saw his escaping air bubbles dance in the gloom, figured which way was up. He kicked off the stony seabed and launched himself towards the surface, exploding from the waves and snatching his breath. For a few dreaded moments he kept bobbing back beneath the surf, the undertow threatening to seize him and return him to a watery grave. But Cormac was strong, back-breaking hours in the smithy having served him well. He reached out over the choppy water, muscular arms working rhythmically, hands cutting through the surging tide, as he began to swim his way back to the shore.

Back to hell.

As Cormac hauled himself onto the rocks at the foot of the cliffs, beaten and bloodied, he looked along the beach.

Unst was in ruins.

Flames churned and black smoke belched from thatched and timber rooftops. Screams rose then died within the burning homes, as those who had sought shelter from the Vikings found nowhere to hide. Here and there the odd villager could be seen, dashing away from the chaos and the killing, only to be felled by a well-aimed spear, or dragged into the darkness by the monsters. Raiders rushed from one building to the next, silhouettes against the inferno, axes raised, axes falling, revelling in their bloody work. The greatest commotion appeared to come from the great hall, which was already partly ablaze.

Pa.

Along with every inhabitant of Unst, Cormac's father had been in the jarlshof. Hamish Tulloch; enemy of nobody, friend to many, father to just the one lad. Cormac tried to push thoughts of what fate had befallen his pa from his mind, but the flames of a burning village were all consuming. Cormac's pals and neighbours: Aidan, Eithne and Erin, and the other young'uns. Brother Benedict, the monk. Jarl Frida and her carls. *How can any of them survive this?*

Cormac let go of the rocks, helpless and hopeless, tears lost within the saltwater that coated his shivering body. He crawled forwards in the sluicing waters of the tide, took hold of a barnacle-covered leg of the shipwright's boathouse. It seemed Blair's shed was one of the few buildings that had been spared so far. That figured, what with it already being a ruin.

Cormac looked back along the beach towards the murder and mayhem. The Vikings were already dragging the spoils of their raid back to their beached longship, a handful of villagers screaming as they were hauled through the tide to the waiting vessel. He had heard of these warships – *drakkars*, the Vikings called them – but had prayed he would never see one. By the light of the burning buildings, Cormac could pick out the details of the ship's prow, a roaring dragon head, tongue rolling over a maw of dagger-like teeth. Its enormous square sail hung loose, clapping as the wind raced across its surface. The cloth was black as the night itself, as was the timber from which the vessel had been fashioned. The fog continued to churn, smoking around the ship's hull, as if the boat had rolled into the harbour on a sea of dragon breath.

Wait it out here. Wait for them to leave, figured Cormac. *But then what?* He could climb the cliffs once more in search of Hilde, who he prayed had survived the melee before the burning God Tree. The image of his friend was burnt into his mind, lying beside Mikko the Silent, the pair covered in blood. Whose it was, Cormac didn't know.

Hands were suddenly upon him as he was seized from behind, grips like iron, fingers digging into his shoulders like knives. Before he could react, Cormac was thrust face-first into the boathouse stilt, his head pressed against the rough and rotten timber. He spluttered, trying to speak, scream, cry out, but he got a mouthful of briny and splinters for his troubles.

"Got some stones on you, young pup, but you bit off more than you could chew this night."

The voice in his ear was unmistakably that of Frostmark.

Cormac was turned about violently, the Viking smashing him against the timber leg of the boathouse once more. In the half-light, Cormac got a good look at his foe, Frostmark somehow defying death's dark embrace. The remains of Mikko's spear were still skewered through the Viking's torso, the back of the shaft now broken after he'd been dashed against the cliff face. The bones of his left forearm had broken and burst from the skin, standing proud of the ruined flesh and muscle like snapped cornstalks. And lastly, his face; lost in shadow, but for his one remaining eye. *That eye.* It glowed like that of a wolf at night, a sphere of eerie silver light that flickered and danced like a distant lantern.

Frostmark's hands were around Cormac's neck, squeezing tight. The Viking carried him by his throat, wading deeper into the darkness of the shipwright's boathouse, striking the boy against pillar and post as he went. With each blow the timbers of the rickety building groaned. Carpentry tools were dislodged from brackets, saws and hammers splashing into the sluicing waters around man and boy. Cormac squirmed, scratching at Frostmark's face, clawing in desperation but to no avail. Something threatened to pop and crack in the blacksmith's boy's neck – his windpipe?

As Cormac's vision lurched in and out of focus, sheet blackness interspersed by stars, he caught a movement behind Frostmark. Another figure had landed in the water behind them, having peeled away from the shadows in the boathouse above, wearing nought but a pair of filthy old britches: *Blair*.

The shipwright suddenly grabbed the splintered shaft of Mikko's spear, yanking the Viking away like a fish on a line and sending the raider careening into another leg of the boathouse with a juddering slam. The boathouse shuddered once more with the impact, more tools and timbers showering the melee from above. Frostmark lurched back towards him, all sense for self-preservation seemingly lost. Blair went with an old-fashioned punch, his big fist hitting the Viking's face dead-centre with a pulping hammer blow. The raider tumbled away in a rage, the water frothing red around him as he collided with a stilt, splintering it. Cormac made to move, away from both men, only for Blair to reach back and place a restraining hand upon his chest, gentle but firm.

"Stay," said the shipwright, his voice a dry rasp as he frantically fished around in the water for something.

The Viking was already thrashing back towards the old man, snarling as he came, gnashing teeth and spitting curses. Frostmark should have been dead, three or four times over, yet here he came! That one eyeball still shone with a malevolent light, a madness having seemingly overcome the raider. *Bloodlust?* Cormac had heard about such a thing, the fabled *berserkers* of Viking legend. These warriors were the most feared in a warband, driven into a murderous rage when unleashed in battle. It seemed the more they wounded this one, the more terrible and ferocious he became.

Cormac watched as Blair rose from the water to face the onrushing Viking, having retrieved what he was searching for. The rusty carpenter's axe arced out, the heavy head striking one of the boathouse stilts, but not before it had separated Frostmark's head from his shoulders.

So powerful was the blow from the axe upon the stilt, the timber split and buckled. In an instant, the boathouse was collapsing in on itself, floorboards and beams tearing free from their fixtures, crashing into the water around the shipwright and Cormac. With one great, gnarled hand, Blair grabbed the blacksmith's boy by the tunic and gave him a mighty, desperate shove, propelling him out of the collapsing building and to safety.

Cormac rolled in the churning breakers as the boathouse broke apart, crashing in on itself. He watched on in horror as the shack was demolished in a matter of heartbeats, burying the shipwright beneath its ruined, twisted timbers.

Everything was gone and destroyed, his friends and family, his home; there was nothing left. The boy floated with the wreckage on the tide, praying for the frigid water to take all the pain away. Closing his eyes, Cormac waited for death, half expecting the cold fingers of the *Nordsær* to seize him and take him down at any moment.

Only it wasn't death that came for him. Least, not in the form he had hoped for. It was the scowling face of one of the Vikings who appeared beside him in the shallows, snatching the broken boy up and throwing him over a broad shoulder. The giant's left hand was missing, the stump capped by a brass cup, and as he waded through the foam and flotsam he called out Frostmark's name in vain. The world turned as Cormac was carried away to the waiting longship, fires burning before him and the screams of the dying behind him.

CHAPTER ELEVEN
FRIDA

The years were many numbered since Jarl Frida had swung a sword in anger. That woman was a relic and had been left in the past, relegated to a dim and distant memory as Frida sought out a new life, far away from those dark, damned deeds. There were sagas written about Frida Blackheart the shieldmaiden, none of which painted her in a fair light. Hers were songs and tales that no soul would be proud of, exploits that kept her in the company of monsters and madmen. Blackheart was a well-earnt name, for sure.

This night, however, that past had caught up with her.

"With me!" she yelled, striking the wall of her longhouse time and again with her sword, the wattle and daub cracking and crumbling with each frantic blow.

With each swing of the steel, Frida's thoughts returned to her daughter. If Unst was doomed, what fate had befallen Hilde? *Has Mikko managed to protect her?* The old Norseman had sworn his life to his jarl, and her child too. If Hilde lived, that was all that now mattered.

Others began helping her, a handful of merchants and villagers alike coming to Frida's aid. With raiders flooding in, there was no leaving the jarlshof through the entrance, so Frida's guests had to create their own exit from the hall. They used whatever was to hand to break down the rear wall, be it plates and bowls from the feast, cutlery, furniture, even their booted feet and bloodied fists. The jarl stood aside, no longer able to swing her sword for fear of striking one of the desperate souls who gathered around her in close proximity. Instead, she returned her attention to the battle.

The battle that was being fought, and lost.

The air was thick with choking smoke, as trails of fire criss-crossed her once great hall. Bundles of burning thatch fell from the roof, sparks and embers showering the jarl as she strode forwards. Frida stepped over the bodies of the dead and dying as she advanced along the length of the longhouse; women and children and old folk. She might have cried for them, but tears had never come easily for Frida.

Is this my doing? Did I bring this doom upon these people?

The sound of fighting rose a notch now, iron against steel, sword upon shield. Frida could still hear the screams, within the hall and beyond it, over the din of battle and the roaring flames, but they were fewer in number now. Dwindling. She shifted the sword in her grasp. It felt heavy, weightier than she recalled. It was strange and alien in her hand, as if this were the first time she had ever held such a weapon. She could feel her energy being sapped, as if the steel was somehow gorging itself upon her very essence. There was a time when Frida could make a sword sing.

Where is that warrior now?

Two men remained standing against the Vikings, the ground around them littered with their fallen companions. Harald Arneson, Frida's youngest carl, who was just a lad when he had come to Unst with his family. The young man's father lay slumped across the firepit, his body burning, the stench of scorched flesh mixing awfully with that of the roast pig on the spit. Beside Harald stood Rab Erskine, a meat cleaver in one hand and a stool in the other, the small wooden seat acting as a makeshift shield. Sweat streaked the butcher's sooty and bloodstained face as he desperately faced off against the laughing, jeering raiders. Erskine was no warrior, but he fought with the desperate tenacity of a cornered wolf.

"Harald! Erskine!" shouted Frida. "Get back. There's nothing more you can do here."

Both men withdrew from the melee, falling back to flank the jarl. The Vikings were spread out, half a dozen of them, shadows in the smoke, slowly prowling closer. Frida saw the whites of their eyes and teeth through their bloody masks, heard the joy in their laughter at the carnage they had created.

"I won't leave you, chief," said Harald, clutching an axe in one hand and a broken shield in the other. "If it is the will of the Gods that we die here, then it would be an honour to die here with you."

"It's *my* will that you protect those villagers," said Frida, gesturing to the rear of the hall with a nod of the head, her attention still fixed upon the advancing raiders. "Go to them. Try and get them to safety."

Harald nodded and was gone, leaving only Erskine beside Frida. He was a big man, barrel-chested, and though she and the Pict came from different worlds, they had always shared a grudging respect for one another.

Erskine turned and spat in her face.

"You did this, you witch. You brought this horror to my home. I curse you tenfold for what you have delivered upon this island."

With that, he was gone, stumbling after Harald. The Vikings parted before Frida, their leader stepping forward.

"Little late in the day for you to be picking up curses, isn't it?" said Hydyr the Hungry. "He rather missed the boat there, eh?"

Frida jutted her jaw at the black-haired Viking, felt the glob of bloody spittle roll down her cheek.

"He's every right to curse me for what's happened this night."

Hydyr went on his toes, craning his neck to look past Frida, watching after Erskine.

"He's a strong one. Mean streak too. If he could learn to swing an axe as well as he does that cleaver, we might even make a Viking out of him. Perhaps there's a Harrowed Man hiding inside your butcher, eh?"

Frida snorted. "Erskine would sooner die than sail aboard the *Sea Wolf*."

"We'll see about that."

Hydyr paced back and forth, his men behind him, as burning timbers collapsed in on themselves. The jarlshof was now a deathtrap, the fires spreading fast, devouring all in their path. Frida clenched the handle of her sword tight, knuckles popping, palm sweating, as Hydyr twiddled with the ring in his beard.

"Wasn't too keen on you, was he?"

"I guess I must be an acquired taste," said Frida, watching the other Vikings as they slowly fanned out, looking to encircle her.

"Aren't we all?" said Hydyr with a shrug of dismay. "Look, Frida. I'm not here to fight—"

She looked around. "Could've fooled me!"

"For one, I'm here to bring you back into the fold."

Frida shuddered, repulsed by Hydyr's proposition.

"Why in Odin's name would I do that?"

Hydyr wagged a slender finger at her. "There you go again, calling upon the Gods. They deserted us long ago. And worse. You can't have forgot, Frida Blackheart. I was by your side on that red day."

Frida's gaze flitted from side to side, the sword clenched in her fist. A few moments more and she would be surrounded. Small price to pay if it meant that handful of survivors could escape. If her sacrifice bought them time, then it would be worth it.

"You think your friends will fare any better when they break out of this burning midden?" asked Hydyr, as if reading Frida's thoughts. "What's the expression? *Out of the frying pan and into the fire.* There's no way this ends well for them, old friend. My battle-crew are out there waiting, crawling over this cesspit of a village, stripping it for what it's worth."

"We have no wealth here, Hydyr!" shouted Frida, despair and anger getting the better of her. "We're fishermen and farmers! There's no secret hoard of gold on Unst!"

More chuckles from the chieftain of the Harrowed Men. "Who said we were here for gold, my love? There are other riches on this rock which are worth far more to my battle-crew. Isn't that right, my friends?"

A chorus of guttural agreement from the Vikings. Beyond them, in the far corners of the burning hall, shrouded in smoke, Frida saw some of the raiders hunched double over the dead and the injured. She couldn't see what grisly business they were engaged in, but there were muffled cries and wet, ripping sounds, sickening noises that sent her mind spiralling and her stomach churning.

"As I said, I'm here for you, Frida Blackheart," said Hydyr, extending a hand of friendship over the flames. "Hiding away on this forsaken island, denying your true calling. You have been missed."

Frida winced. Her own life was forfeit, as it had been since that terrible day, that *red day* of which Hydyr spoke. Whatever awaited her, she knew as sure as night followed day that it wasn't Valhalla.

"But I think you know the other thing I seek, my love," continued Hydyr. "You took it, from Uppsala. And it was *mine*."

A shiver snaked down Jarl Frida's spine, and it took all her nerve not to show it.

"I don't know what you mean," she lied.

"Guess we'll have to jog your memory then."

The Vikings closed in. She knew these men, had stood in shield walls with them. Knew their names, their tales, their deeds. All dark and dread. The Harrowed Men.

Jarl Frida lifted her sword.

It was Hydyr's turn to pull a face.

"Weighs heavy, doesn't it? An ungodly burden, not like before, shieldmaiden. You look so very tired. Old, one might say. Do you not wish to have the strength of your youth returned? Be the power you once were?"

Hydyr's eyes sparkled with terrible promise. "I have such a gift to share with you."

Frida lunged to her right, the sword plunging between the axe and shield of the nearest Viking; Lief the Laggard, slow as ever and caught off-guard. It found the man's chest, punching through ring-mail, in and out like a seamstress' needle. Lief's eyes went wide with shock, but Frida was already moving.

The raider to her left had seized the initiative, jumping forwards with his trusty spear. Dagfinn Bearclaw was a big brute but clumsy with it, and the spear found nothing but air. Bearclaw realised the error of his ways just as his throat was opened by a slash from Frida's sword, a claret bib showering his heaving chest.

As quick as that, in a couple of heartbeats, two of her foes were cut down, and she was springing over the firepit to her next enemy when the first arrow hit her. It caught her in the hip, knocking Frida off balance and sending her tripping over the corpse of one of her carls. She steadied herself, tried to turn the misstep into an attack opportunity, only for a second arrow to strike her. This one came from behind, a bowman having manoeuvred through the shadowy depths of the longhouse until he'd found a vantage point. Frida felt the arrowhead emerge from the front of her right shoulder; the iron head was there, beneath her jaw, in her eyeline, caught in the thick fur trim of her cloak.

Is this my end at last?

It was a sword that struck her next, striking hard across her back, sending the jarl to her knees. A seax followed, one of her former companions darting in, finding a gap in her ribs where his long knife could find a home. She heard Hydyr's voice barking out commands over the noise of the fire and the collapsing of timbers.

"Turn this hovel over. Search her bedchamber. If it's here, she will have kept it close. She's no fool."

Frida rolled over, coughing blood, looked up as the Vikings drew back, letting their chieftain come to the fore. He loomed over her, face hidden in darkness but for the chill, eerie glow of his eyes.

"Frida Blackheart," said Hydyr the Hungry with a weary, disappointed shake of the head. "Why do you always have to make things so difficult?"

His kick came out of nowhere, as did the darkness that accompanied it.

CHAPTER TWELVE
HILDE

It was a hungry gull that yanked Hilde free of her nightmares, in the most painful and frightening fashion. She felt the bird's jagged beak peck her bloodied brow, striking skull as it fished around the open wound for a morsel of meat. Hilde cursed loudly, tried to bat the gull away, but it was a game old bird. It squawked angrily, flapping its broad grey wings as it hopped on her chest from one foot to another, not prepared to ditch its meal just yet. Hilde raised a hand to shield her face, only for the gull to stab her palm, its beak as sharp as any knife. It took the arrival of a second bird to send the gull on its way, Siv swooping in to collide with the assailant with a frantic beating of black feathers, the raven's taloned feet raking the other's throat. Then it was gone, swooping away from the clifftop to where grislier pickings lay in the cold light of dawn.

Hilde turned her head, saw the body of Mikko the Silent beside her, laying where he had fallen. Her clearest memory of the aftermath to the fight with the Viking was holding onto the slain huscarl, as the cold and shock slowly overwhelmed her. She remained numb now, struggling to comprehend the night's events. Beyond Mikko's corpse, the God Tree had been reduced to a pile of smoking ash, the slate-grey sky and miserable drizzle only making a grim day that bit grimmer.

Siv's feet worked upon Hilde's bruised breastbone, the raven demanding the girl's immediate attention. Hilde brought her face back front, looked up at the nightbird's beady black eye. Siv's chest heaved, followed by her gullet, before she retched up the contents of her stomach onto Hilde's face.

The jarl's daughter instantly tried to wipe the bird vomit away, only for Siv to rap her knuckles with her shiny beak.

"Stop protesting, child," squawked the bird.

"What is it?" asked Hilde, inspecting the gloop on her fingertips. She gave it a sniff, turned up her nose. "Smells sweet, spicy.'

"Tis a poultice of yarrow and lady's mantle," said Siv. "Should help the wound start to heal, though I fear you'll yet need stitches."

Hilde winced but let Siv work, the raven's touch surprisingly delicate as she gently packed the gash with the mixture of herbs. The girl attempted to glance over at Mikko once more, only for the bird's talons to grip her chest.

"Keep still," said Siv. "You, I can help, but there's nought to be done for Mikko. Let us pray a warm welcome awaited him in Valhalla."

Overhead, gulls circled, drawn to the huscarl's body. These were opportunistic scavengers, carrion feeders, and Hilde knew fine well that they had their collective eye on Mikko's corpse. Poor Mikko; the old warrior had surrendered his life defending Hilde's. The girl's heart was broken, her only solace being that one day she would meet her old mentor again in the feast hall of Valhalla. Hilde sniffed back a tear.

Judging by the death and destruction that had been visited upon Unst, that time might be right soon.

"We need to take care of his body," said Hilde as Siv hopped clear, her work done.

The raven fluttered over to the cliff edge as Hilde followed on unsteady feet, unable to look away from her old guardian. The gothi's ceremonial sword still lay upon Mikko's chest. Hilde bent and picked up the blade, wondering if the priest had survived the night.

"A pyre for the dead is the right thing to do."

"It would need to be a big pyre," said Siv as Hilde turned her attention to the ruins of Unst.

Of the drakkar, there was no sign. Hilde leant out from the clifftop, looked down to the rocks below, expecting to see poor Cormac's body, dashed and mangled on the rocks, tugged by the tide. Brave, bold Cormac; her closest friend, the one person Hilde trusted above all others. The one who made her heart tremble, could her reduce her to fits of hysterics and caused her pulse to quicken when she was with him. Foolish though it was, Hilde hoped fate had been kind to Cormac. Perhaps he had survived the fall. Perhaps he had been taken by the Vikings. Perhaps he lived.

Perhaps.

The village had been reduced to rubble and charred timbers; nothing had escaped the Vikings' axes and torches. The jarlshof was a smoking shell, the wattle, daub and thatch all gone, a blackened husk all that had remained of the hall of Jarl Frida. Hilde's heart panged with the realisation of her mother's fate. The shieldmaiden; *she would have been in the building, defending it, defending* her people, *against the invaders, wouldn't she?* Jarl Frida's carls would have done everything in their power to protect the people of Unst.

But it had all been to no avail.

"You need to leave Unst," said Siv, poking Hilde's heel by way of warning. "Find people, any people. Get away from this cursed island."

"But it's my home."

"Not any more," said the bird.

Siv scurried clear, out from under Hilde's feet, as the girl stumbled towards the path that descended the cliffs. Her steps were staggered and clumsy, her ankles buckling, knees failing as she grabbed the gorse bushes for support, to stop from tumbling off the trail. The waves still crashed below, relentless, oblivious to the horrors that had played out upon the island. The remains of the shipwright's boathouse bobbed on the tide, washed in and out, the timbers clattering as they jostled one another.

Arriving at the gothi's hut, Hilde stopped short of the entrance, hoping her voice would carry beyond the deerskin door.

"Gothi?"

"He'll be dead, child," said Siv, scratting at the earth outside the hut. "They all are."

Hilde shot the bird a filthy look. Summoning her courage, she drew the animal hide curtain back, her eyes adjusting slowly to the gloom.

There had clearly been a melee, the contents of the single-chambered hut in disarray. Portions of the simple structure had been broken from within, daylight filtering through the splintered wooden walls. The various bird and mammal remains, such as skulls, bones and feathers that had decorated the gothi's hut, now littered the floor, transforming the holy man's home into a bestial lair. Most shocking of all was the sight of the gothi's corpse, sprawled against his overturned cot. His hands were pressed together as if in prayer around the white-chalked flesh of his chest, the lattice of fingers holding a dark glistening wound closed. This had been the handiwork of the Viking, Frostmark.

A rasping moan emerged from the gothi's bony, butchered chest. It was so sudden and unexpected that Hilde almost stumbled through the battered wall of the hut. The man's bloody and cracked lips trembled as he struggled to make the word.

"... *Draugr.*"

Hilde called Siv before dropping to her knees beside the gothi. The bird slipped warily under the ragged curtain and skipped closer. The gothi was motionless, just as before, a corpse to all intents and purposes.

"He's alive," said Hilde.

"He doesn't *look* alive."

"He just spoke."

"What did he say?"

"One word: *draugr.*"

For a ponderous moment Siv didn't move. The raven was a statue.

"What's a draugr?" asked the girl.

That jolted Siv back to life. "The gothi is delirious, child."

Hilde reached out, placed a hand over the gothi's knitted fists that were still pressed against the awful deep chest wound. His knuckles and fingers were cold as ice, as was the blood that coated them. *Has he held his hands, clenched together, over his breast all night? Keeping himself alive?*

"Can you help him, Siv? Like you helped me?"

Hilde turned to the raven who wouldn't meet her eye. No amount of yarrow would save the gothi now, and girl and bird both knew it. It was a miracle the holy man had survived this long.

"Neither living . . . nor dead . . ." said the gothi, his voice weak, teeth chattering with the effort.

The gothi coughed, spluttered. His fingers were separating, his strength abandoning him at long last. Hilde dropped the sword, clasped both of her hands around his, held them together over the mortal wound, willed him to keep death at bay.

"Stay with me, gothi. Please. I don't understand any of this!"

The holy man's head dropped forwards, his words slurring. His voice was quiet, just a rasp.

"Danger . . . shieldmaiden. The red tide . . . comes for you . . ."

The gothi's hands went limp, falling away from the hole in his chest. Try as she might, Hilde could no longer hold them in place, lips curling with anger as she tried in vain to hold death back. But it was no use. The holy man was gone.

Hilde turned and regarded Siv. The raven hopped and squawked when she saw the look of murderous intent upon the girl's face. Hilde's fingers closed around the handle of the ceremonial seax once more. She raised the elegant long knife, looking upon it with fresh and admiring eyes, turning it this way and that before wiping the streaks of blood from it.

"I intended to return it to the gothi," Hilde said, considering the seax. "That would be the right thing to do, wouldn't it?"

The precious metal within the steel glimmered, flashing along the length of the seax, momentarily bringing the blade to life in Hilde's hand.

"It belonged to your mother, once," said Siv, as if reading the girl's mind. "The gothi was only ever its custodian, should Jarl Frida ever want it back. By rights, that long knife belongs to you, child. A great prize to any man, that seax, only to the gothi it was especially significant."

Hilde shot a questioning glance at the nightbird.

"The *blót* offering is an important sacrifice," continued Siv reverentially. "Such a blood ritual warrants the kiss of a special blade. You use silver, the Gods might just answer your prayers..."

Rising from her crouch, Hilde shoved the seax into her belt and yanked the tattered curtain to one side.

"Are we leaving?" asked Siv, following to heel like a faithful hound.

Hilde was back outside, facing the elements, the cold drizzle spattering her face as she set off down the winding trail with new strength and purpose. Siv flapped after her, jumping from one rocky outcropping to the next as Hilde traversed the cliffs.

"Don't go down there," warned the raven. "You won't like what you find!"

Hilde had heard enough, shooing the bird away. Siv swooped off, screeching as she went, leaving the jarl's daughter to descend the path with only dark thoughts for company. With every step, she was left wondering what barbaric fate had befallen her mother. Hilde was no fool; she knew what Vikings were capable of.

Bodies littered the length of the muddy lane that ran through the settlement, each already covered in bickering gulls. Hilde spied the charred remains of those who had burnt alive in their homes and farmsteads. They were the lucky ones. It was those who had died in the street, by sword, axe and worse, that brought her legs to buckling, the nausea overwhelming. They hadn't just been cut down but slaughtered in the most horrifying manner. If Hilde didn't know better, there appeared to be *bite marks* taken out of them, limbs missing, torn or chewed away. What kind of beasts had the Vikings brought with them to Unst, that could do such unimaginable things? Hilde had *known* these poor people, seen them every day, grown up alongside them. And now they were gone, butchered like pigs, snuffed out like candlewicks.

Will I find similar in the jarlshof? Jarl Frida had been a mighty warrior in her youth. *Was my mother able to hold her own against the monsters?*

A handful of bodies lay in the ashes of the longhouse. Hilde paced across the scorched earth, but there was no sign of Jarl Frida. In fact, there were fewer bodies than she was expecting to find. Most surprising was the fact that she couldn't find the corpses of any Vikings in the devastation.

There was a clap of wings as Siv landed on Jarl Frida's toppled and burnt throne.

"Not a single Viking amongst the dead," said the raven.

"Quite the magic trick, you reading my thoughts," said Hilde as she approached the fallen chair, its once-polished timber legs now reduced to hunks of charcoal.

"There's no magic to it," said Siv. "I'm just observant. A blind raven is about as much use as a one-legged man in an arse-kicking contest."

Hilde snorted. She might have laughed at the bird's wit another time, but not today. She reached down, grabbed a burnt leg of the throne and heaved, turning the crumbling seat over. By some miracle, the object of Hilde's childhood fascination had survived. She bent down, tugging it loose from the back of her mother's seat. The leather bindings were blistered and tarnished, but it had remained intact. Hilde slid her arm through the straps and straightened. The weight felt good.

"Shieldmaiden," said Siv, impressed but also fearful.

Hilde marched back through the ruined hall, out over what had once been the threshold, guarded by her mother's most loyal carls. All dead. All gone. For a moment she thought she saw Jarl Frida's body in the mud and blood beyond the longhouse, only to realise it was just her mother's wolfskin cloak. Hilde crouched, ran her hands through the grey fur. She lifted it, buried her face in it, breathed in a great lungful of air. That was Jarl Frida she could smell. Hilde turned it over, inspected it. The wolfskin was bloodied, where blades had found their way through the cloak.

My mother fought.

Hilde let her fingers play over the churned-up mud, inspected the countless trails leading off down to the beach. The tracks told their tale; the booted feet of Vikings, the heels of prisoners dragged to the waiting longboat. Siv landed on Hilde's shoulder.

"Does she live?" asked the raven, once more giving voice to Hilde's thoughts.

Hilde was about to ask the bird which way the Vikings might have headed, when she saw a figure walking up the lane towards them. She hefted the shield, which suddenly felt heavier than a plough, and drew the silver seax from her belt. As the figure drew closer, she recognised the man. He was a bedraggled and filthy mess, all scarred skin and buckled bone, naked but for a pair of weathered leather britches. His scraggly, matted beard matched the tangle of grey hair upon his head, but it was the shipwright all right. He carried a bucket with a rope handle in one hand, its wooden lid clattering with each step, as if whatever was inside was trying to break out.

Blair came to a halt before the jarl's daughter and placed the lidded bucket upon the mud between them. His rheumy red eyes regarded the raven briefly, before settling upon Hilde. The gaze of the shipwright, this shambling shell of a man, was one that put a grip on her heart. There was a menace about him.

A sound emanated from the bucket, not unlike a low murmur.

"What's in there?" asked Hilde.

And Blair reached down and lifted the lid.

CHAPTER THIRTEEN
CORMAC

For a lad who had spent his entire life in a fishing village, Cormac had never got used to the sea. The blacksmith's boy and boats were an awfully ill fit. The rocking motion, the tilting horizon, the groan of the timbers; even on the calmest of days they would all combine to leave Cormac's stomach in knots. On a stormy day such as this, where the waves struck the prow of the *drakkar*, sending it pitching up and down, the contents of Cormac's belly made an explosive reappearance. The intermittent showers of sea spray washed much of it from the lad's face and body, but the taste of bile and vomit remained lodged in his throat. It was his worst nightmare. Or rather, he had always imagined it to be his worst nightmare. All that had changed last night though, as Cormac got a full appreciation of what horrors the world could throw his way.

A woman sobbed nearby, but she wasn't alone; there were plenty of fearful murmurs rippling around the deck of the longship. Cormac was sat between a pair of rowing benches, knees drawn up tight beneath his chin, his hands bound together by rope. This thick length of hemp connected him to more poor souls who had been captured in the raid upon Unst. Brother Benedict sat to Cormac's left, gripping his simple crucifix in white-knuckled fists. Breathless prayers fluttered from his mouth, his lips repeatedly brushing the cross in hope, seeking divine intervention.

"*Domine, protege me,*" whispered the monk. "*Domine, defende me.*"

To Cormac's right, slumped against the hull of the longship, was a portly trader from Alba. The merchant had been at the jarl's feast, where he had appeared jovial and rather drunk. The gold chain he had worn was now missing, as were the rings that had decorated his pudgy fingers. One of those digits was now absent, a bloody stump all that remained after one of those precious pieces of jewellery had been removed from his hand. His face was white, shock still gripping him after the events of the previous night. Beside the trader sat Rab Erskine. His hands may have been bound at the wrists, but that wasn't stopping the butcher from surreptitiously picking away at the rowing bench in front of him, his fingernails digging into the rough wooden seat. Erskine's eyes met Cormac's briefly; they were hard and emotionless, passing over him before scouring the longship for the approach of their captors.

Beyond the rowing bench, the woman's sobbing hitched up a notch.

"Someone tell her to quit her mewling," said Erskine, his voice low but loud enough to be heard by the other prisoners in their small group.

"She's scared," said another woman, her voice disembodied, her location unplaceable across the lurching deck. A queer mist hung over the longship, and had been there since dawn, blotting out the sun as the vessel pitched upon the waves. The fog put Cormac in mind of a mourner's shroud, only adding to the unshakeable sense of dread that hounded them, haunted them.

"We're all scared," said the butcher gruffly.

"Where's the harm in letting her cry?" said the woman, still comforting the grieving mother.

Cormac watched Erskine grit his teeth, the whiskers on his chin bristling as he battled with his temper.

"The more she weeps and wails, the more chance there is that these godless Vikings come cast their eye over us."

"She lost her bairn in the raid," added the woman. "Show some humanity and leave her be."

Erskine stopped picking at the rowing bench. He twisted where he sat, his face a grimace as he talked over his shoulder, leaving any niceties out of his words.

"We all lost somebody back there. I lost my son."

He paused to glower at Brother Benedict, who avoided the butcher's eye contact.

"You got anything to say about him being in a better place now, holy man? Didn't think so."

Erskine squinted as he looked along the length of the longship. Cormac followed his gaze, difficult though it was to see through the strange fog that swamped the boat and surrounding seas. After the attack on Unst, the drakkar had taken straight back to sea, cutting a path east across the waves, its crew focused on chasing the *Nordsær* winds. That industry had dropped a notch during daylight, a skeleton crew working the deck and sail, keeping it moving while their sword-brothers and shieldmaidens rested. Cormac could just about discern the indistinct outlines of slumbering raiders, many of whom had found places around the ship to lay their heads. They hunkered down beneath cloaks and skins, seemingly exhausted by the bloodshed and butchery of the night before. Not all of them that rested slept, though. Shadows shifted in the front of the longship, where a small group of Vikings were huddled together. Cormac heard a strained, gurgling cry followed by the wet and hungry sounds of feasting.

"Trust me," said Erskine grimly, returning to his labour, scratching at the timber seat. "Last thing we want is them coming over here. Now shut her up."

The weeping woman's cries lessened, as her companion urged her to quieten down. On cue, one of the Vikings materialised through the mist, slouching down the deck from the prow. As he passed by Cormac and Erskine, he glanced their way, his lips and jaws glistening wet and dark.

Cormac had already guessed where the drakkar was bound: Norðvegr, home of the Norsemen. By the dim sunlight that had found its way through the blanket of fog throughout the day, he could surmise that they were sailing east, away from his home and the Hjaltland Isles. He had expected to see the deck littered with the spoils of their raids, battle chests brimmed to overflowing with stolen artefacts from Alba and its neighbouring lands, but that wasn't the case, and it got the boy to thinking. Perhaps it wasn't gold the Harrowed Men had come to Unst in search of. Perhaps it was something else.

Cormac was left staring at Erskine, whilst beside him Brother Benedict continued his incantation.

"Domine, protege me. Domine, defende me."

Cormac found Brother Benedict's prayer reassuring and wondered if the butcher might need some words of comfort too.

"You know, he might not be dead."

Erskine stopped what he was doing and looked over, as if surprised the boy could speak. Cormac could see the man's fingertips were bloody from where he had been picking at the bench.

"Say what?"

"Aidan," said Cormac. "He might be alive. I saw him, last night. Before the attack."

The butcher sniffed, turned his attention back to the rowing bench.

"He's dead. Feel it in my bones. Nobody escaped the sacking of Unst, but for them that have been taken as slaves. Trust me, boy; death would be a kindness compared to the fate these Vikings have in store for us."

Cormac shook his head. "I'm just saying—"

"Saying what?" snapped Erskine. "That my feckless, idiot son somehow found the smarts to outwit a Viking war-band? The lad got beaten senseless by the jarl's wee whelp; what chance do you think he had against a raider? Pull your head out of your arse, young Tulloch, and give it a shake. My halfwit son is dead."

The butcher took a breath, fixed his eye on the boy. "Dead as your old man."

It was a knife to Cormac's heart. Jabbed in deep and twisted. His mouth was dry suddenly, lips cracking as he struggled for the words.

"You're lying," he managed to say. "Lying, just to shut me up."

"It's the truth," said Erskine, raising his bound hands to point a dirty, bloody fingertip at his eyeball. "Saw it with these here eyes, boy."

Cormac dragged his gaze away from the butcher, wishing the crashing waves of the *Nordsær* might drown out Erskine's awful words, but he wasn't done talking.

"Cut Hamish down in the street, they did, as we tried to run. Didn't go down easy, mind. Had some fight in him. Took an axe to the back before they stuck him with a spear. He suffered, did the blacksmith."

Cormac squeezed his eyes shut. Still, Erskine's voice cut through.

"That's when I decided the battle was lost. I stood beside Jarl Frida and her carls; I did my bit. I fought those Viking dogs as hard as the next man, but when those next men fall – and fall *hard* – it's time to call it a day. Hell, if Hamish Tulloch gets himself stuck like a wild boar, what would they do to me? And so, the blacksmith's dead, and the butcher lives to see another day. Least for a while, anyway..."

Cormac stifled a sob of his own, decided he would save that for a time when he was safe, if it ever came. If Hamish Tulloch was indeed dead, those tears would have to wait. If Cormac was to live through this, he would have to be strong. He clenched his jaw and was left wondering why Erskine would behave this way. *How can he be so cruel?* Then Cormac remembered the man in Unst. He recalled the beatings Aidan would receive, the cuts and bruises that would regularly appear upon his friend's face. Sure, Hilde had given Aidan a thrashing only yesterday, one that he probably deserved, but it was nothing compared to the beatings his father handed down to him. No, Erskine might have been a Pict, but the similarities between the butcher and the blacksmith's boy ended there.

Beside Cormac, Brother Benedict's chant continued, over and over, as if his prayers might somehow banish all the horrors that had befallen them. Cormac stared at the mast, where the black sail was rolled up and lashed to the yardarm, as it had been for the entire day. How many Vikings made up the crew of the drakkar? Did more of Cormac's friends and neighbours live, bound and beaten across the decks of the pitching ship?

"Domine, protege me. Domine, defende me."

"What's he saying?"

Cormac looked up and saw a figure leaning against the mast, staring straight at him from beneath the heavy cowl of a great long cloak that kept his entire body shrouded in shadow. Beneath the thick robe, the man wore a suit of leather, the breastplate of which was studded with bolts of iron. His black beard was tied beneath his chin by a single golden ring, and although he had never seen one in the wild, his bright white smile put Cormac in mind of the snarling teeth of a wolf. He recognised the man too, had seen him in the jarlshof at the feast, just before the world had gone to hell. He had to be their leader – their jarl.

"You'll get no sense from him," said Erskine, shifting where he sat, his tattered fingers no longer picking at the seat.

"It's gibberish. The monk speaks in tongues."

"A holy man, eh?" said the Viking, dropping down to straddle the rowing bench Erskine leant against.

He spoke quietly, as if he were nursing a sore head. The jarl's movements were slow, laboured and considered, as if he wasn't at his best. Furthermore, Cormac couldn't help but notice the Viking was avoiding the light where possible. It all put the lad in mind of his father after he'd had a night on the ale. Hamish Tulloch, God protect his soul, was always tender the morning after.

The jarl nodded respectfully at the butcher.

"Saw you fight on Unst. Got some steel in that arm, Pict. If I didn't know better, I'd swear there was some Viking blood hiding in you somewhere."

Erskine smiled before spitting at the Viking, the phlegmy glob hitting the man's cheek and rolling into the whiskers of that jet-black beard. The Norseman chuckled and, raising a thumb within his cowl, gave it a slow wipe and flick.

"It's Latin," said Cormac.

"Come again, lad?" said the Viking, standing once more.

"The words are Latin," repeated Cormac. "They're prayers. He seeks protection from God."

Blackbeard nodded, impressed. "You speak the language of the Christ-god?"

"A little," said Cormac, which was no lie. Say that for Cormac Tulloch; he had an ear for different tongues. "I pick things up quickly."

"Like a thief, only with words. Cunning little Pict, aren't you?"

The Viking winked and Cormac blushed.

"They call me Hydyr the Hungry. What name do you go by, lad?"

"Cormac Tulloch."

Hydyr balled his fist and punched his breast slowly.

"Good to meet you, Cormac the Cunning."

Then the man was strolling away on the pitching deck, returning to the stern, the weird mist following him. Cormac felt a shiver run down his spine as he thought on the encounter.

Is Hydyr impressed with me? Or mocking me?

Erskine's chuckles made his head snap back round towards the butcher.

"What's so funny?" asked the boy.

"You just stuck your head in the wolf's jaws," said the butcher, returning his attention to the wooden bench. "This doesn't end well for you, *Cormac the Cunning*."

Now that's *mocking,* thought Cormac. He leant against Brother Benedict, let his head fall against the shoulder of the monk's thick, damp habit. The mumbled prayers continued, but Cormac got the distinct feeling that if there was a God up there, they were falling upon deaf ears. Added to that, the woman had started sobbing once more. And Cormac felt like joining her.

CHAPTER FOURTEEN
HILDE

"This has to be some kind of trick," said Hilde, staring in horror at the contents of the bucket.

The severed head of Finn Frostmark, the Viking with whom she, Cormac and Mikko the Silent had tussled and fought the previous night, sat nestled within the wooden pail. A dirty rag had been shoved into his mouth, the frayed ends tied off behind the back of the head. Frostmark's single good eye watched them, swivelling in its grubby socket, blinking, while the Viking's nostrils flared with fury. All the while, a guttural growl emanated from the raider's throat; no mean feat considering the vocal cords were essentially attached to nothing. And there really wasn't a throat to speak of.

"No trick," said Siv, pecking the top of Frostmark's head with that shiny black beak. "Draugr."

"There's that word again," said Hilde, as Blair watched on impassively. "*Draugr:* what does it mean?"

Frostmark's filthy teeth chewed on his gag while his solitary eyeball turned this way and that, fixing his captors with a vengeful glare. A gaggle of gulls had gathered nearby, showing a great deal of interest in the contents of the bucket, always on the lookout for their next meal.

"It's like the gothi said," replied the raven. "The draugr are neither living, nor dead. They are caught between worlds, cursed to never enter Valhalla and feast in the hall of the fallen. They will never know glory in death."

Hilde dropped the shield and seax and crouched, buttocks resting on her heels. As she craned closer to inspect the head, she saw Blair's hands twitching. The shipwright was clearly anxious, and wary of what the head might do to her.

"Did you do this?"

His shrug was an admission of guilt.

"I've seen some queer things in my life, lassie, like talking ravens, but never seen anything like this." Blair gave the bucket a kick, which set Frostmark to growling again. "That's some dark magic right there."

"How does a man survive such a thing?" said Hilde, as much to herself as the others, her mind battered. "His head cleaved from his neck, and he still spits and snarls? Who cursed him? Why was he damned?"

Siv jumped onto the bucket rim, giving Frostmark's scalp a belligerent peck.

"Why don't you ask him?"

Hilde didn't need telling twice. She reached into the bucket, fingers feeling round the back of the Viking's head.

"Careful, lass," said Blair warily.

She tugged the knot loose and whipped the cloth away, leaving Frostmark spluttering and coughing within his small, circular wooden cell. When he was done spitting, he looked up at them, lip curling with derision.

"Why, you filthy, motherless scum—"

As quick as a blink of the Viking's sickly eye the gag was back on, yanked tighter than before. Hilde tied the knot off, rocked back onto her heels.

"This can go one of three ways, Frostmark," she said, slapping the bald head of the undead raider. "You play nice and answer our questions, then we play nice. You get nasty, and the gag goes back in your miserable mouth. And if you say anything that *really* upsets me – and we all know you could – well, you get hoyed into the sea. Let the fish eat what's left of you. I don't give a rat's stinky arse."

She grabbed him by the ears and lifted his head from the bucket, brought it close to her so they were almost touching noses.

"So, what's it gonna be?" asked Hilde. "Blink once if you're going to play nice."

Frostmark's lonely eyelid descended slowly, before rising back into place. Hilde managed a surly smile, though in truth she was utterly repulsed, and it was taking every nerve she had left not to vomit.

"Good. That wasn't too difficult, was it?"

Hilde flipped the bucket over and stood the draugr's head on its upturned base. The torn flesh of his neck stuck to the wood like the foot of a snail, holding it in place. As Hilde once again removed the gag, she felt Blair's eyes upon her, watching her every move, tension emanating from his ragged frame. The nearby gulls hopped about excitedly at the sight of the severed head, recognising an easy meal when they saw one.

"Let's start again," said Hilde.

Frostmark squinted and hissed at the sky, which remained choked with storm clouds, the rain a constant miserable drizzle.

"Aye," said the draugr, "but get the big fella to stand in front of the sun, would you. Don't like the feel of it. Hurts, it does."

Blair looked up at the bruised heavens, utterly perplexed. "What sun?"

"Humour him," said Hilde, and the shipwright positioned himself between the draugr and the faint light of day.

"So," said Hilde. "Why did you come to Unst, Finn Frostmark?"

The severed head sniffed, hocking up something nasty and rotten, spitting it into the mud.

"One rock's as good as the next."

"There's no treasure to speak of on Unst," said Hilde. "You should have raided Alba if it was gold you sought. We fish and we farm here. We don't hoard."

"Gold isn't the only treasure that the Harrowed Men covet."

"So, you took our people as slaves?"

A smirk appeared upon Frostmark's scarred and weathered face. "Something like that."

Hilde shuddered and was about to press him further when Blair cut in, rapping the draugr's bald pate with his knuckles.

"The men and women of Unst, them that lie dead in the street, they have been ... *disfigured.* Violated. Throats torn out, limbs ripped off, flesh eaten. Savaged as if by a pack of wild dogs. Does the same fate await those you've enslaved?"

Frostmark blew his cheeks out as if he had nought to do with the horror.

"I've no control over my crew's behaviour. You're right

though, some of them are like bloody wolves."

For a moment, Hilde feared the bile that had risen in her throat might suddenly make way for vomit. This was the confirmation she had feared, that the raiders had fallen upon the wounded and the dead of Unst and begun devouring them. It was all she could do to hold her nerve in front of the grotesque, severed head, whilst Blair continued his questioning. She saw the white of his teeth through his filthy whiskers, as the old carpenter struggled to remain composed. His voice was a whisper when it emerged through his clenched and set jaw, spittle frothing on his furious lips.

"Where have your friends taken our kin?"

It occurred to Hilde that this was the first time she'd ever interacted with the shipwright, let alone heard him speak. His accent was different to that of his fellow islanders. Softer, more like that of a man of Alba.

"Forget about your kin, Pict," said Frostmark with some delight. "They're as good as dead already."

"Not the answer I was seeking, Norseman," said Blair, and kicked the head off the bucket, sending it rolling into the gulls.

The birds took flight momentarily before swooping back down to earth, pecking at Frostmark's helpless head. The draugr's scream was surprisingly high pitched as the gulls nipped at his flesh, tearing strips loose and gulping down morsels.

"For the love of Hastur, get them off me!" he screeched.

Blair trudged over, swinging his boots at the birds, before stooping to pick up the head. His thumb somehow found its way into the empty eye socket as he returned to the girl and the raven, dropping it on its side upon the base of the bucket. As much as the severed head of an undead Viking was able to, Frostmark looked deeply upset.

"Praise Hastur," said the draugr, gasping for air that it didn't need. "That was a rotten trick, Hjaltlander. Sticking your filthy finger in my eye socket crossed a line!"

"I'm no Hjaltlander, devil, and I can do far worse than that," said Blair. "Speak fast, lest we return what's left of you to the birds."

Siv cackled, the raven clearly enjoying the show the shipwright was putting on. This wasn't the man Hilde thought she knew, and truth be told, she was both impressed and afraid. There was something frightening about him, as well as comforting. Hilde had known Blair to be a hermit, had glimpsed sight of him lurking around his boathouse, but she'd dismissed him as being shy and afraid of people. Hilde prided herself on knowing everyone on Unst, from those folk who lived in the village to the crofters who worked the land and tended their sheep, but here was a man who had remained a stranger to all. Hilde couldn't remember a time she'd ever seen him in the jarlshof. Blair was a stranger in his own backyard, a threat to no one. But now, there had been a transformation.

Shy and afraid of people. How wrong had she been?

Blair placed his broad, calloused foot onto the side of Frostmark's head and applied enough pressure that the bucket began to groan. The draugr whimpered, gums splitting, teeth loosening.

"Our loved ones; where have they been taken? Talk, fiend."

"They sail to my homeland!" squealed Frostmark.

Blair's bushy eyebrows plunged into one another, forming an arrowhead of grey whiskers. "Norðvegr?"

"Aye," said Frostmark, surprised by the Pict's use of his native tongue. "Spoken like a Norseman. So, you've heard of Norðvegr?"

"'Tis the land of the Vikings," said Blair with a grimace. "My people call it Norway."

Though there was a talking, severed head lying on the bucket before her, Hilde couldn't take her eyes off Blair. She was finding him increasingly fascinating. The shipwright knew things, not least the tongue of the Vikings. How many more secrets he had kept from his neighbours was yet to be discovered. Mention of Norðvegr had Hilde on her toes now, for it was where her mother hailed from, and Hilde had been taught well.

"Ruled over by our king, Harald Fairhair," said Hilde proudly. "We may be many leagues from Norðvegr, but the Hjaltland and Orkneyar Isles remain part of that great kingdom. My mother has been a loyal servant to the king, ruling in his name, just as her fellow jarls on these islands, Gudrun and Rognvald, do. Why would King Harald permit you to raid us on Unst?"

Siv hopped forwards and pecked the draugr's head.

"Answer her, you wretched ball of rotten flesh!" crowed the raven.

The Viking simply grinned at Hilde, who felt a fresh and foul wave of nausea ripple through her as the realisation dawned on her.

"This had nothing to do with King Harald, did it? You never had his blessing."

Frostmark chuckled, dark blood oozing between his yellow peg teeth.

"No, child. My chieftain, Hydyr the Hungry, serves a greater lord than that fool Fairhair."

Blair picked up the head by the ear, prompting a fresh chorus of yelps from Frostmark, and dropped it back into the bucket. He grabbed the wooden lid and was about to clatter it back into place when Hilde stayed his hand.

"I've one more question for Finn Frostmark," said Hilde.

"Fire away, girlie," said the severed head in the bucket. "I've nowhere to be."

She cleared her throat, afraid to voice the question now, though it had to be asked.

"The rest of Jarl Hydyr's battle-crew, your Harrowed Men. Are they all . . . like you?"

Frostmark's sickly grin was all the answer he needed to give. Blair slammed the lid down on his head.

"There you go, devil," said the shipwright. "No more nasty sun. Enjoy the darkness."

It was suddenly very quiet inside the bucket. Perhaps the head was indeed content now to be back in the tub, away from the daylight.

"What do we do with him?" asked Hilde, eyeing the bucket with deep suspicion. "He's a monster, right?"

"We take him with us," said Blair. "He's more useful to us alive than dead. Or whatever the hell he is. He knows this

Hydyr the Hungry, knows how his chieftain thinks, and a great deal more, I warrant."

The shipwright began to march down the lane, back towards the remains of his home, which choked the far end of the shoreline beneath the cliffs.

"Where are you going?" Hilde called after him.

"Fetch my gear," replied Blair without looking back. "Then we burn our dead, them what the flames spared last night."

"And what then?"

"You tell me," shouted the man. "I'm just a shipwright. You're the jarl's daughter."

Hilde strongly suspected he was teasing her. She held no authority, not any more anyway. And she was pretty sure that Blair was more than *just a shipwright*. Siv stood atop the bucket, squawking at the gulls which were creeping ever closer, wanting another taste of its grisly contents.

"We get a ship?" said Hilde, as much to herself as the raven. "That's what we do. Head to Scatness and beg for Jarl Gudrun's help. We get a ship, and we go after our family."

Saying it out loud made it no less ridiculous. A girl, an old man and a nightbird. Somehow, they were expected to take on a battle-crew of undead Vikings and free their friends and family? Hilde watched the shipwright disappear into the wreckage of his boathouse. She frowned.

"What's the matter, child?" asked Siv, hopping up and perching upon her shoulder.

"Blair said the Vikings took his kin too. I thought he was a loner. Who do you think he meant?"

Hilde might have mulled that question over further had

she not been distracted by a call for help, out beyond the skeletal, blackened remains of the stable block. She was running instantly, heart soaring with hope as she followed the cries.

Others had survived. Others had outwitted the horrors of the Harrowed Men.

"I'm coming!" she shouted, throwing all caution to the wind.

Hilde skidded to a sudden halt, arms flailing, and narrowly avoided falling into the latrine pit. Down below, neck deep in a bog of stinking feculence, was a boy. The whites of his eyes were all that was visible through his mask of faeces, and it wasn't until he spoke that Hilde realised who she was rescuing.

"You got a rope?" asked Aidan Erskine.

For the briefest moment, Hilde considered dropping a load of her own on the butcher's boy.

Then she went to fetch that rope.

CHAPTER FIFTEEN
CORMAC

Though many of the Harrowed Men slept like the dead throughout the day, they came alive at night. Once the sun had slipped below the western horizon, it was as if a spell was cast over the crew, rousing all of them into life. They were suddenly a hive of industry, rushing about the deck of the black drakkar. The strange mist that had shrouded them during the day dissipated with nightfall, the moon banishing all trace of the sickly fog. Most alarming, at least to Cormac, was the fact he couldn't see land, in any direction. The Harrowed Men were done with the Hjaltlands. Silver waves that reflected the moonlight were left in the longship's wake as it continued its passage east into strange waters.

Cormac lay back against the rowing bench, shoulder to shoulder with Brother Benedict, and stared up the mast towards the blackness beyond. Gemstones glittered in the endless heavens, a million treasures scattered across the night sky.

"Have faith, Cormac," whispered Brother Benedict beside him. "We are being tested, just as our Lord Father's son was tested."

"Is he up there now, watching us?"

The monk stared at the void. "God the Father is everywhere, Cormac. He's with us now."

Cormac huffed and sighed, feeling like the butt of a cruel joke. "He's awful quiet."

Brother Benedict smiled, the first time since their terrible ordeal had begun. There was something disturbing about that smile, for the rest of his face didn't match the expression. A sheen of sickly sweat shone upon his skin, whilst his eyes were wide and wet with tears. There was a madness there, like the monk had stepped out of himself and was no longer truly present. It left Cormac unnerved and concerned for the young man.

"There is a purpose to everything, difficult though that can be to see," said the holy man. "All that happens is part of His plan, no matter the pain and hardships our mortal flesh faces. One just needs to have faith."

Cormac gave the young monk a sideways look. He got the distinct feeling that Brother Benedict was talking to himself as much as the blacksmith's boy.

"With respect, I'll put my faith in myself. Your God hasn't done much good for me so far. I only took him into my heart two days ago, and my entire world has turned to crap. Perhaps he isn't the God for me after all."

Brother Benedict's odd behaviour did little to put Cormac at ease. He suspected the monk wanted to lecture him further on the previous day's baptism, and the serious nature of the ceremony. He didn't need to, of course. Cormac knew exactly what the purpose was of the baptism, how the immersion in the tide washed away his original sin, transforming him into a Child of God, symbolic or otherwise.

Cormac spied Rab Erskine in an agitated state, shifting

where he sat and looking about as the Vikings busied themselves across the deck.

"What's the matter?" asked Cormac.

Erskine glowered at him, as if he'd been rumbled doing something terribly secretive and shameful. Then he shuffled a touch closer, bumping into the fat merchant who lay in a fitful sleep between the butcher and the blacksmith's boy. They all remained connected to one another by the same length of rope; butcher, trader, boy and monk.

"We've lost two more," said Erskine once he was in whispered earshot of Cormac. "I counted thirteen of us brought onto this boat when we left Unst, tied to this length of rope. Those two women, the sobbing one and her pal, they've gone now as well. We're down to ten."

Cormac twisted and checked for himself. Sure enough, the two women couldn't be seen.

"My numbers ain't great, but thirteen take two is eleven," said the lad. "That ain't ten."

Erskine's mood didn't lighten any. "I'm counting the poor sod who they did in first. You know; the one they had in the prow?"

Erskine's choice of words made Cormac's empty stomach lurch once more.

"What do you mean, *had*?"

"Come on, boy, you're not blind. Or maybe you're just daft. You heard them doing him in, just like I did. You sure as hell saw one of them walk by with gore dripping off his jaw, because I know I did. Reckon these Viking dogs were hungry when they awoke and needed to break their fast with some fresh meat. Your weeping lassie and her friend must have caught their eye."

Cormac shook his head, though he knew what Erskine said was true. God knows, he had tried not to think about the strangled, gurgling cries they had heard in the day, and the wet ripping noises that had accompanied them, but those sounds still lingered in his ear and in his memory. They tormented him.

"No, you've got to be mistaken. Perhaps they've taken them—"

"Taken them *where*?" exclaimed Erskine, voice louder now. "You think they're being entertained, wined and dined somewhere? We're on a godforsaken boat in the middle of the sea."

Spittle flecked the butcher's ugly, twisting lips. "We're not here as slaves, Tulloch. We're the *larder*."

As utterly unpalatable as the suggestion was, there was no avoiding the ugly truth: those poor souls the Vikings had seized on Unst served no other purpose than being food for the raiders. These weren't slaves to be traded when they arrived home in Norðrvegr; they were fresh provisions for the journey home. *Cannibalism.* It wasn't unheard of. Cormac knew tales of wild men who lived on the frayed edges of the map, hidden in caves on Alba, or marooned on storm-ravaged rocks, who had turned to human flesh in order to survive. But for men and women such as the crew of the *Sea Wolf,* to willingly choose to eat folk, to slaughter and consume innocents like cattle . . . What monsters were they?

Erskine turned back to the seat that he'd worried and

worked at throughout the day, digging those ruined fingertips and broken nails into the wood, twisting them this way and that. Cormac watched as fresh beads of blood ran down Erskine's knuckles. What *was* he doing?

"Spent my whole life handling livestock and chopping up meat," muttered Erskine, gritting his teeth as he pulled hard at the surface of the bench. "Never imagined it'd ever be me on the menu."

He let loose a long, drawn-out sigh of relief as he slowly began to withdraw the object of his obsession from the rowing bench. Cormac watched as it emerged, sliding from the timber like a sword from its scabbard; a thick, iron carpenter's nail, not unlike the kind Hamish Tulloch would fashion in his smithy. It had to be maybe half a foot long, the shank's end coming to a perfect and quite deadly point.

Cormac felt something quite unexpected, as Erskine smiled at him triumphantly: hope.

"It's all change," said Erskine, carefully placing the makeshift blade in his lap before drying his bloody fingertips on his britches. He turned to Cormac, his eyes wide and wild.

"The sooner you get your head around that, boy, the better. Unst is gone. It's in the past. You lost your pa, and I lost my lad. There's no going back to the world that was. It's changed forever. And you need to change with it. If you don't, well . . . you might as well dive overboard now and join Aidan and Hamish with the rest of the dead."

All feelings of optimism were banished in an instant from Cormac's mind as he watched Erskine throw the rope around the neck of the sleeping merchant and yank it tight. The trader, now rudely awakened, let loose a squawk of horror, his own bound wrists pulled up high and over his shoulder. His hands grasped for the butcher, pudgy fingers, including the stump waggling desperately where one had been severed by a Viking, but he couldn't reach Erskine.

"Stop!" screamed Cormac, but the butcher paid him no heed.

Erskine looped the rope around the merchant's neck a second time, the two collapsing into the hull of the longship as they wrestled desperately. Erskine raised a knee and braced it against the small of the man's back, muscles bunching in his arms as he took the strain. The Vikings began to gather, whooping and hollering as they watched the men struggle, taking great delight in the awful spectacle. The rest of the prisoners screamed and panicked, huddling behind or clambering over one another to stay clear of the violence.

Cormac was dragged nearer to the melee by the connecting rope, a stray boot from the merchant catching him across the jaw, sending his head bouncing off the bench. He lay concussed on the pitching deck as the men scrapped with one another. This was no fight. It was an execution. Saltwater sluiced across Cormac's face as the merchant's wheezing gasps were cut short and his struggles gradually ceased. A couple of trembling quivers from his feet, heels rapping on the hull, and then he was still.

The shouting and jeering suddenly subsided as the Vikings looked down at the jumble of bodies between the row benches. Whereas moments ago they had looked like a group of revellers in their cups, they now resembled a pack of wolves, hungry ones at that. As Brother Benedict tried to help a stunned Cormac to his knees, the pair found that the binding rope was caught up around the merchant's dead body.

The largest of the Vikings stepped through the assembled spectators. A big fella with a bloated belly that hung over a straining belt, he only had the one hand, his left arm capped by a brass cup over the wrist stump. A dark tattoo encircled his wobbling throat, appearing to illustrate a serpent swallowing its own tail. Cormac vaguely recognised him; yes, this was the one who had carried him to the ship, calling out for his dead friend, Frostmark.

The Viking pointed at Erskine.

"Cut the big man free. He's earnt himself a trip to the dragonhead."

The crew whooped at this. *The dragonhead.* That was at the prow of the longship, where the grisly deed had taken place during the day, blanketed in fog. It was likely where the two women had met their end. And now it was Erskine's turn. Cormac felt no sympathy for the butcher as he was hauled to his feet, the rope that connected him to the murdered merchant untied. The man was a killer, as bad as the Norsemen, worse to turn on his own people.

"Wait!" said Erskine, warding the Vikings back with open and pleading hands. "You don't understand; he was looking to attack you. Tore a great long nail from the deck. Said he was going to shiv the next one of you came close. There, see!"

Erskine pointed at the deck and the eyes of the Vikings followed. The one-handed man crouched and picked up the iron shank from the boards. He held it between his thick fingers in a surprisingly delicate manner.

"This nail?" he asked.

Erskine nodded excitedly. "I saved your life, pal."

A ripple of laughter passed through the crowd of Vikings.

"You saved *my* life?" said the fat warrior, to which the butcher nodded.

As quick as lightning, the big Viking punched the iron nail, all half-a-foot's length of it, directly into his own breast, likely skewering his own heart. Erskine gasped, whilst many of the onlooking prisoners screamed in horror.

"You saved *this* life?"

Erskine had no answer to that, his lips trembling as he searched in vain for a reply, but it was the one-armed raider who hadn't finished speaking.

"Why would you do that, Pict?" he asked suspiciously.

Erskine nudged the corpse. "He was a fool, would've got us all killed."

"That will likely still happen," said the one-handed man.

"I could be more use to you alive than dead," said Erskine, his voice taking on a pleading tone that made Cormac's skin crawl. The butcher gulped, or at least tried to, nerves threatening to get the better of him. "I have certain . . . *skills* that could be of use to you."

The one-handed man's eyes narrowed as he appraised Erskine. He nodded towards the stern.

"Take this Hjaltlander to the chief. It ain't my call to make.

Let Hydyr the Hungry decide his fate."

A pair of Vikings seized hold of Erskine and sent him stumbling along the centre of the longship, back towards the rear of the drakkar. Two dozen Norsemen remained standing around and above Cormac and Brother Benedict, their gaze fixed upon the merchant that the pair remained bound to. Cormac shivered. Wolves was right. Hell, even their eyes glowed, this pack of predators staring hungrily at the fresh kill at their feet.

"What do we do with him?" asked one of their number, unable to take his eyes off the body.

"Take him to the dragonhead, of course," said the one-handed man. "Waste not, want not."

The Vikings fell upon the body, tearing the merchant loose from his bindings and proceeding towards the prow with their prize. Cormac looked away, embracing Brother Benedict while the familiar, awful sounds of feasting commenced once more. Not even the sobs of the other prisoners could drown out the horror that followed.

To the east, sheet lightning lit the distant night sky as thunder rumbled over the *Nordsær*. Cormac prayed to any God that might listen as the *Sea Wolf* sailed straight and true towards turbulent waters.

CHAPTER SIXTEEN
HILDE

As they climbed the muddy road that rose through Scatness, drizzle dogging their every step, they made for an unusual trio; the old man, the butcher's boy and the girl with the handsome shield.

Blair was much transformed from the man Hilde had encountered in the ruins of Unst. He wore clothes, for a start. Bare feet were now booted, and a battered leather breastplate adorned his torso. A finely made sword sat proud of its scabbard on his left hip. With its bone white handle and bronze pommel and cross-guard, it was wrapped in dirty rags lest it catch the eye of a footpad. Of course, none of this was visible thanks to the fur-trimmed black cloak he wore, drawn tight about himself. Even the handsome shield strapped to his back had been disguised, its embossed leather and bronze boss now hidden behind animal hide. Whilst a cord-bound sack was slung over one shoulder, he carried a simple lidded bucket in his free hand.

Aidan Erskine trudged along, head down, dressed in the oversized clothes recovered from a butchered fisherman. A rope tied about his middle kept the britches from falling down, and though the outfit stank of fish guts it was better than the alternative. Once Hilde had hauled him out of the latrine pit, Aidan couldn't shed his crap-coated gear quick enough. A dook in the sea had cleaned him up good, but Hilde couldn't shake the stench from her mind. That kind of grim business could scar a soul for life. Unsurprisingly, beyond moaning at the texture of his itchy hessian smock, Aidan had very little to say.

Hilde looked every inch the shieldmaiden, only in miniature. Jarl Frida's shield was slung across her back, in much the same fashion as Blair carried his, while the silver seax was tucked snugly through a thick strap of leather on her belt. Again, not ideal for such a fine weapon to be on show, but scabbards were thin on the ground in the wreckage of Unst. Her mother's wolfskin cloak hid the blade from the most intrusive of eyes. The grey fur still held Jarl Frida's scent, and whilst comforting to Hilde it was also a constant reminder of the girl's mission as she strode up the torch-lined street towards the jarlshof of Skatness.

An eerie song rose up from the harbour below where a large Norse ship was moored. Hilde was relieved it wasn't a longship and recognised it for being a merchant *knarr*. *But that melody*. The tune and voice were at once enchanting and disturbing, accompanied by the rattling of chains, and Hilde felt the hairs rise, up and down her arms, goosebumps mottling her flesh. She looked back down the hill towards the knarr, scouring the ship for signs of life. A single, shadowy figure shambling around the stern.

Aidan saw it too.

"What the hell is that?"

Hilde recognised his unease and leapt upon it. "Don't know, but it sounds like it wants to lure a halfwit butchers' boy to his watery doom."

The seed of fear sown in her sparring partner, she turned her attention to Blair.

"How are you doing, old man?" asked Hilde, glancing at her senior companion as they climbed the hill.

"Just dandy, little girl," replied Blair. She could tell by the strain in his voice that this was, in fact, untrue.

"Just holler if you need me to carry anything. Don't want you throwing your back out."

"Don't you worry your pretty little head about me, lassie."

Hilde sniffed.

Pretty.

There was little chance she'd ever be described as that again. She reached a hand up to her brow, where the poultice of yarrow and lady's mantle remained packed into the wound. It had dried now, forming a crust, while fresh blood still pooled beneath the dressing.

"It'll look good that, once it sets in," said Blair.

"Huh?" asked Hilde.

"Your scar. Proper fierce. Like a real shieldmaiden might sport. Any man will think twice before crossing you, mark my words."

"Why would I believe anything you tell me?" she asked, her suspicions about Blair still hanging around like a bad smell.

He sighed and shook his weary head. "Comes to something when a bairn can't believe an old shipwright."

Shipwright.

So long as Hilde lived and breathed, there was no way

Blair was a shipwright, least not originally. There was more to the old man's story than he was letting on, and she'd be damned if she wouldn't get to the bottom of it. Hilde had lived her entire life on Unst, in a village of a hundred or so people, and not once interacted with the hermit. And she couldn't think of a single occasion when he'd ever built a boat.

"Shipwright, my arse," she muttered aloud.

"Whassat?" said Blair.

"Nothing," replied Hilde.

Scatness was the principal settlement on the isle of Meginland, the closest thing the Hjaltlands could consider to a capital. However, it was no city, not like the ones Hilde had heard about in travellers' tales. The population of Scatness was around three times that of Unst, at least before the Harrowed Men had paid Hilde's home a visit. That said, there was little evidence of those numbers this night. The cottages and huts either side of the road appeared empty, shrouded in darkness, doors swinging on hinges as if freshly abandoned. Hilde heard the distant croaking of Siv, harsh but unmistakable, as the raven cried out three times. She knew what that call meant, her mother having taught her the bird's tongue.

Beware.

"You feel it too?" said Blair quietly, stroking his wild nest of whiskers thoughtfully.

Hilde shivered. "Aye. Where is everyone?"

"This place is sick."

Finn Frostmark growled within his bucket, gagged as

he had been since they had questioned him that morning. Hilde eyed the container warily.

"He needs to quit that."

Blair gave the tub a rattle, the head bouncing about within. "Pipe down in there before I feed you to the rats."

It had been a long and traumatic day. The three had burnt the dead first, fashioning a funeral pyre out of whatever timbers had been spared by the Vikings. Hilde had begun the task keeping a tally but soon gave up, the head count spiralling in horrific fashion. By the time they put a torch to the bonfire there had to be fifty bodies on the pile. Many had been desecrated in an unholy fashion; bones broken, flesh torn, throats ripped apart. Once the corpses took the flames, the survivors couldn't get away fast enough, the smell unimaginably awful.

Salvaging a small fishing boat from the harbour, they took to the water, skirting the cliffs as they sailed northwest around Unst before bearing south. Siv circled overhead, scouting their passage, ensuring the way was clear. As for the old man, considering he was supposed to be a shipwright he was next to useless, finding new and exciting methods of getting in the way whilst the two youths handled the vessel together. All the while, Frostmark gnashed and seethed in his bucket, as the rickety boat battled its way through the channels, following Meginland's rugged coastline. When they could face the dangerous currents no more, they found a spot where they could beach the vessel, continuing the rest of their journey on foot.

"When we get to the jarlshof, leave the talking to me,"

said Blair as they approached the imposing longhouse at the head of the settlement.

"Why would I do that?" said Hilde. "Jarl Gudrun was a friend to my mother, I was introduced to her when I was a bairn."

"You're still a bairn."

"I'm no bairn," she replied defiantly, thumping her chest.

Blair cowered briefly as he walked, raising his hands in a mock show of fear.

Idiot.

"I've been here before," insisted Hilde, recalling the beautiful, blue-eyed chieftain. "She knows me. We can use that."

"We don't know what we're walking into, lass. What happened on Unst makes for an incredible story. The kind that folk won't dare to believe, and even if they did it would likely cause a panic. I don't think we should be telling Jarl Gudrun any of that. We're here to get safe passage to Norðvegr, that's all. And I've enough to pay our way for that."

Blair shifted the sack that was across his shoulder, and Hilde heard the metallic grating sound within. What he proposed to buy passage with, she had no idea. Maybe he'd been rooting around through the remains of Hamish Tulloch's smithy and had found a clutch of nails that he could barter. Hilde smiled: *that would've made Cormac laugh.*

As quick as that, the smile was gone. Poor Cormac. The last sighting of her friend was by Blair, just before the boathouse collapsed upon him. As Cormac's body hadn't been recovered in the sacked village, Hilde had to assume he'd been taken by the Harrowed Men, along with her mother. Whether either was alive remained a mystery.

"You said you had family taken in the raid," said Hilde, eyeing the old man suspiciously. "Who, exactly?"

There was no answer forthcoming as they arrived at the entrance to the jarlshof, where a pair of carls awaited them. The corpses of over a dozen crows hung from the rafters around the edge of the thatched longhouse, a sure sign that nightbirds were not welcome in the hall of Jarl Gudrun. Hilde glanced about but saw no sign of Siv. Clearly the message had been received by the raven. Neither of the carls stood to attention, one of them slumped on the wooden steps that led up to the great doors, his head in his hands. His companion slouched against the wattle and daub wall, scratching at his throat as a dog might worry a flea. This Norseman stepped forwards and looked the three visitors up and down. There was something off about the man, least to Hilde's eye; his skin was so drained of colour as to be almost grey.

"What do you want with the jarl?"

"We're here to trade," replied Blair.

He unhitched his sword and left it on the steps, all under the watchful eye of the standing guard.

"I got to leave my sword too?" she asked the men.

The seated carl looked up at last, his bloodshot eyes regarding Hilde with scorn as he brayed like a donkey.

"Nah. Somehow, I don't think Jarl Gudrun's afraid of a bairn."

Hilde felt the colour in her cheeks as Aidan shouldered

past her. Unless she was mistaken, the boy chuckled. She gave Blair a filthy look, the shipwright's eyes twinkling with rare mirth.

"See?" he said. "Bairn."

Passing between the carls, the three entered the hall of Gudrun Rognvaldsdottir.

From Hilde's recollection, it was much changed. Larger than the jarlshof on Unst, it lacked the heart and hospitality of Hilde's home. Jarl Frida's longhouse had been a busy, bustling place, the doors always open to villagers and guests alike. Hilde may indeed have only been a bairn when she last visited Scatness, a half dozen years back, but there had been music, and laughter, and merrymaking. All of that was now gone.

Though her head was dipped, Hilde's eyes were up, as she scoured her surroundings. Say that for Jarl Gudrun's hall; it was warm. Two huge iron braziers stood either side of the doorway, loaded with burning timbers and glowing coals. A fire pit crackled in the centre of the hall, blooms of filthy smoke rising and spreading about the chamber like amorphous black tentacles. Straggling sheafs of hay and straw hung loose up and down the length and breadth of the ceiling, the thick thatch of the jarlshof in sore need of maintenance. It was a miracle the building hadn't sprung a leak. The trestle tables that ran the length of the longhouse were mostly empty, bar dour-looking carls here and there. Some lay upon the detritus-littered floor, passed out through one overindulgence or another, great clumps of fallen thatch providing makeshift cots for them. This granted the interior the feel of a barn, where one might keep livestock; hell, it even had the smell of a stable, foul, sweaty, and stinking. More figures moved through the shadows around the hall's edge, flitting in and out of torchlight as they flanked the visitors. Hilde was under no illusion; all eyes were on the trio from Unst, at least those belonging to them that were conscious.

Behind the chieftain's chair at the head of the hall, a broad wooden staircase rose to a galleried landing in the dark rafters of the roof, likely leading to the private quarters of Jarl Gudrun. Nearing the throne, the visitors found their host already in conversation with a peculiar-looking woman, who was flanked by a grim-looking pair of bodyguards. These men wore leather breastplates and thick woollen cloaks that marked them as men from Alba. Their mistress had to be as tall as Blair but half his age, and her suit was fashioned from some kind of black animal pelt. Upon her head she wore a colourful headscarf that was decorated with golden coins, and on her hip a curved knife in a mother-of-pearl scabbard.

Guess she doesn't pose any threat to Jarl Gudrun either, mused Hilde.

Six fair-haired, pale-skinned youths stood behind this woman, three lads and three lasses, and each of them wore a thrall collar about their throat. Hilde had heard of these. Jarl Frida had received visitors on Unst who would customarily have brought slaves with them, but not in her hall. Her mother avoided the practice, and whilst she hadn't been in the habit of criticising the customs of others, she forbade the wearing of thrall collars in her jarlshof. By the looks of things,

Jarl Gudrun had gone firmly in the other direction.

One of the housecarls stepped forwards to receive the six youths before leading the slaves away up the staircase. As they departed, Hilde recognised the faded remains of black ash and blue woad paint upon their skin, marking them unmistakably as Picts. Hilde heard a brief but low growl emanate from Blair beside her, which he struggled to keep in check.

Jarl Gudrun brought her attention to the visitors from Unst.

As jarls went, Gudrun was young, her age somewhere between that of Hilde and her mother. She hadn't claimed stewardship of Scatness through might, cunning or charisma, but rather had benefitted from her father being Jarl of all the Islands of Hjaltland and Orkneyar. Rognvald Eysteinsson ruled over these far-flung rocks in the *Nordsær*, charged with protecting the islands in the name of King Harald Fairhair. Frida had sworn fealty to Jarl Rognvald. Gudrun had done the same and acted as her father's proxy.

"What business do you have in my hall?" she said at last.

"We come seeking passage to Norðvegr, Jarl Gudrun," said Blair, clumsily saluting her with a fist to his chest, as was the Norse way. "I was told that you could secure such a journey."

"For the right price," said Jarl Gudrun, her voice a tired drawl.

The woman in the headscarf had moved to the side of the jarl's throne and was looking Hilde up and down with eyes of the deepest, darkest green. Hilde had never seen eyes like them. The girl gave the stranger a hard stare, but it wasn't enough to halt the woman's appraisal of her.

"Aye," said Blair, swinging the sack from his shoulder

and drawing loose the tied rope. "For the right price."

He shoved his gnarled hand into the sack and pulled out a fistful of treasure. There was no better way to describe it. Between clenched fingers he held strings of necklaces, a couple of bracelets, a torc and a bolt of silk. How in the world the shipwright had got his hands on such trinkets, Hilde could only imagine. *Is he a pirate? A bandit?*

Jarl Gudrun leant forwards upon her throne, and suddenly others in the room began to pay attention. The slaver's bodyguards appeared extremely interested in what the shipwright held in his hand – or perhaps, Hilde wondered, they were intrigued by Blair himself. They whispered to one another, eyeing the wild looking hermit and his treasures. Hilde and Aidan were painfully aware of the animated reaction of the onlookers, but Blair only had eyes for the chief.

"Can you help us, Jarl Gudrun?"

Hilde watched as the jarl's attention shifted from the booty to the shipwright. There was something about the woman's expression that was troubling. Her wan complexion suggested she had a fever, droplets of sweat beading across her brow. And Jarl Gudrun's eyes. The bairn in Hilde had remembered them as brilliant blue, yet now they seemed grey and milky, almost silver, as if the light and life had gone from them and she was old before her time.

"Whose hoard have you stolen from, Pict?" she replied at last.

"I'm no thief, Jarl Gudrun," said Blair. "What you see here is mine. And it can be yours, if we have a deal."

The jarl reclined in her chair. "Maybe it can be mine

anyway, Pict. Deal or no deal."

Hilde heard the men preparing for a fight before she saw them; swords and seaxes being drawn from scabbard, staves and spear-ends dragged across the flagged floor. The carls of Scatness materialised through the smoke, peeling away from shadows and rising from their seats. Hilde reached inside her wolfskin for her weapon, fingertips finding the handle of the silver seax.

"Why must this end with bloodshed, Jarl Gudrun?" snarled Blair, his words infused with anger.

"*Your* bloodshed, Pict. My carls will cut you down like a cornstalk if I so much as sneer at you."

"And I might leap up to your fancy chair and snap your brittle twig of a neck."

Hilde shook her head, willing things to deescalate – and swiftly – but the jarl wasn't done sparring.

"A clapped-out old dog like you might leap?" Her laughter was shrill, and she clapped her hands. "It appears my hall now has a jester!"

Hilde turned to Aidan. The butcher's boy's face was drained of colour as the carls approached from all sides. Hilde grabbed him by the elbow, drawing him close as she prepared to draw her blade. The jarlshof was quiet but for the steady rain that hammered the roof and the sparks that sizzled and spat in the firepit. And all the while, the shipwright stared down the jarl of Scatness.

"Just say the word, woman," said Blair, eyes twinkling with murderous promise. "Just give me that sneer."

CHAPTER SEVENTEEN
CORMAC

As the *Sea Wolf* crested a vertiginous wave, Cormac felt his insides curdle within his chest. Had his jaw not been clenched and teeth gritted, he feared his guts might have scrambled out of his mouth and scurried away to safety. Only there was nowhere to hide as the world dropped out from under him, the longship dipping back towards the surging sea, prow first. Cormac hunkered down, wedging himself into the footwell between the rowing benches, bracing himself against Brother Benedict. The impact sent his head bouncing off the monk's shoulder, his lip splitting, the blood instantly washed away as a wall of spray showered the drakkar's pitching deck and its luckless passengers.

Whilst the captives remained in a huddle, clinging onto one another and the groaning timbers for dear life, the crew showed no such fear. Cormac opened one bleary eye, squinting through the squall as the Vikings ran up and down the deck, tightening ropes, bailing water, securing chests and running repairs. That the longship seemed in danger of capsizing at any moment and being dashed to smithereens bothered them not one bit. They laughed, they sang, and they cursed at the exploding heavens as thunder, rain and lightning lashed down on them from on high.

From where Cormac crouched, his fellow slaves screaming

as one, willing their collective nightmare to end, it felt like they were sailing straight to hell.

"Pater noster, qui es in cælis, sanctificetur nomen tuum!" shouted Brother Benedict, his prayer carrying over the crashing of waves and the joyous cheers of their captors.

Cormac had seen a change in the young monk. The holy man was finally showing a nerve that had been missing the previous night, when the raiders had come calling, butchering their brethren and throwing their prisoners aboard the longship. That was when his flock had most needed him, and Brother Benedict had been lacking. Fear would do that to any man. Now, as the horror heightened, he had stepped up, burying his own terror to battle with later. There was no doubt in Cormac's mind that the monk remained afraid – hell, they all were – but for now he needed to give the survivors of Unst some hope. He did that through the power of prayer.

"Et ne nos inducas in tentationem, sed libera nos a malo. Amen!"

Brother Benedict was on his knees, straining against his bindings, shouting his words of praise at the same heavens that the Vikings cursed. Cormac raised his own bound hands, grabbed the monk by his cassock, and hauled him back into the hull of the drakkar.

"All well and good if you want to get yourself thrown off this damned boat, pal," shouted Cormac into the older youth's ear. "But do that when you're not tied to me, eh? I ain't ready to meet my maker just yet."

Brother Benedict gave Cormac an odd smile, as if he was only half hearing him and had been stricken delirious.

He looked almost ecstatic, which did nothing to calm Cormac's nerves. Their fellow prisoners reached for the monk with roped hands, dragging him back into their midst. The blacksmith's boy followed, attached as he was to the other, as Brother Benedict began to repeat his prayer, his congregation now joining him.

"More Latin?"

Cormac looked up from where he clung to the hull like a limpet, raising his bound wrists to shield his eyes from the spray. Hydyr the Hungry stood over him, watching the prayer group with what appeared to be fascination.

"It's called *The Lord's Prayer*," said Cormac, struggling to hear his own voice over the din of the storm and the sea.

Hydyr seemed satisfied with the answer.

"Good for him," said the jarl, before lunging into the footwell and straddling Cormac, whipping his seax from its scabbard.

The boy's hands were still up, and he now raised them even higher to repel the man. Cormac let out a cry of shock as the Viking's blade darted forwards, quick as a striking snake. Only it didn't hit the boy. It came up behind Cormac's wrists and with a couple of swift and sure movements, the binding ropes were severed, setting him loose from the other prisoners.

Hydyr clambered back towards the centre of the drakkar's deck, pausing to look back at a bemused Cormac. He reached a slender hand out, beckoned, and the boy followed.

It was no easy task, traversing the deck of the drakkar as it rose and descended, pitching back and forth. Cormac found himself on all fours, going from one bench to the next, on his belly at times, as spray hit hard and water sluiced over him. Hydyr faced no such problems, progressing with ease as he made his way to the stern of the longship. If he had seemed weary and sickly during the day he was the opposite now, almost dancing across the deck of his ship, hailing his crew and thoroughly in his element.

Finally arriving in the rear portion of the ship, Cormac found sheets of canvas and animal skins had been stretched and pinned over the deck, this makeshift tent providing a small degree of shelter for those beneath. The material flapped and clapped as the wind hit it from all sides, threatening to rip it free from the drakkar and send it flying into the night sky. It was merely a token protection in a storm such as this – it did little to stop the driving rain and explosions of salt water that periodically hammered the ship – but it was something.

An enormous war chest dominated the stern deck, positioned beside the tiller, set apart from all else. Fashioned from black wood like the rest of the ship, it was perhaps eight feet long, and a few feet wide and tall. Cormac noticed its surface was etched with runic symbols, impossible to read from this distance, whilst the chest's base appeared to be bolted to the boards. It was an impressive piece of carpentry, and left the lad wondering what Hydyr kept inside of it.

Then Cormac spied the hulking figure at the tiller, the long wooden beam held fast in the crook of his crippled arm. The one-armed ox stared ahead into the storm, his remaining hand scratching at his bloated gut where it hung over his leather belt. He might have been sailing on a pond, so at ease did he appear as he guided the drakkar over the turbulent sea.

"Boy!"

Hydyr had raised the edge of the tarpaulin and gestured for Cormac to head under. The boy from Unst duly obliged, slipping and sliding his way past the jarl before collapsing against one of the covered rowing benches. Hydyr had his back turned to him and was busy prising the lid off a small barrel. Cormac could make out the vague outlines of figures around him in the gloom, also sheltering from the storm as best they could. There was a strange smell under the canopy that reminded Cormac of the stench of the sick or dying. This had to be the resting place of the injured Harrowed Men after the attack on Unst. Cormac hoped there were a good number of them enduring lingering, painful deaths.

"A word of advice, Cormac the Cunning," said Hydyr. "You shouldn't stare at Einar the Small."

"Who's that then?" asked Cormac. "The brute who steers your ship? The giant with one paw?"

He heard the jarl chuckle at that.

"The man grieves for the loss of his shieldbrother, Finn Frostmark. He misses the bald fool."

Cormac felt his skin crawl. He knew the man that name belonged to. He was the Viking at the Gods Tree who took a tumble into the sea with him. The same man who had his head removed by Blair the shipwright. Cormac tried to swallow, his mouth dry but for the blood that welled from his busted lip.

"I saw Finn Frostmark die."

Hydyr stopped what he was doing, half-looked over his shoulder at Cormac. "Is that right?"

"Aye. Saw his head fly off. Your man does right to grieve him."

Another chuckle from Hydyr the Hungry that left Cormac unnerved. "I definitely wouldn't mention that to Einar."

The lid came off the barrel and Hydyr's hand dipped inside, removing a slippery silver fish.

"You should eat," said Hydyr, tossing the pickled herring to Cormac. "You'll need your strength."

Cormac stared at the fish in his grubby hands, his stomach gurgling at the sight. *You'll need your strength*. What in the world did Hydyr have in store for Cormac? The man had seemingly taken a shine to the boy from Unst; perhaps it was Cormac's sharp mind that interested him. Either way, Hydyr was happy to see Cormac eat whilst the other captives, still bound together, went without. Once more, his belly growled. He hadn't eaten since Jarl Frida's feast, and that was well over a day gone by. He was about to take a bite, when his thoughts returned to those prisoners who had disappeared. Had Rab Erskine been right? Had those poor souls really been *eaten?* Cormac presented the fish back to the man who now settled opposite him on the lurching deck of the longship.

"Won't you join me, Jarl Hydyr? You're the hungry one, correct?"

Cormac saw the man's shoulders jiggle up and down: *is he laughing?* Hydyr dismissed him with a wave of the hand.

"I've already eaten."

That made the boy shudder – just *what* had he eaten? But Cormac could fight his hunger no longer. He tore into the flesh of the fish, tearing great chunks of the vinegar-soaked meat from the bone and gulping it down, head and all. Hydyr the Hungry watched all the while, thumb and forefinger playing with the golden ring of his jet-black beard. He appeared to be enjoying himself far too much.

"Why did you set me free?" asked Cormac, wiping the grease and scales from his face with his sleeve.

"You're about as free as dog in a jarlshof. The dog has a job to do. He's there to hunt, be it deer or wolves, or mice and rats. He has a purpose. But he still belongs to the jarl."

"I'm the dog?" asked Cormac glumly.

"You're not free, lad. Not by any stretch." Hydyr pointed at the boy. "You have jobs to do, Cormac. You have purpose. But you still belong to me."

Cormac stripped the last bits of flesh from the fishbone. Hydyr saw this and pushed the small cask forwards. It slid along the deck as the drakkar rolled, and Cormac threw his hands out to catch it. More herring slopped about in the barrel. He reached in, snatching another.

"And what jobs would you have me do?"

Hydyr relaxed where he sat, holding on to the hem of the canvas covering and idly keeping it in place.

"The tongues you speak – Norse, Pictish, Latin – they would be of use to me, especially the latter. Where I mean to travel I expect I shall have need of one such as yourself to translate for me."

Cormac swayed from side to side, the ship seeming to steady a little, the waves not quite so fierce as before. Perhaps it was just a lull, but with a bit of luck they were clear of the worst of it.

"Where do you think you're going to need Latin?"

"In the lands of Christ, of course. I'm not such a fool that I expect the men of the southlands to speak my crude barbarian tongue."

The southlands. Hydyr meant Europe. What business the jarl had there was anyone's guess, but Cormac doubted any of it was pleasant.

"You could use Brother Benedict if a translator is what you need. My knowledge of that language has its limits, unlike the monk's."

"Your gift of the gab isn't the only thing that intrigues me about you, Cormac the Cunning," said the jarl, encouraging him to keep eating with an approving nod of the head. "You've a trade too, have trained as a smith is my understanding. My crew are always in need of a man with such talents."

"What? To make more weapons so you can kill more people?"

Hydyr looked offended, but it was clear to Cormac he was being mocked.

"Why, we need nails for our ships, shoes for our horses, hooks for our fishing lines and locks for our chests." Then that smile was back, the wolf's grin. "And weapons, of course."

Cormac wagged a half-eaten fish at the man. "How do you know I'm a blacksmith?"

"I'd like to say your strapping frame told its own tale,

but that would be a lie. Erskine told me."

Cormac choked. *Erskine.*

"What have you done with him?"

The jarl frowned, and his eyes appeared to glow for a moment beneath that dark, knitted brow.

"So very many questions. I want you to remember this conversation, lad, how I humoured you, how good natured I was, for I cannot promise to always be in such a cooperative mood."

There was no mistaking the threat there. Cormac shivered, nodded, dropped his gaze, unable to hold the chieftain's fierce stare.

"I know, Jarl Hydyr, and I thank you."

Then the man was pleasant once more, his voice almost cheery.

"Erskine came to me willingly. I thought it would take much longer to bring him over to our way of thinking, but it never ceases to amaze me how quickly a man will switch his allegiance if it means saving his own skin."

Hydyr craned his neck, looking deeper into the shifting shadows beneath the clapping tarpaulin. Cormac squinted, his eyes unable to adjust to the gloom. He caught sight of vague shapes, heard coughs. Then he spied the heavy-set frame of Rab Erskine, sitting hunched, his back to the boat's groaning frame. His bullish bravado from earlier was now gone. Erskine's eyes were open, staring intently off into space, his chest, arms and hands spattered with fresh blood.

"What . . . what happened to him?" asked Cormac, fearful of the answer he would receive.

"He's been busy," said Hydyr casually. "Butchering. Tending. Feeding my brothers."

"Whose blood is he covered in?"

"His neighbour's. His own."

The blacksmith's boy pushed the barrel of fish back towards the jarl, fighting the urge to vomit. Cormac's mind felt fogged, as if a veil of confusion had descended upon it. How quickly he had allowed himself to fall under Hydyr's spell; the easy conversation, the charm, the food, the shelter. It was all an act, and something else, something unnatural. There was a power in Hydyr's words, and in the man's gaze. There was a magic there. The man was a monster, no doubt about it, only he was yet to physically show it to Cormac.

"I know what you're thinking," said Hydyr, rising tall and rolling the tarpaulin back. "*These are bad men.* And you'd be right. We are. And so long as you do as I say, Cormac the Cunning, you and I shall get along famously. But do not think to cross me. Do what I ask when I ask it, and you'll know favour like no other man. I like you, lad; I find you intriguing. There's more to you than just hammers and nails. I suspect we're only just scratching the surface."

Whilst the longship still battled with the *Nordsær*, it was no longer the fierce contest that had raged earlier. The rain still fell, the thunder still rumbled and the lightning flashed, but the sea itself appeared calmed, like a wild stallion freshly broken.

"It will be dawn soon enough," said Hydyr. "When the light rises in the east, I must rest. We still have many leagues to cover as we sail for Norðvegr, though I fear we shall not see land before dawn. You may busy yourself fixing any tears in the sails. You're good with a needle and twine, I assume?"

Cormac nodded, and Hydyr opened one of the chests that was secured to the deck. He removed a ball of hemp and threw it to Cormac. A black metal needle the length of his finger was buried in the middle of the ball of string. The sight of it immediately had Cormac's mind spiralling back to the sight of Einar the Small sticking Erskine's nail into his own heart. His shiver was missed by Hydyr.

"Good. Once you're done with the sails, there's armour to mend. A stitch here. A fix there. Nothing too arduous, I can assure you. Every ship, every crew, needs a lad like you. Initiative, Cormac. Thinking for yourself."

The jarl placed those long, slim fingers beneath Cormac's jaw, lifting the boy's head so he could look him in the eye. The touch of the jarl was chill, and it was all Cormac could do to stop from recoiling. Hydyr let his thumb brush the broken skin of Cormac's mouth, coming away painted red. The blacksmith's boy shuddered, unable to hide his revulsion as Hydyr licked his thumb clean of blood, smacking his thin, dark lips.

"I suspected as much, little cuckoo. You're not like the rest of them."

He brushed Cormac's hair from his eyes. "And for what it's worth, I am truly sorry for what happened to the man who raised you."

Hydyr turned to walk away, but Cormac wasn't done talking. He let his defiant words chase the jarl away, recovering some pride in the process.

"That man had a name: Hamish Tulloch. And that man was my father."

Hydyr didn't look back, but he raised a hand, wagging a finger as he went, the boat rising and falling over the uneasy sea.

"He wasn't your father."

Cormac was momentarily flummoxed, left struggling for a retort.

"That's... that's my Pa you're talking about!"

"He may have raised you, Cormac the Cunning," repeated Jarl Hydyr, "but that man was not your father."

Crouching beneath the tarpaulin, Cormac watched Jarl Hydyr return to his crew. They met him with cheers, hailing his name as he joined them in their labour. Cormac could see how the jarl was well-liked by his sword-brothers and shieldmaiden sisters. The man was charming, quick-witted, and spoke with passion and purpose. What that purpose was, Cormac had no idea, but he already feared it was something terrible.

The Vikings worked, and the blacksmith's boy watched. Cormac sucked his lip, swallowing the blood that the chief of the Harrowed Men had tasted moments earlier. Who was Jarl Hydyr to say such a cruel thing to him?

"You don't know me," Cormac snarled to himself. "You know nothing about me, or my Pa. You're a liar, Hydyr the Hungry. A damned liar."

Cormac near leapt overboard when he felt a hand seize his wrist, a grip of cold, hard iron. From out of the shadows beneath the canopy, a familiar face materialised, drawing herself closer to the boy whilst also pulling him in. She reeked of death. Her lips were close to his ear when she spoke, her voice a threadbare rasp.

"He's many things," said Jarl Frida, "but Hydyr the Hungry is no liar."

CHAPTER EIGHTEEN
HILDE

In that frozen heartbeat, Hilde was left in no doubt that the jarlshof of Scatness was about to erupt in an orgy of violence. Blair meant every word he had said, had near enough sworn an oath to Jarl Gudrun that he'd kill her if she so much as looked at him wrong. He may not have had many more summers left in him, but the shipwright wasn't about to back down in this fight. Hilde glanced upon Aidan's panicked face and realised that the butcher's boy might die of a heart attack before one of Gudrun's carls got a chance to cut him down. She had to act quickly.

"Jarl Gudrun," she said, stepping forward.

Blair cursed. Carls advanced. Hilde continued.

"It's been many years since I last visited Scatness as your guest. I fondly recall the hospitality you showed myself and my mother, Jarl Frida."

She let that hang there, like a worm on a hook, waiting for the woman to take the bait. Jarl Gudrun's pale face was fixed with an expression of confusion. To Hilde's left and right she saw the Norsemen closing in, felt Aidan bump into her back as they approached from behind. Blades reflected firelight.

"Stop!" commanded Jarl Gudrun loudly.

Her house carls withdrew, though the looks on their faces

revealed their disappointment. The slaver's bodyguards continued to glare at Blair, the shipwright having firmly attracted the interest of the men from Alba. The jarl's expression softened as she pointed at the girl with a wavering finger, a smile quivering upon her trembling lips.

"It's... ah..."

"Hilde, Jarl Gudrun," said the girl from Unst, bowing respectfully. "Hilde Blackheart."

Tense though the moment was, Hilde allowed herself a fleeting sense of pride. Was that the first time she'd ever taken her mother's battle name? Perhaps it was the shield, the wolfskin, and the silver blade upon her hip.

"Your mother is a dear friend of mine," said Jarl Gudrun. "How does she fare?"

Hilde looked to Blair, as if seeking permission to talk, but the old man still glared at the jarl.

"She's fared better, Jarl Gudrun," said Hilde. "Unst is destroyed, many slaughtered and those who were spared enslaved."

She glanced at the woman in the headscarf, who suddenly chose to avoid the girl's gaze, before turning back to the jarl.

"My mother was amongst those taken."

Upon receiving the news, for the merest heartbeat, Jarl Gudrun stared at Hilde, as if awaiting more information. Then she recoiled in her seat, throwing her head back in dismay.

"Then it is as my father, Jarl Rognvald, feared. We are no longer safe from our own kin."

"This attack was expected?"

Jarl Gudrun's expression was fierce. "We are at the very

edge of King Harald's realm, exposed to attacks from pirates and Picts alike. No offence," she added for the benefit of Blair.

"None taken," said the shipwright, though Hilde sensed he was still steaming.

"Then you are without home and shelter, little bird. Come. Sit by my fire."

Mention of birds had Hilde thinking back to what had awaited them at the entrance to the jarlshof.

"I noticed the crows you'd hanged out front, Jarl Gudrun. Suffering a plague in Scatness?"

"Merely a favour for my guest, Mistress Zaleska," she replied, gesturing to the woman in the headscarf. "She guests with us frequently and has no fondness for the nightbirds."

The woman with the green eyes stepped into the firelight, and when she spoke, flames appeared to dance within her mouth. Her teeth were fashioned from precious gold, and the accompanying words were as sharp and hard as her chiselled face.

"They are a filthy, sneaking creature. I do not trust the nightbirds. When I was a child, it was foretold that one would bring about my downfall. Since then, I've never taken any chances."

Not their biggest fan then, mused Hilde, but kept her quip in check.

"Scatness appears unexpectedly quiet, Jarl Gudrun," said Blair, watching her reaction carefully. "I was expecting lanterns and laughter lighting up the town, but we encountered quite the opposite. Didn't see a living soul on the walk to the jarlshof. Has the town been stricken with some kind of illness? Or has your flock of sheep been scattered?"

The woman arched an eyebrow in the shipwright's direction.

"My flock hasn't gone anywhere, Pict. I can assure you, Scatness is still very much their home. But enough idle talk."

Jarl Gudrun clapped her hands and called out into the shadowy recesses of the hall, having effortlessly shifted from untrusting chieftain to genial host.

"Agnes! Fetch food and drink for my guests and be quick about it. They have been through a terrible ordeal and must be exhausted."

Hilde clenched her hands together by way of thanks. "It's a kind offer, Jarl Gudrun, but one we have to pass on."

"I won't hear of it," said the chief firmly. "It's rare that I receive visitors these days. You would turn down this simple hospitality, Hilde Blackheart? You would offend me?"

As an old woman hastily cleared a cluttered table behind them, Hilde looked up at Blair. He didn't seem taken by the idea, his attention still focused on the various armed men that surrounded them. The tension in the room remained and, despite Jarl Gudrun's apparently welcoming overtures, Hilde was struggling to shake the initial ill welcome.

"Thank you, Jarl Gudrun."

Grabbing Aidan by the elbow, Hilde took a seat on a bench beside the trestle. Blair followed, taking up position on the opposite side, ever mindful of the carls. They milled about, always close by, never fully retreating. Their very presence was a constant reminder that violence was only an ill-advised word away. Hilde chanced a glance at the chief and saw she was leaning around the side of her throne, in quiet conversation with the slaver. Unless Hilde was mistaken, the woman in the headscarf was still looking her way.

Are they talking about me?

"I don't like this," whispered Blair. "Something ain't right. We should think about taking our leave, sharpish."

"I'm with him," said Aidan. "This place gives me the creeps."

"Scatness is a ghost town," added Blair.

They were both correct. Hilde felt it too. She kept her voice low and spoke under her breath.

"Let's keep it brief then. Get this ship secured and we can be on our way. Don't think any of us want to be here any longer than we have to."

Her two companions grunted their agreement, just as Agnes deposited a platter of food onto the table between them. Hilde tried to smile at the servant by way of thanks, but the old woman wouldn't meet her eye. Instead, Hilde turned her attention to the fare that had been provided; the heel end of a loaf of bread, accompanied by a scattering of oatcakes and a gnarled cut of roast pork. None of it appeared especially appetising.

"I count ten of 'em," said Blair as he grabbed the hunk of bread. He tried to break it, found it impossible, and when he rapped it on the table top it made a sound like stone upon boulder.

"Ten of what?" asked Aidan, confused.

"Carls," said Hilde, her eyes narrow as she watched the shipwright toss the bread aside.

"They ain't all Norsemen," grumbled Blair. "I'm including

the men from Alba who are taking that slaver's coin. Spotted them the minute I walked in, and pretty sure they spotted me. Thought I was going to get propositioned for a dance for a moment."

"Don't be thinking of starting anything, old man."

A snort from Blair. "Ain't none of 'em on their toes, and that includes the pair of arselings on the front door. Most of these fools look like they've been in their cups all night. Don't think there's one of 'em playing with a full bag of bones."

"Does he mean to fight them?" asked a concerned Aidan.

"No," said Hilde. "He does *not* mean to fight them. Isn't that right?"

"I like to know the odds is all," said Blair.

The old timer flicked a weevil off one of the oatcakes and gave it a tentative nibble. Spitting the crumbs away, he turned up his nose.

"We can't trust this woman."

Hilde grimaced. "But Jarl Gudrun was friends with my mother."

"*Was* being the operative word, lassie. I can't imagine the glassy-eyed lunatic who plays host to us presently much resembles the woman your Ma knew."

Hilde reached for the piece of pork, only for Aidan to smack her hand away.

"What the hell—"

"Look," said the butcher's boy, eyeing the steak, "at the meat."

"We call this pork," she said sarcastically. "Thought you'd recognise that much, *butcher's boy*."

"Look," repeated Aidan.

"What am I looking at?" asked Hilde, sighing as she examined the piece of pork by the firelight. It seemed like a regular cut, if a little discoloured. "It's a bit grey. Probably a leftover from an earlier supper. Maybe yesterday?"

Aidan rolled his eyes. "Look closer, you silly cow!"

Hilde was about to strike him, but then she saw it. The meat rippled ever so slightly as something moved beneath its surface. Hilde's nose was already turning up, as Aidan reached across and flicked the old meat, the pork splitting as a bloated maggot squirmed out of its hiding place. Hilde put the back of her hand to her mouth, fighting the urge to hurl.

"Maybe yesterday, you say? Try last week," said Aidan, his voice an angry whisper. "This meat is as rotten as everything else in this bloody town."

Blair took hold of the bad meat and tore a strip off it.

"The hell you doing?" asked Aidan. "I just told you it's bad. You eat that, you'll be sick."

The old man gave the boy a sneer as he shoved the greyed pork into his pocket.

"It ain't for me, ya wee numpty. It's for the head. The Viking. Reckon he'll be peckish later."

Hilde and Aidan both glanced at the covered bucket that was perched on the bench beside Blair. They shivered in unison, unsure of how that feeding time might play out. It was certainly something Hilde wasn't keen on witnessing.

The shipwright was already rising from his bench, and the two youths followed, the trio returning to the jarl's throne.

Once more, the carls followed, just out of reach, yet near enough that they might spring if called upon. Blair eyeballed those closest to him, nodding at them as if to say: *whenever you're ready.* Hilde shook her head.

A shipwright. Sure.

"You're done eating?" asked Jarl Gudrun, disengaging from her conversation with the woman in the headscarf. "My, you must have been hungry!"

Hilde looked over at the platter of untouched food. It very clearly hadn't been eaten. *Is she being wilfully blind, or just mocking us?* Did Jarl Gudrun *know* her staff had just served her guests spoilt and rancid food? Just how disconnected with events was the Jarl of Scatness? Jarl Frida had a saying for folk like this: *they're away with the fey folk.* A fine way of describing their host, figured Hilde, though there was something more. Aidan wasn't wrong. There was something truly rotten about Scatness, and Hilde was already looking forward to seeing the back of the place.

"Thank you for your kindness, Jarl Gudrun," said Hilde. "However, nothing changes from what my friend here said earlier. We still require passage to Norðvegr, at the soonest opportunity. And our gold is good as payment. Just name your price."

Jarl Gudrun's nod was slow and considered.

"You're an impressive one, young shieldmaiden. Your mother would've been proud of you."

"She *is* proud," corrected Blair gruffly. "We don't believe she's yet dead. Hence the urgency of our journey if we're to catch these bastards. Vengeance really doesn't permit us to remain here any longer. You understand?"

The atmosphere in the jarlshof felt dangerous, as if lightning charged the air of the smoky hall. The chief leant forwards and kept her response directed to Hilde. Seemed she was done speaking with the old man for the foreseeable.

"Little bird, you may have noticed there is only one ship in Scatness harbour, and that is the knarr of Mistress Zaleska."

Jarl Gudrun tipped her head in the direction of the woman in the headscarf beside the throne, who opened her golden mouth once more.

"My knarr is no longship. It is no vessel of war. I am a simple trader. We talk tomorrow about that price, girl. You and I, we trade. Yes?"

Cadavers held more warmth, and there was something about Zaleska's choice of words that left Hilde even further disturbed, on a night of many disturbances. *No mean feat,* figured the young shieldmaiden.

But it was Jarl Gudrun who spoke next.

"You three shall rest in my hall this night. I shall not accept no for an answer. My only condition is that you remain in your guest quarters until dawn. Once I retire, this hall becomes the playground of my carls. It is no place for bairns and old men."

A chorus of lairy and lascivious chuckles echoed around the jarlshof, which set Hilde's already frayed nerves on edge.

"It's only fitting that I allow my men some indulgences in the dead of night, and afford them privacy in the process," said Jarl Gudrun. "I am a gracious host, but do not take advantage of that generosity. I shall not be tested. Then tomorrow we decide what can be done with you. Perhaps we may secure you passage to Norðvegr."

A rumble of thunder growled overhead, right on time. Jarl Gudrun smiled.

"Thor's temper permitting, of course."

CHAPTER NINETEEN
CORMAC

Cormac squinted at the tear in the tarpaulin, wishing there was an alternative way to harvest the precious resource. The rainwater drizzled through the ragged hole, dripping into his cupped hands. All the while he kept his legs braced against the rowing benches, trying not to shift position. Convinced he had gathered enough, he scooted back on his knees, doing his best to remain upright in the process, desperate not to spill a drop of water.

"Jarl Frida," he said, almost colliding with his chief where she lay crumpled upon the deck. "I need you to drink. Please, raise your head."

With great effort, her face contorting with pain, the woman managed to lift her head, just enough that Cormac could bring his hands to her mouth. He raised his elbows, tipping his hands and letting the paltry contents of his makeshift cup dribble between her lips. This was the sixth time he'd attempted such a trip, and in total the jarl had managed maybe two mouthfuls, and even then she coughed it up. It wasn't much, but it was something.

"I can see why my daughter was so fond of you," said Jarl Frida, collapsing back into an awkward heap.

Cormac shuffled alongside her, not sure of what to do. He glanced over at Rab Erskine, considered asking him for help, but the butcher remained in some strange catatonic state, as if whatever horrors he'd witnessed had yet to sink in. Drawing himself up close, Cormac lifted Jarl Frida's head and shoulders, turning her torso enough that he could manoeuvre himself beneath her, so she could rest upon him. The black drakkar rocked and rolled, as did the jarl's almost lifeless body, before Cormac found himself supporting his broken chieftain.

"Would it be too much trouble," said Jarl Frida, "for you to drag me yonder and toss me over the side?"

Cormac patted her shoulder affectionately.

"Maybe we'll feed you to the fishes when you're dead, Jarl Frida. Until then, I'll do everything I can to keep you alive."

Jarl Frida managed a feeble smile. "I'm afraid that ship sailed long ago."

In the darkness beneath the tarpaulin, Cormac could feel where her breastplate was torn and bloodied. The Harrowed Men had done a job on the chief, no doubt about it.

"I'll get you up and well again, my jarl, I promise."

She raised a hand, wincing with the effort, and brushed his cheek once before it collapsed back against her butchered chest. Cormac turned his head this way and that, trying to count the points where Jarl Frida had been struck. There was a hole in the belly of her leather corset, dark blood welling within it. An ugly arrowhead stood proud of her right shoulder, the tarnished metal tangled in the tresses of her blonde hair. The rest of the missile was still buried within her chest, muscle and sinew packed around that splintered shaft of misery.

"You think I'm joking, lad," said Jarl Frida. "But I mean it. You get me overboard, that makes you a hero in my eyes. There's nothing left for me here."

She fumbled for his hand and, upon finding it, gripped it tight. There was still some strength there.

"And the minute you get off this boat, you run, Cormac. You run hard, fast, and as far as you can, and you get away from Hydyr the Hungry and his Harrowed Men. Y'hear?"

He patted her hand, prised her fingers from his. "Save your grim words for a darker day."

"A darker day than this?" she scoffed. "My daughter's dead, my people slaughtered. If worse is to come, the Gods have discovered ever more cruel ways of tormenting Frida Blackheart."

Cormac lowered his head along with his voice. "Hilde lives, Jarl Frida. Least she breathed when I last saw her, back on Unst."

Jarl Frida's eyes met Cormac's. "Do not jest, boy."

"I swear, she's alive."

Her gaze drifted, as did her words. "Then I still have a purpose." Then her urgency returned. "There is still hope. I thought this world was doomed, and everyone in it, but if my Hilde still breathes then I have a reason to fight on."

Jarl Frida grimaced as she lifted her arm and planted her hand upon the deck of the drakkar. Then she began to rise, forcing herself upright off Cormac's lap.

"What do you want me to do?" asked the boy, feeling suddenly rather useless as the jarl found hidden reserves of energy.

"I heard you say to Hydyr that you were good with a needle and thread," said Jarl Frida, picking at the ties that kept her breastplate fastened. "Let's see how good you are, Cormac Tulloch."

The boy squirmed clear of the woman as she tugged the leather laces loose and the armour fell away. She cried out as it caught around the arrowhead. With a nod of her head and wide, earnest eyes, she gestured to it.

"Pull it through, lad."

The metal head of the arrow was inches from the boy's face. Cormac shuddered, unsure of whether he could do it or not.

"I might cause more damage if I—"

"Do it!" snapped Jarl Frida.

Cormac gripped his fingers around the dark metal, felt his nails dig into the edges of the wound, and then pulled with all his might. Jarl Frida gritted her teeth, ignoring the accompanying pain, as Cormac drew the arrow shaft through her shoulder with a wet, sucking *pop*.

"Good," said the jarl breathlessly, shaking the leather breastplate off. "Now get to work."

Cormac stared at the wounds upon Jarl Frida's torso. There were many old ones, but it was the fresh ones that made Cormac feel faint. Sure enough, in addition to the arrow's ragged hole there was a deep gash in her stomach around the bottom of her ribs, the flap of flesh yawning open where she was doubled over. He inspected her back, saw another cut that matched the one in her belly where a blade had passed clean through. There was also a savage cut that passed diagonally over her back, revealing the unmistakable white bones of her spine. The boy feared he might pass out, so terrible were the injuries.

"The needle," said Jarl Frida calmly. "And the thread. I need you to stitch me up."

He reached down, picked the ball of twine up in a trembling hand. The woman reached her hand out, placing it over his. Cold though her flesh was to the touch, she somehow managed to radiate reassurance.

"Calm yourself, Cormac. You can do this. I have every faith in you."

Cormac took a breath. Then he set to work.

He was no seamstress, that much wasn't even up for debate, but he'd done a fair bit of stitching over the course of his fifteen winters, carrying out the tasks a mother might have done whilst his father slaved away in the smithy. Darning clothes, hemming sheets, repairing sacks; he could punch a needle, no problem. Getting one through skin though, that proved markedly more difficult. Jarl Frida's flesh was cold, clammy, had a texture to match the pickled herrings he'd scoffed earlier that night. And try as he might, he couldn't get past the fact this was Jarl Frida he was stitching up, not a threadbare pair of pants.

"You should be dead," he muttered as he bit and tied the thread, closing shut the arrow's entry wound in her shoulder blade.

"Don't I know it?"

"How is it you're *not*, Jarl Frida? Do you have the protection of your Gods?"

Her laugh was guttural. She stared at the drooling Erskine as Cormac sent the needle and thread in and out of the slash across her back.

"I sailed with this crew, many years ago, lad. I *led* them, was their chief. I was one of the Harrowed Men. Still am, truth be told. It's a family one never truly leaves."

"I don't follow."

Jarl Frida looked over her shoulder at the young man as he worked.

"There is no God in any faith who can protect me now, Cormac. I am cursed, just like all the Vikings on this forsaken ship."

Cormac was having none of it. "You're Jarl Frida. I've seen your kindness firsthand, the great things you've done for the people of Unst, be they Norse or Pictish." He shook his head. "I see a good woman. Not a cursed one."

"You're blind," muttered Jarl Frida. "You see the truth with your own eyes yet still disbelieve it. Two nights ago, a man ran a seax through my belly, while another cut my back open with his sword. I've been felled by arrows, kicked and drowned, stabbed and strangled, yet do I appear dead to you?"

Cormac said nothing. The more Jarl Frida spoke, the more difficult he found it to deny what she was saying. Even her flesh had the feel of a corpse, and yet she *lived?*

"Draugr," said the woman, the word escaping her lips like life's final breath.

Cormac's hand slipped, the needle piercing deep into the flesh of his thumb. As Cormac cursed he heard Jarl Frida gasp in immediate response to the injury. Cormac withdrew his thumb quickly, almost put it to his mouth to suck it but then thought better of it. The memory of Hydyr and the blood, and all that surrounded him on the drakkar, put paid to that impulse. He wiped the puncture wound on his thigh and returned to work.

"Restless spirits," said Cormac in quiet response.

That earnt him another glance from the jarl.

"You've heard of the draugr, then? Hilde always said you were learnt, especially for a blacksmith's lad. She didn't lie. How do you know of such things?"

"I listen and I remember," he replied, tying off another stitch, biting its ends with his teeth. "I've always loved the tales of your people, passed down by the old folk."

"My people?"

"The Norsemen. I'd sit with the elders on Unst whenever I could, helping mend baskets or bring the catch in if it meant hearing another piece of a saga. Tales of ancient monsters and warrior heroes, of scheming witches and warlocks who whisper in the ears of jarls and kings across our world and beyond. It was the stories of the *vættir* that fascinated me the most, the faerie races, and how the jarls bent them to their purpose. Siv the raven once snickered in my ear that you fought alongside an elf, back in your day."

"She did, did she?" said Jarl Frida, her eyes staring off wistfully, briefly lost to a time long gone. "Valdir. He was a brave and beautiful one. Too good for the Harrowed Men."

As she reminisced, Cormac continued, enthusiastically sharing what he knew.

"And there is a jarl in Norðvegr who has a dwarf shipwright building her longships, if you believe it? Rumour has it the Jarl of Hedeby has a sea-trow, to keep his harbour clear of storms. They even say that King Harald Fairhair has a frost giant in the ranks of his guard. And it wasn't just the elders who shared these stories. Hilde was always rabbiting on about the Norse myths, and I was ever happy to listen."

Cormac shuffled around to Jarl Frida's stomach, stared in bewilderment at the gaping wound.

"I'm not even sure I can fix this," said the boy. "I can sew the flesh together, but the sword ... it passed straight through you. Your innards ... they can't—"

"Just stitch me up, lad. Let me worry about the rest."

And so, he continued with his work.

"They're not myths if they're true, Cormac," said Jarl Frida. "And they are true, for the most part. Occasionally the odd human might be mistaken for huldufólk or other vættir – a lofty man passing for a troll, a short, ugly woman taken for a duergar – but some of those faerie folk did indeed live alongside us. Those races had all the strengths and flaws that humans have, but other beings haunted Midgard that were devoid of any goodness or decency, who were rotten and wicked to their very core haunted Midgard."

Cormac's hand trembled as he laced the needle and thread through the skin of Jarl Frida's torso. The stench of death had suddenly permeated the deck, as if seeping out of the very timbers the *Sea Wolf* was made from.

"The Harrowed Men are draugr," said Cormac, sharing what he knew. "Cursed to haunt the world of the living, forbidden to ever enter Valhalla. I've heard the tales."

"You're smart."

"I'm scared," he replied swiftly. "It all makes sense now. I saw what happened to Finn Frostmark in Unst, saw the wounds dealt to him that would have felled the strongest warrior, but he fought on regardless. I watched as Einar the Small drove an iron nail the span of my hand into his own heart, and he simply grinned. There's no way a human could live through such horrific injuries, which also means..."

Cormac stopped sewing the hole in Jarl Frida's stomach. There was only one more stitch to make. The chief tenderly took the needle from Cormac, and pushed it through the cold, dead skin of her own belly. She drew it tight, tied it off and snapped the thread.

"I too am draugr," said Jarl Frida. "But then, you knew that the moment you saw these wounds. Which I thank you for repairing."

She shifted, tried to straighten her back, wincing with discomfort. Cormac heard her muscles cracking, popping, her limbs stiff. He had heard that noise before, when his father and others had handled a recently deceased elderly crofter. Whilst Hamish Tulloch and his friends prepared a small barrow, a couple of old fishwives had washed the dead farmer's body. Cormac had watched in ghoulish fascination and had run away fearfully when he'd heard the dead man's arms groan and creak as the women handled his corpse.

"How can you all be draugr?"

"We were cursed for a terrible deed we carried out, an act so blasphemous and heinous there would be no redemption. And so, the Harrowed Men now wander Midgard, continuing the awful acts they committed in life, only now in death."

Jarl Frida reached a hand out for her leather breastplate, and Cormac hurried to help, sliding it back over one arm and tying it off beneath the other.

"The wounds I've sewn shut. Will they mend?"

The jarl grimaced as Cormac pulled the leather thongs tight, securing the breastplate.

"In their own way. A draugr's wounds will remain upon their flesh, marking them until the end of time, when their physical form will finally cease to be. Furthermore, the Harrowed Men have found a way to lessen the effect of their injuries. The consumption of certain foods can stave off the effects of decomposition, allowing them to pass off as mortal men."

Cormac didn't need to ask what those foods were. He knew fine well, looking across at the motionless Erskine, spattered in gore.

"Blood, flesh, and bone," said the boy.

Jarl Frida nodded. "The Harrowed Men worked this out very quickly and found that humans provided the best source of sustenance for them."

"They're cannibals."

Jarl Frida shrugged. "I'm not sure that's entirely true. That would be people feeding on one another. The draugr are no longer human. To the Harrowed Men, the prisoners aboard this drakkar are merely cattle, unless you can provide some service to them. And it looks to me like you've endeared yourself to Hydyr the Hungry."

Not for the last time, Cormac felt his insides turn in on themselves, flipping and coiling at the memory of the jarl tasting his blood. What would happen when the rest of the prisoners had been devoured? Would he be next?

"Jarl Frida," Cormac gulped, "you're weak. If what you say is true, about the draugr needing to feed to replenish themselves, then the same goes for you, right? Well, I know what you favoured on Unst; people talk, not least your own daughter. It was no secret that your diet consisted of red meat, and that you preferred blood in your goblet to mead."

The woman's face was deathly serious, the full ramifications of the boy's words sinking in.

"Look around, Jarl Frida; there's no sheep or swine aboard this longship. You said it yourself; we're cattle. And you need to eat if you're to recover."

Cormac's heart beat wildly in his chest. He could feel it rattling his ribs, threatening to punch its way out of his breast, as he edged closer to his jarl. He raised his hand, presenting the bloodied thumb to her, a fat, ruby-red droplet welling from the wound.

"You could—"

"No!" gasped Jarl Frida, striking Cormac's wrist so hard that he feared it might snap. He held his bruised arm to his chest, clenched the bloody thumb and fingers into a fist.

"Do not tempt me, Cormac." She choked on the words. "If I start . . . I don't know if I could stop. I won't be like them. I'd sooner starve." She looked at him, eyes wet with tears of regret. "I'm sorry, lad."

Cormac nodded, nursing his arm. "And Hydyr is like the rest of the Harrowed Men?"

Jarl Frida considered that, her head lolling as the drakkar found smoother waters. She looked out from under the tarpaulin, along with Cormac, the pair watching the black-bearded chieftain as he laughed and worked the deck with his fellow Vikings.

"No," mused Jarl Frida. "Hydyr is changed somehow, different to the man I knew. He appears to have embraced his condition, and more. His appetites have changed too; he has forgone the consumption of flesh. Now he only drinks blood. He's thriving. He's up to something."

She gripped Cormac's wrists with corpse-cold hands, so sudden the boy almost shrieked.

"Whatever you do, do not trust Hydyr the Hungry."

"I don't."

"You say that now, but he is luring you into his confidence, winning you over, one tiny act of kindness following another. Whatever he offers, you must decline it. He'll promise you great things, but the cost is too grave! When the chance comes, you run, do you hear me? *Run!*"

"I'm not stupid—"

"I know you're not, Cormac, but that silver-tongued wolf has a way about him. He'll win you over, play father to your son."

Father.

The word was a dagger-blow to the boy's soul. He pointed

at Hydyr angrily.

"He said Pa wasn't my father..."

"I know what he said, Cormac, and it's true. I'm sure it hurts like an arrow to the heart, but it's the truth."

Cormac felt the tears now, racing down his dirty cheeks, his chest shaking as great sobs threatened to erupt. Jarl Frida grabbed him, shook him, her eyes darting about the shadows that surrounded them beneath the canopy and on the tilting deck.

"Calm yourself, lad. Steel yourself, for worse is to come."

"Hamish Tulloch—" began Cormac.

"Was a good and honourable man, who took you in when nobody else would. He provided for you, taught you a trade, treated you like his own. But I'm afraid he was no more your father than I am your mother. I'm so sorry."

All those happy memories came back to Cormac in a surging tide, flooding his mind and crushing his broken heart to pulp. Hamish was the only family he had ever known. He had never doubted for one moment that they were kinfolk. Which prompted a question from the boy.

"If Pa took me in . . . from whom? Who delivered me to him? How did I end up in the village?"

Jarl Frida gave him a stern look, as if considering how she might word her reply.

"No sense in keeping secrets any more, and I reckon fifteen winters is long enough, looking at where we've ended up. It was Blair who brought you to Unst. Brought you to the island from Alba."

"The shipwright?" Cormac was stunned. "But I don't

even know the fella. He scared all hell out of me. You're saying *he's* my family?"

Jarl Frida shook her head irritably. "I don't know what you are to him, only that he brought you to us, safe and swaddled. He must have had his reasons to bring you to Unst. Or maybe he was putting distance between you and a problem on Alba. We'll likely never know."

Cormac rocked where he sat, gnawing on his split lip, wracked with questions that remained unanswerable. What business did the shipwright have with him? Why would Blair cross seas and brave storms, just to bring Cormac to a rock on the edge of the world? What – or who – in the wide world had the man been running from?

Another question niggled Cormac, picking away at his mind like a nail upon a scab.

"Hydyr the Hungry knew. He said Pa wasn't my father, was adamant. How would he know that?"

Jarl Frida looked away. "He must have been able to tell by the taste of your blood."

Cormac frowned. Something wasn't adding up. "But . . . if he knew my blood was different to Pa's, that would have to mean . . ."

He left his conclusion unvoiced. No words could help him rationalise or make sense of his father's grisly fate. Not only had Hydyr killed the man, but if he knew Cormac's blood was different to the blood of Hamish Tulloch – by *taste* – then he must have *fed* off him.

If Cormac had been in any doubt regarding Hydyr the Hungry and the possibility he was a monster, they were now banished. The jarl of the Harrowed Men could flatter him all he wanted, woo him with compliments and play mentor to Cormac's apprentice, but the blacksmith's boy now had a very clear purpose in life, however brief that might prove to be.

He was going to end Hydyr the Hungry.

CHAPTER TWENTY
HILDE

The clap of thunder and the flash of lightning struck in unison, each seemingly seeking dominion over the other, whilst below, in the sorry settlement of Scatness, a torrent descended. The jarlshof trembled beneath the onslaught, rivers of rain seeking a way through the thick thatch that covered its roof. For the most part, the longhouse appeared waterproof, but not the guest quarters. The cramped room in which the visitors had been deposited was situated midway along the length of the longhouse's southern wall and bore more resemblance to a store or a gaol cell than a bed chamber. Rain broke through the thatch here to shower the grotty chamber below. Hilde stared glumly at the ground, counted seven puddles that were growing steadily, the earth and straw floor gradually turning into a muddy swamp. She had to wonder: if this was where Jarl Gudrun put her guests, what kind of pit had her slaves been sent to?

"This keeps up we'll likely drown to death before we even get on a boat," she said miserably.

Hilde sat cross-legged on a cot, their belongings beside her, the mattress bowing beneath their collective weight. Blair knelt before the exit, hard at work. He was using a fancy silver candlestick as a makeshift lever, waggling it between the door and its frame to try and lift the bar beyond.

These were no guest chambers; this was a holding cell. The candlestick had been retrieved from the shipwright's bag of booty. Blair was a dark horse. There had been more treasure and gold in that handful he had presented to Jarl Gudrun than Hilde had ever clapped eyes on before. *Where in Odin's name had he got it from?*

The splash of a boot in a puddle brought her back to the present.

"Quit your pacing, already," Hilde snapped. "Back and forth, back and forth. Odin help me, I'm getting sea-sickness just watching you."

"Can't help it," said Aidan as he turned at the door and marched back across the room, which was only a dozen paces across. "I don't like this place. It's giving me the chills. We should get gone and sharpish."

"Get gone where, you niding fool? There's the mother of all storms blowing out there, in case you hadn't noticed!"

Aidan paused and clutched his stomach, which made an audible growl. "Blooming starving too."

"You? Starving?" scoffed Hilde. "Don't make me laugh. You've got plenty of puppy fat. Could live off it for weeks."

"I haven't eaten since the feast."

Hilde snorted. "You had a mouthful of something when I found you in that latrine pit."

He shot her the filthiest of looks. "Wind your neck in, ya wee walloper. You would've fared no better in my predicament. I've lost count of the number of times I've hurled since that night."

"There's a pork chop going free in the main hall if you

still fancy it? Have to pick the flies and maggots out of it, but Erskines have eaten worse."

She saw him clench both his fist and his jaw. The bruising around his face was beginning to die down, as were the colours, shifting from bluish-purple tones to browns and yellows. The marks from her fingers were faintly visible around his throat, gifts bestowed upon the butcher's boy from when she had throttled him, that awful red mist having descended. She could feel it bubbling up now, rising in the pit of her belly, summoned forth by the predicament she found herself in. Last thing she wanted to do was look at Aidan Erskine's ugly mug. Hilde considered saying something more to antagonize him further, but it was Blair who spoke.

"If you two are going to kiss, just bloody well get on with it. Pair of you are doing my head in."

Hilde spluttered. She wanted to admonish Blair for saying such a ridiculous thing but was unable to form or find the words. Instead, she felt a shiver dance up her spine as her cheeks flushed warm and red. The briefest glance to her side revealed that Aidan was equally embarrassed by the shipwright's words, as he averted his gaze from his erstwhile nemesis. Before the moment of awkwardness could extend any further, Blair waved a hand.

"Make yourselves useful," he said, gesturing towards the rough-textured exterior wall. "See if you can find a way through that."

Hilde headed over to where a narrow slit in the wall allowed a little air into the chamber. Drawing her seax from her belt she set to work hacking at the thick mud and straw, set hard as baked clay over the years. She brought the blade back, driving at the wattle and daub with the weapon, working it wider as best she could, but it was slow going. Aidan came over to help, adding his assistance begrudgingly. They worked in tandem, Hilde chopping, Aidan ripping at it with his hands, tearing clumps of the structure away. It was perhaps big enough for Hilde to stick her head through the aperture when there was a movement outside, swooping towards them out of the darkness, causing the two youths to yelp and jump clear.

In came Siv, entering the room through the small makeshift window, alighting upon a post at the foot of the cot. The raven ruffled her feathers, shaking the rain from her plumage.

"Nice weather for ducks, but no fun for a raven," said Siv with a shiver. "And I've been to more welcoming places."

Hilde came straight over, stroking the bird's head affectionately. It was good to see her.

"Jarl Gudrun and her friends ain't so keen on your kin," said Hilde. "That Zaleska woman said something about a prophecy involving nightbirds. Clearly, she's not taking any chances."

The raven's glassy eyes blinked three times. Hilde thought she saw fear in them.

"No. I saw how she treats my cousins, the superstitious wretch."

Blair paused from his labour, put his ear to the door. "Hall sounds as quiet as a burial ground. Maybe the jarl and her friends have either headed to bed or left for the night."

"What on earth did Jarl Gudrun mean?" said Hilde. "*Tomorrow we decide what can be done with you* – what's to decide? They either help us or don't. None of this feels right."

"Aye," agreed Blair. "We ain't guests; we're prisoners. If there was some other way of getting off the island, I'd suggest we take it, but as things stand, that slaver's ship is the answer."

"There must be other boats," said Hilde.

"Fishing boats, bairn," said the shipwright. "Nothing that will get us over the *Nordsær* in one piece. That storm could sink any ship. We need that slaver's knarr, and a crew, if we're to stand any chance of safely reaching Norðvegr."

"Do we not wait and see if Jark Gudrun can negotiate passage for us with Zaleska?" Hilde asked hopefully.

Blair gave her a pitying look, and she didn't like it one bit.

"What?" she said.

"You need to open your eyes, lassie,' said the shipwright. "There will be no negotiation. This jarlshof feels like a tomb. Stinks of death, and I know that smell all too well."

Hilde let that go. There was a glint in the man's eye, a fevered way in which he talked that suggested he was in no mood for questions. He turned back to the door and the task in hand but continued to speak.

"What's it like out there, raven?"

"I've got a *name*," replied Siv haughtily. "The entire town suffers the same apathy as you mention. Homes appear empty, abandoned. So far as I can tell, families must have departed Scatness, fled to outlying villages across Meginland."

Blair twisted the candlestick, grimacing as the bar beyond the door began to shift. They heard it clatter in its bracket, and Blair cursed. Aidan appeared by his side, taking the candlestick from him and taking a turn with the door, leaving the shipwright to join Hilde beside the cot.

"Your mother's pal, Jarl Gudrun, already knew that it was Vikings who raided our village."

"How do you know that?" asked Hilde.

"You told her we'd been attacked, and people had been taken prisoner. Well, of course it *could* be Vikings who carry out such a raid, but not exclusively. There's a long history of other islanders raiding one another up, as well as pirates from Alba. How could Jarl Gudrun have definitively known who was responsible? She *knew* about the attack. She knew it was Vikings who painted the sands red in Unst."

Hilde considered what Blair had said. It made for a convincing argument, undoubtedly.

"If I'm to call Jarl Gudrun out for being a liar, I need to be absolutely sure of my accusation. There's no room for error."

"So, let's be absolutely sure," said Blair, and he reached under the bed and withdrew the covered bucket.

Flipping the lid open, he reached in and grabbed Finn Frostmark by his ears, removing him and placing him neck-first into one of the muddy puddles. The severed head had taken on a grey pallor since they had departed Unst, and the smell of putrefying flesh was as pungent and unpleasant as Hilde had expected. The shipwright tugged the gag loose and took a step back. Frostmark smacked his puckered lips and cleared his throat, his one good eye swivelling from shipwright to shieldmaiden, glistening with grotesque mischief. When he spoke, the words emerged like a gargle, bubbles rippling across the puddle from beneath his stumped neck.

"You know, you could've just asked me in the first place if you wanted to know Jarl Gudrun's deal."

"Speak, head, or go back in the bucket," said Hilde.

Siv hopped forwards and gave Frostmark's ear a peck for good measure, hard enough that the head nearly toppled over.

"Peck me all you want, pigeon, but that won't get you any answers. I want something in return first." He smacked his lips. "I'm hungry."

"You'll get no such—" began Hilde, but Blair cut in.

"Hang on," said the shipwright, fishing the piece of grey meat from his pocket.

He held it out under Frostmark's nose. The draugr's eyebrows rose with slow suspicion as he regarded the morsel. Blair gave it a waggle. Frostmark didn't react. Blair slapped him in the face with the hunk of pork, and the draugr just spat, his face twisting with clear disgust.

"I don't know what that is, but by Hastur's breath, I won't be eating it."

Hilde gave the Viking's bald head a slap with the flat of her hand.

"Ayez!" yelped Frostmark.

"You said you were hungry. So, eat. Be thankful we haven't tossed you onto a fire yet, you miserable arseling."

"I *am* hungry, child! But just not for that."

Hilde looked confused, but Blair caught on quickly. He held his hand open to Hilde.

"Your seax."

She withdrew the weapon and handed it to him, handle first. Without hesitation, the old man turned his forearm over and drew the blade across the sinewy skin. A red ribbon appeared instantly and was accompanied by a low gurgle of feverish anticipation from the draugr. More ripples emanated from around the neck of the severed head, the muddy water's surface trembling, as Blair held his forearm over Frostmark. The Viking's mouth opened wide, his tongue extended as far as it would go, as Blair turned his arm, allowing the blood to steadily drip the short distance to the draugr's slavering lips. It spattered his brow and his sharp nose, before finding its way to Frostmark's hungry, mewling mouth. He lapped at it hungrily, eyeball rolling in that single socket, purring like some monstrous kitten. After a few moments, Blair pulled back and, taking a strip of cloth from the bedding, dressed the wound.

Hilde stared at the Viking's head in disgusted fascination, as his purple tongue fished around his own face, trying to lap up any stray drops of blood. He appeared blissed out, like he'd just enjoyed the finest mead. His eye settled on Blair and gave the shipwright a wink.

"That's some good blood you've got there, Pict."

Blair sneered at the severed head. "Enough blathering, demon. Talk."

Frostmark sighed, as if disappointed by Blair's tone, but talk he did.

"Jarl Gudrun has lied to you, from the moment you arrived in her hall. There's a good reason why she knew that Hydyr the Hungry and the Harrowed Men attacked Unst;

she sent us there. We arrived in Scatness over a week back, and though many men stayed aboard the *Sea Wolf,* a handful of us accompanied the chief to the jarlshof. Greeted us well, did Gudrun Rognvaldsdottir, far better than the likes of us deserved. Typical, though, considering her father, Jarl Rognvald, is such an arselick. The apple didn't fall far from the tree."

Frostmark chuckled but realised his audience wasn't laughing with him. If Hilde didn't know any better, she could've sworn that wee dram of Blair's blood had put some colour into the undead Viking's cheeks. The draugr's face went serious once more.

"For seven nights, she entertained the chief. Seven nights she fell under his spell. None of you will know what he's like, but Hydyr the Hungry could charm the skin off a snake. He obviously saw something in Jarl Gudrun to give her his blessing."

Hilde frowned. "What do you mean, *his blessing?*"

Frostmark's eyeball looked down, and then all around.

"Wasn't so long ago I had a bit more about me. That's before yon Pict over there took my head from my shoulders, of course."

Blair gave him a small salute, as Frostmark continued.

"We Harrowed Men all considered our terrible fate to be a curse, least at first, to never be killed in battle. No glorious deaths for me and my brothers. And should the day ever come when we are truly silenced, with no return, we will never enter the Hall of the Slain. We may never join our kin in Valhalla. There are none more damned than the Harrowed Men."

"What was it you actually did?" asked Hilde. "To be cursed in such a way?"

A sickly grin creaked across Frostmark's face, like a crack might appear upon ice.

"You have heard of Uppsala, girl?"

"Aye, who hasn't?"

"And who told you about it?"

Hilde turned to Siv. The raven dipped her head and spoke with great reverence.

"It was my place to educate the child, as directed by her mother. I schooled Hilde on her history, and the politics of her people. I told her about the importance of Uppsala to the Norsemen. And not just the Norsemen, but to all the races across Midgard. It is that most holy of places, the spiritual home for many of the *vættir*, the faerie folk, as well. It is a place of great beauty."

Frostmark gurgled. "I'm guessing Jarl Frida didn't talk much to you about the place, girl?"

There was nothing Hilde could say. Her mother was a closed book about so much. There were a host of questions about Frida Blackheart's saga that remained unanswered. This was one such chapter in that tale, but not for long.

"Figures," said the draugr. "Every good Norseman knows that Uppsala contained the finest treasures in all of Midgard. This is the place where kings and queens brought their greatest gifts in tribute, where the mightiest warriors gave their lives in willing sacrifice to the Gods. No offering was too generous to the High Priest of Uppsala. These holy men and women, these emissaries of Odin, were paid in blood and gold. Those priests and priestesses guarded those treasures in the name of the All-father and His many offspring. So many children, none of them legitimate, each as corrupted as Him what sired them. And we are expected to worship Him?"

Another wet laugh from the draugr, his solitary eye sparkling like a precious stone.

"Well... could there be any greater hoard for a battle crew to seize than that which belonged to Odin?"

If Hilde wasn't mistaken, the temperature in the room seemed to drop at that moment, as the hammering of rain died down. She looked across at Blair, but the old man was staring at Frostmark. *Are the Gods listening to us?*

"Uppsala was unprepared for the *Sea Wolf*," said Frostmark. "The Harrowed Men marched through the forest to that temple in the dead of night. There were no guards, no carls, no warriors ready to defend it. This was Uppsala, for Hastur's sake! Who would try and steal from the Gods? Who would dare!"

Frostmark winked at Hilde, that awful grin lighting up his death mask again. She shivered, her own skin now as cold as a corpse's.

"Frida Blackheart led our battle-crew right into the heart of that temple. It was the gold she was after, see. All that glitters, all that wealth, with which she might build a kingdom of her own, the like of which Midgard had never seen. The Gods would be impressed by such a bold deed, she said. They would respect her for such a brazen act of thievery. Only, not everyone amongst the Harrowed Men was aligned with Jarl Frida's way of thinking."

That single eye stared off into space, or rather, back through time, to the night in question. Frostmark was calm now, almost reflective.

"So much killing. Slaughter the likes of which I ain't never seen before or since. It was like a sickness had taken us, a bloodlust like we'd never known. And it was Hydyr the Hungry who led it, your mother's right hand. He was the one to draw first blood, cutting down the High Priest after making him beg for mercy. Course, the old man didn't die right away. He had to watch on whilst we butchered the rest of 'em, cut 'em down like stalks of corn. There was no fight from them, no screams, no terror in the priests and priestesses. Perhaps that drove us into ever deeper, darker acts of violence upon them. I guess we'll never know. But with his dying breath, it was the High Priest who cursed all them what were there, every one of the Harrowed Men, to a life – an *un-life* – of damnation. Our world was never the same again."

Hilde could no longer look at the hideous head, instead fixing her gaze upon her hands in her lap. Anything but look at her companions. How could her mother have done such a thing, carried out such a blasphemous act without thinking of the consequences?

"You say Hydyr the Hungry gave Jarl Gudrun his blessing," said Blair, changing the subject and bringing it back to Hilde's earlier question. "How?"

Frostmark's brow creased. "Hydyr ain't like the rest of us. He's changed, changed in a way we haven't. He's guided by a higher power."

"You said you were cursed by the Gods," said Siv, threatening to jab him with her shiny beak. "Stop speaking in riddles, draugr. What higher power is there beyond the Gods?"

The Viking flinched. "A *greater* God. An Old One. A God that is older than all those who call Asgard their home. And so we fight in His name now, preparing Midgard for His coming."

There was a rumble from Blair which matched the thunder of the storm. In one hand he still held Hilde's silver seax. He hooked the thumb of his other and aimed it at the door.

"That still doesn't explain the blessing Hydyr bestowed upon that woman in there. Speak, head, and speak clearly, lest I bury this seax into your rotten skull."

Frostmark closed his eye and spoke quickly. "Think of Hydyr as Hastur's first disciple."

"Hastur?" said Siv. "This is your new God?"

"He is the oldest God," corrected Frostmark. "The Unspeakable One."

"And?" said Blair, his knuckles cracking around the handle of the long knife.

"There is power in Hydyr's blood that sets him apart from the rest of us. He's shared that blood with Jarl Gudrun, and now she's in his thrall."

"She's his *slave?*" asked Blair.

"She's bound to him, as sure as any collar of iron. If it's anything like Hydyr's influence over the Harrowed Men, he can bend her to his will, control her."

Hilde looked up. "Does Hydyr control you, even now? Are these your words or his?"

Frostmark's lip curled. "His reach has waned. I almost can't feel his presence any more."

"Almost?"

"Oh, he's left a stain upon my mind for sure. But he's gone, at least for now, perhaps never to return. I swear to Hastur, I'm telling you the truth."

Blair levelled the seax at the head, spittle frothing across his bared teeth and trembling whiskers.

"Swear to this forsaken God of evil one more time, and I swear to you, Finn Frostmark, that we'll see the inner workings of that head of yours.'

Hilde slid down off the bed, her booted feet landing in a filthy puddle. She'd seen drier pig pens than Jarl Gudrun's jarlshof. It was all so horribly clear to her now. The Jarl of Scatness had known what was transpiring for over a week and done nothing to help Hilde's people.

"Jarl Gudrun didn't even warn us," said Hilde. "She's as responsible for what happened on Unst as any of the Harrowed Men. What does she stand to gain from this betrayal, beyond Hydyr's favour?"

"You're not listening to old Finn, child," said the draugr. "She's sworn fealty to Hydyr the Hungry, taken an oath to him that foregoes any loyalty she has to any other jarl, be that her father or even King Harald Fairhair in Norðvegr. She serves Hydyr utterly. And a little bit of his power has been passed on to her."

"Passed on how?" asked Blair.

"If Jarl Hydyr is Master of the Harrowed Men, then Jarl Gudrun is the Mistress of Scatness," replied Frostmark. "Just as Hydyr holds the draugr to his will, so Gudrun does the same with her carls. It's all in the blood, see? Gudrun has passed this disease on to her people, cursed them just as she was cursed by Hydyr. Only them who serve Gudrun, they ain't the same as the Harrowed Men. They ain't draugr. They're . . . something else."

"Something new?" asked Hilde.

"Something *old*."

Frostmark's tone was grave, his one good eye red and rheumy. To Hilde, it appeared his mask had slipped, and they were seeing something else now. Was it fear?

"What aren't you telling us?" asked Blair, suspicion etched in his voice.

"You smelled the stench of death in there, Pict, heard you say it yourself. That's the corruption. The poison that pumps through Gudrun's corrupted heart now courses through the veins of her carls. That's how Hydyr's power spreads, that's how his reach grows. It branches, like forked lightning, in every direction. The Hjaltlands aren't the first place Hydyr has visited. His influence grows daily . . ."

Siv clacked her beak, causing Hilde to jump. "Hydyr is a spider at the heart of a dark web."

"And that web is growing," said Hilde. "His followers are multiplying."

Blair cracked his knuckles, the sound as harsh as branches breaking.

"We need to leave. It's clear we're no longer safe here.

I thought it bad enough there were men of Alba working for her, but if she's in league with the draugr, it's far graver than that."

Hilde snatched up the cloth gag and moved towards the Viking's head.

"You know, you don't need that," said Frostmark, his voice strangely earnest and unthreatening, and quite out of character. "I'm good now. I'll behave myself."

She looped it around his jaw, cutting short the blasphemous expletives he began to blurt out. Hilde tied the knot. Tight. Then dropped the draugr back into the bucket, popping the lid back into place.

Hilde stopped what she was doing, her shoulders sagging. She shook her head, muttered a curse of her own.

"Hell's teeth."

"What is it?" asked Blair as he grabbed the handle of the bucket.

"Aidan," she said, nodding at the silver candlestick upon the floor, and the open door that creaked on its hinges. "He's gone."

CHAPTER TWENTY-ONE
AIDAN

He had never known hunger like this. Truth be told, Aidan Erskine had never gone without. When you were the butcher's son, it was rare to miss a meal. Not that folk on Unst couldn't butcher their own food; life was tough on the islands, and people had learnt to fend for themselves. But Rab Erskine had been smart enough to make himself invaluable to his neighbours. He raised swine of his own, slaughtering them and trading every scrap of their carcasses to his friends, from snouts to trotters. Rab was a dab-hand at skinning and tanning, and his crude leathers were picked up by those hardy fishermen. And he built a smokehouse, which he maintained for those very same seafarers, preparing their catches for a price. Rab Erskine was known across the Hjaltland archipelago for being tough and uncompromising, a man of action, a man who kept his word. He was hard as nails. It was true that Aidan Erskine had never known hunger. But he had known hate.

Aidan could no longer hear his companions. He'd left them bickering with that hideous head in the bucket. All he heard now was the rainfall upon the longhouse roof and the crackle of the firepit in the main hall. He kept in a crouch, crabbing his way along the wall, bent double and staying out of the torchlight. It wasn't the best position for his protesting belly. His stomach groaned and grumbled as a host of hunger pangs attacked it.

Sure, that slab of pork they had been served had been rank, as were the accompanying foodstuffs that Agnes woman had brought them. That didn't mean to say there wasn't something else in the larder, back in the bowels of the jarlshof. Surely the old bag had to be keeping the good stuff back there, right? Dishing up that rotten fayre to her guests was just a cruel prank Jarl Gudrun had played.

The hall appeared empty at first glance, but Aidan was taking nothing for granted. He'd seen the shady figures prowling its edge when they had arrived earlier that evening, watching the visiting trio from the shadows. It felt good to have Blair by their side. At first glance, the old hermit appeared held together by gristle and whiskers, but there was a steeliness about the man, a toughness that one missed at first glance. When he'd faced off against Jarl Gudrun and her carls, Aidan had been in no doubt that Blair had meant every word of his threat; if the jarlshof were to descend into violence, the shipwright would be at the heart of it.

Aidan was less pleased to have Hilde tagging along with them. His skin still smarted from the various injuries she'd dealt him on Unst, busted nose, split lip and black eye providing constant reminders of that altercation. Most of all, it was his pride that hurt. Aidan was the biggest lad in the village, unsurprising considering the brawn of his father, and was used to throwing that muscle and weight around. He enjoyed his position as self-proclaimed leader of Unst's young'uns. Hilde Blackheart had always been the dissenting voice though, sparring with him verbally and physically at every opportunity. Cormac Tulloch tried to temper Aidan's willingness to throw his fists, had warned him that no good would ever come from it, but would Aidan listen? Not even the beatings his father dished out, after every occasion where Hilde had got the better of him, had dissuaded him from going back for more. The butcher's boy and the jarl's daughter would fight until the end of days, as sure as night followed day. It was their destiny.

Directly ahead, illuminated by the half-light of the dwindling firepit, was Jarl Gudrun's throne. Empty, as was the rest of the hall. The heavy doors at the front of the longhouse were closed, and, as there were no guards, for a moment Aidan wondered whether it had been abandoned for the night. That couldn't be the case, though. This was the jarlshof. This was Gudrun's home. The jarl was likely in bed asleep now. Perhaps her carls were doing a patrol of the longhouse, indoors and out. With that in mind, Aidan kept moving, as quickly and quietly as was possible.

Though different to the one on Unst, there were elements to the jarlshof of Scatness that were similar, not least the fact that the hall's kitchen would be situated at the very rear, along with servant quarters. But where were the slaves kept? Aidan wondered what had had become of the six thralls delivered to Jarl Gudrun earlier. None of those unfortunate Picts were that much older than Aidan and Hilde, just young'uns themselves. Where had Mistress Zaleska seized them from? What right did the strange woman have to take people from their homes, throw collars of iron around their throats and claim them as chattel? Say that for Jarl Frida; she'd never held with that Norse tradition. Anyone who came to Unst was always considered a free man or woman, lest they step out of line.

Aidan was no fool. He knew that his father had his demons. It had always surprised him that Rab Erskine had never been on the receiving end of the jarl's justice. Aidan had seen his father beat a man bloody over a raw deal one market, stopping short of killing the fellow. Enough witnesses had stepped forwards to defend Erskine's story, back up his version of events, but Aidan had always suspected they were folk who'd owed his pa a favour or two. Aidan had been there. He'd seen how the argument had played out firsthand. It was Pa who was the welch, robbing the merchant twice over.

Rab Erskine. He was a liar, he was a bully, and he was Aidan's father.

Once more his expectant stomach cramped, as if realising a meal was imminent. Aidan passed beneath a staircase behind the throne, the steps ascending into the eaves of the longhouse. That had to be the jarl's bedchambers up there, and it was the last place he wanted to explore this night. Deeper through the jarlshof he went, fearing that he might stumble into one of the carls at any moment, but there were no movements within the longhouse. It felt abandoned and did nothing to calm Aidan's already fractured nerves.

Directly ahead, the faintest of flames flickered, reflected off the wall of a short corridor. Aidan crept along, still low to the ground, close to the wall, mindful of the noises his feet and his stomach were making. He held his hands out before him, fumbling around as he went, the light so dim it was near impossible to see. Turning a corner, he arrived in what he recognised was a kitchen, a large stone firepit dominating its centre. A spit and iron pot were suspended over this, but the hearth remained unlit, the only light coming from a single lantern that sat atop an enormous trestle table. The flame within was dying, the fat reserves it fed off almost spent, its wick drooping and slowly burning away to nothing. Refuse cluttered the table, gnawed bones and rotten fruit, more rancid meat and ruined vegetables. A leg of lamb sat neglected, flies teeming in the air around it, drawn to the rotting joint. The floor was equally littered with detritus, where pots, pans and plates had been discarded, dropped or shattered, and left where they had fallen.

By that dim and dying light, Aidan spied a wheel of cheese on the far side of the kitchen, sat on the top shelf of an apparently empty larder. There was something that wouldn't have spoilt, its thick rind preserving it from one season to the next. His belly instantly began burbling and bleating when it realised what his eyes had seen, and Aidan nearly struck it to shut it up. He crept carefully around the filthy trestle, traversing his way across the room. He was a couple of strides from the shelves when he realised he wasn't alone in the kitchen.

Kneeling upon the floor behind the table was the old serving woman, Agnes. The fading light of the candle didn't entirely reach her, leaving her blanketed in darkness but for the nest of thin white hair upon her head. She was hunched over, rocking, seemingly nursing something in her arms. Aidan considered ignoring her, grabbing the cheese wheel and getting the hell out of there, but he felt a pang of sympathy. He had heard the way Jarl Gudrun had spoken to the woman, had seen how downtrodden she had been. Aidan shuffled slowly forwards, squinting through the gloom, manoeuvring around the crouching servant until he was in reaching distance.

As Aidan's eyes gradually adjusted to the lack of light, his hand stopped short of tapping Agnes on the shoulder. He could now see what the old maid was nursing, or rather whom. One of the Pictish slaves, sold to Jarl Gudrun earlier that night, lay sprawled upon the floor, her eyes staring up at the cobweb-covered roof above. Her mouth was open, gasping slowly like a dying fish, as Agnes's head remained buried in the girl's shoulder blade, deep in the flesh. A bib of claret had spread out from the young woman's throat, spilling down over her chest as she lay limp and dying in the old servant's clutch.

Aidan took a step back, followed by another one, horror at what he was witnessing propelling him backwards with growing force. His heel hit a pan, sent it clattering into the shattered remnants of a plate. Agnes's head whipped up from the body of the Pict and turned sharply to look at the butcher's boy. Her eyes were twin pools of deathly black darkness, and as she saw the boy they widened, shining bright for a moment. Her scrawny jaw was wet with blood, and those teeth . . . those teeth. They were the teeth of a shark, a ridge of terrible serrated blades that gnashed together in a snarl.

Aidan tripped over more of the broken crockery, tumbling back onto the kitchen floor. He felt something hard crack against the small of his back, paralysing him for a moment as his spine went numb. He rolled over, pushed the offending pot aside and began to drag himself across the kitchen floor. He glanced back.

Agnes was upright now, dropping the Pict's body with a thump. Still enveloped in darkness, all Aidan could see was the sparkling lights within those awful, black eyes. She dropped her head suddenly, raising her shoulder blades sharply. The action reminded Aidan of how a hawk might move. And sure enough, the old woman began to stalk forwards. She ducked and weaved, gauging her prey, her movements sharp and erratic and utterly at odds with her venerable appearance. There were no missteps, as she stepped and hopped easily through the wrecked kitchen.

Aidan scrambled away, fast as he could, powered on by fear. He grabbed the pots and plates, the smashed crockery, and began hurling them at the old hag as he went. She dodged a few of the missiles, but let the others bounce harmlessly off her. Then she pounced.

The butcher's boy was ready. He brought his legs back, knees bent as he took her entire weight upon his feet. Monstrous though she was, she still had the weight of a little old lady, and Aidan was able to support her, his legs compressing against his chest. She clawed at his face with her hands, fingers scratching his cheeks, tearing at his hair, teeth gnashing and spitting blood onto the boy. Then he launched her back with a great heave, sending her flying across the room.

Agnes hit the shelving with great force, shattering the remaining shelves, including the uppermost one that held the cheese. The great wheel of dairy goodness fell like a boulder from the heavens, smashing the servant over the head and felling her, before rolling over to Aidan. He struggled to his feet, picking up the cheese and tucking it under his left arm, just as the monstrous maid leapt back to her feet.

Once more, she was almost upon him before Aidan's reactions saved his bacon. The festering leg of lamb was in his hand, his fist closed around the shank's bone, as he swung it with all his might. Aidan was no warrior, but just as Cormac Tulloch had the arm of a blacksmith, so Rab Erskine's boy had a butcher's brawn. The joint of lamb struck Agnes hard against her head, the accompanying *snap* convincing Aidan that the woman's neck had been broken. That sent her staggering to one side like an awful marionette, where she then collided with the iron pot over the firepit. She went down in a dead heap once more, the spit and heavy cauldron landing on her with a sickening *crunch*.

Aidan breathed a deep sigh of relief, desperate to get the air back in his lungs. He suddenly realised the rot of the lamb had got up his nose, the stench unbearable. Tossing it aside, along with its accompanying swarm of bloated bluebottles, Aidan wiped the stinking meat juice on his thigh. He took two steps towards the exit from the kitchen and heard a series of strange noises at his back.

Clattering. Groaning. Gurgling.

He turned slowly.

The old woman had risen from the ruins of the firepit, head crushed, broken ribs poking out of her smock, shark's smile lighting up her nightmarish face.

Aidan screamed.

CHAPTER TWENTY-TWO
HILDE

It was his scream that got them running.

Hilde was no fan of the butcher's boy – the Gods knew the pair of them had sparred over the years – and Aidan was hardly shy about his dislike for the jarl's daughter. Regardless, Hilde didn't want to see him come to further harm. It was only a couple of days ago that she'd given him a beatdown that he'd never forget, and since then his home had been destroyed, his father likely killed, and everything he ever cared about snatched from his miserable grasp. But for now, Aidan Erskine had suffered enough. Siv screeched at the sudden commotion, taking flight in a flash of black feathers and swooping out through the hole in the wall. Hilde made a silent prayer as she and Blair ran from their jail cell into the main hall of the jarlshof, dashing headlong into madness.

If any more pain is to come Aidan's way, Blessed All-father, let it be by my hand and nobody else's.

Blair led the way, sack of gear across his left shoulder and the bucket swinging from his hip. His sword-hand was empty, the shipwright at pains to give the seax back to Hilde. Seemed at first the old man fancied his chances with his bare hands, before Hilde realised he just wanted her to live. Best opportunity for that happening was if she had that silver blade in her hand.

Aidan came scrambling out of the darkness behind the jarl's throne, tripping and stumbling, bouncing off the walls in a blind panic. Hilde had to do a double-take when she saw the wheel of cheese he was carrying in the crook of his left arm, but any amusement at that sight was short-lived. Aidan's face was streaked with fresh blood where it looked like he'd been raked by fingernails or claws, and hot on his heels came a horror.

Initially, Hilde didn't know who or what she was looking at, for the attacker's head appeared to have been smashed and battered, glistening dark by the light of the firepit. Within that blood-red mask dread-black eyes flashed, while the monster's jaws opened impossibly wide. So many teeth – too many for a human mouth – each one sharp as a razor and long as a pine needle. When she leapt through the air (for Hilde now realised exactly who had appeared before them) they could see her broken torso, ribs exposed and poking clear of her smock. Agnes, the tired old servant who had delivered a platter of rotten food to them earlier, had transformed in spectacular fashion.

She landed on Aidan's back, catapulting him headfirst into the back of the jarl's throne. The two went down in a tangle of limbs, the wheel of cheese rolling comically away. Agnes twisted atop the struggling boy, trying to find a way to the tender, exposed flesh of his neck. Blair was there quickly, his boot catching the monster across her jaw, sending her skittering away across the hall.

Another clap of thunder shook the jarlshof, though its accompanying lightning had no way of penetrating the gloomy interior of the longhouse.

"Quickly," said Blair, grabbing Aidan by the elbow and pulling him to his feet. "To the doors!"

He propelled the lad forwards, only for the young man to take the slightest diversion, pausing to reclaim his prize cheese. He rejoined Hilde, clutching the yellow wheel like his life depended upon it.

"You really went looking for food?" shouted Hilde as they ran down the length of the jarlshof towards the exit.

"What part of me starving didn't you understand?" said a breathless Aidan.

They reached the end of the hall, bouncing into the double doors which stood closed to the elements. Two enormous iron braziers stood either side of the threshold, their coals and timbers still burning, a rare source of heat on this cold and terrible night. Blair grabbed the doors' metal ring handles, gave them a firm pull, then a push. Tried again.

"Here," said Hilde, adding her weight to proceedings, the pair of them struggling to shift either door.

"They're barred from outside," snarled Blair. "The whole damned jarlshof is locked down. We're trapped."

"Why would they lock us in?" asked Aidan.

"Because we were never meant to leave," said Hilde.

All three of them turned. Agnes was crouched at the foot of the jarl's throne, hunkered down like a wolfhound, almost unrecognisable from the woman they'd first encountered. A dark tongue snaked out of her mouth and danced along her terrible teeth. Aidan pointed at Agnes, his back flat to the timber doors, heels digging in hard against the earthen floor of the longhouse.

"The Picts . . . them what Jarl Gudrun bought from the Zaleska woman. The old crone killed one of the lasses. Saw her do it, with my own eyes . . ."

Hilde gave Aidan a dig with her elbow.

"You mean *that* lass?"

Shambling out of the shadows behind the throne, stumbling towards the light of the firepit, came a gore-drenched, fair-haired young woman. Hilde recognised her for one of Jarl Gudrun's newly acquired slaves. She was as pale as death, and her inelegant movements put Hilde in mind of a bairn taking her first steps. The Pict came to a halt beside the throne. Her injuries were now fully evident, her neck a mangled mess of scarlet ribbons, torn and tattered where those dagger-like teeth had worried and ruined her throat. Without looking, Agnes raised a bony, bloody hand into the air, and the ghost-white girl reached down with a hand of her own, tenderly stroking the old woman's fingertips.

"What am I seeing here?" asked Hilde, her mind fracturing with every passing heartbeat.

Blair stepped forwards in front of his young charges, horror writ upon his disbelieving face.

"When the butcher's boy said she was dead, I thought these poor wretches were Jarl Gudrun's larder, brought here for her to feed upon. But . . . but it's *worse* than that. They're not here to be eaten . . ."

Hilde finished the sentence for him.

"They're here to be turned."

Agnes made a strange retching sound that caught the attention of the three captives. They watched as she twisted her head this way and that, manipulating her mouth, lips sliding up and down over those innumerate overlarge teeth.

"You..." she began, pained to speak when all she wanted to do was feed. "You... should have stayed... in room."

She snapped her jaws, ground her teeth, regained her composure, those alien, ebony eyes fixed upon her prey.

"The Mistress... awaits His command, for He... He will decide what is to become of you. If that is a blessing... then she means to bless you herself."

"Bless?" exclaimed Blair. He pointed at the pale Pictish girl as she swayed in an undead trance. "What kind of blessing is that? I see only a curse!"

"Jarl Gudrun would share her gift with you," said Agnes. "And you would be grateful. We all serve Jarl Gudrun. And Jarl Gudrun serves Him."

"Him?" shouted Hilde, encouraged by the old man's stance. "You mean Hydyr the Hungry? That black-bearded serpent is responsible for all of this. We know, witch! We know your game!"

Hilde had heard some awful sounds in her life – the death rattle of an old woman suffering from consumption, the noise a pig makes when its slaughtered – but she was unprepared for the laughter that bubbled forth from the serving woman. It bubbled up through her scrawny throat, vomiting forth in a foul eruption of bloody ichor and hideous glee.

"Jarl Hydyr?" cackled Agnes. "The Hungry one is but

His herald. Our Master is the Golden Jarl, the Unspeakable One... *Hastur!*"

"We're not scared of you, demon!' shouted a defiant Aidan, having found his voice at last. "We've fought draugr before; we don't fear your kind! Do your worst, you old hag!"

It was a lie, of course. Neither of the young'uns had actually fought the draugr, though Blair had duelled with Finn Frostmark, ultimately removing the Viking's head from his accursed shoulders.

Agnes leapt onto the jarl's throne and threw her head back, letting loose a guttural cry. Shapes began to shift in the shadows of the loft above her as a host of figures slowly materialised. Hilde counted six or seven of them, recognising them as Jarl Gudrun's house carls. They prowled towards the top of the staircase, remaining on the edge of the firelight. A host of black eyes sparkled in the dark, reflecting the flames, all fixed upon the three survivors from Unst. Hilde was put in mind of the way a wildcat might move when stalking its prey. Though barely visible, the carls had been feasting, that much was clear. Some were in a state of undress, and like Agnes sported red, glistening stains upon their jaws and chests. No doubt the remaining slaves were strewn about the loft, dead, ruined or transformed like the one beside the throne. Hilde didn't want to think about what kind of horrors had taken place in the pitch-dark of the jarl's bedchambers.

"I may have spoken out of turn," whispered Aidan to his companions, his moment of bravado having dissipated like a fart on the wind.

"You think us draugr?" called out Agnes, once more choking down a bilious bout of laughter. "Oh, we are far worse than that!"

Blair turned and threw himself at the doors once more, pounding them with his fists and putting his shoulder into it. The entire threshold shook, dust dislodged from the timber frame as the shipwright struck it with all his might, but it would not budge. Hilde watched as the carls began to descend the staircase, slinking and swaying, snarling at Agnes who waited patiently for them atop the jarl's throne. The creature that had once appeared as a benign old woman snapped back at them, as if speaking in some animalistic tongue, before returning her attention to their three guests. She pointed a bony finger and barked out a throaty cry. Her companions responded in kind, becoming more animated, scuttling down the remaining steps of the staircase and fanning out into the hall.

Dropping his sack and bucket at the threshold, Blair grabbed a torch from the wall and advanced a few paces, swinging the flame this way and that, desperate to keep the undead warriors at bay. They didn't slow, and came darting and dancing along the hall towards them.

"Whatever you do," Blair shouted over his shoulder to the two youths, "you stay behind me, y'hear?"

Hilde dropped her shield and ran.

"Come back, lassie!" shouted Blair as she bolted away from them.

Even Aidan tried to grab her, but the shieldmaiden was too quick for him.

"I'll be back!" she yelled as she dashed across the hall, making straight for the guest quarters where they had been imprisoned.

Three of the carls bounded away from the others, pursuing Hilde as she reached the southern wall of the jarlshof and slipped into the room that had so briefly been their residence. She slammed the door shut behind her, grabbed the cot, flipped it on its end and rammed it up against the iron ring handle, pinning the rough timber frame in place. No sooner was the door secured, she ran to the outer wall, where the rain still lashed in through the opening she had fashioned.

As Hilde hacked at the hard earth and set about widening the window, she heard the trio of undead warriors collide with the door. She chanced a peek over her shoulder, saw the bed frame juddering, threatening to come loose from where she'd wedged it. Holding the seax in both hands, she sawed and jabbed with furious desperation, breaking loose larger fragments of packed clay and prising them away from the wall.

Another look over her shoulder, and she saw a pale arm with sharp, filthy nails squirm through the opening, followed by another, as the cot began to shift. More snarls and barks followed from within the hall, as the gap between door and frame gradually widened. Unable to delay any longer, Hilde tossed her long knife through the opening, out into the night, and scrambled up the wall, looking to follow it. Her head and shoulders were through and out, her skin raked by the shards of clay that snagged her as she wriggled and worked her way towards an exit. She was halfway out when she felt her hips catch against either side of the rough tunnel. *Childbearing hips,* one of the less-than-helpful elders back on Unst had referred to them as. Cursing her proportions, Hilde breathed in, manoeuvred onto her side, just as she heard the bed frame clatter and the door bounce off its hinges.

She fell forwards, freed from the confines of the window at last, falling headfirst back to earth beyond the jarlshof. Self-preservation kicked in as Hilde threw her arms out before her to cushion the landing – a broken neck would be a hell of a way to go for the daughter of Frida Blackheart – and readied for impact. Only she never hit the ground. She was yanked hard, like a fish on a line, a hideous hand having snared her about the ankle. The arm was all the way out of the opening, ink tattoos stark against cold white skin, as it began to haul the girl back into the room. Hilde kicked back with her other foot, striking the undead warrior's knuckles, but the creature was utterly unfazed, relentlessly drawing her in.

Hilde grabbed at the soaking ground, hands coming away useless with fistfuls of mud which she flung aside. There, the handle of the seax, only a hand's breadth away. She quit kicking at the carl's grip and launched her heel against the wall, her body going stiff and straight as she forced herself away from the longhouse. It was enough to steal her a little distance, as her hands closed around the handle of her mother's blade. Then she was rising to meet the monstrous Norseman, the seax scything up through the night.

The offending arm was suddenly spinning through the air, spattering dark goo in its wake. Where the silver had severed the limb, the flesh of the stump sizzled, as if burnt by a white-hot fire. Hilde landed with a splash beyond the jarlshof, as she heard her enemy's screams of despair within. Then she was struggling to her feet, slipping and sliding in the mud, as she dashed breathlessly around to the front of the longhouse.

The carls who had guarded the double doors earlier were no longer present. A wooden beam had been placed into a pair of brackets either side of the entrance to the longhouse, holding the great doors firmly closed. Hilde cursed. How had they not noticed these brackets when they had arrived? Then again, one didn't expect to find barricades on the outside of a jarlshof. Such a defence was ordinarily situated *inside* a building, to keep enemies out, not trap folk within.

She heard a pained cry from inside the hall. May have been Aidan, could have been one of the warriors. Hilde wasted no more time. She went to one side of the door and took hold of the wooden beam's end. She briefly attempted to lift it out of the bracket, which seemed impossible for one person, let alone a girl of fifteen winters. Instead, she pushed the timber from its end, her shoulder pressed hard against the wood, slowly but inexorably forcing it across the entrance. The beam passed over one of the end brackets and, once clear of the fixture, came crashing down onto the ground. She grabbed the timber and pulled hard as if it were an oar, prising the double doors apart enough that she could barge through and re-enter the hellish jarlshof.

Fires had sprung up on the left side of the hall, where one of the braziers had been toppled during the fracas. Burning coals and flaming logs had found their way across the floor of the longhouse, the dry walls and piles of straw having greedily accepted their heat. Both Blair and Aidan were oblivious to Hilde's reappearance, each doing what they could to keep the monsters at bay. Blair was making good use of his torch, scything it this way and that through the air before them, the carls recoiling from the fire, clearly fearful of it. Aidan stayed close to the shipwright, protecting the old man's flank, using Hilde's shield to bash and beat the dead back.

"This way!" she screamed, picking up Blair's sack and Frostmark's bucket.

Aidan turned when he heard her, and unless she was mistaken, he might have even smiled to see her. He kicked his pilfered cheese through the narrow opening before leaping after it. Blair took one more wild swing with the torch, sending the host of strange draugr rocking back, before throwing the burning brand high over their heads. As the torch spun, its flames caught the low-hanging thatch, the hay taking the fire as it got tangled in the roof. Then he ran for the opening, pausing only to kick the other brazier over, sending its blazing contents against the right wall of the longhouse. The monsters roared, but Hilde and Blair were already gone, staggering out of the burning jarlshof.

"Help me," said Hilde, pushing the open door closed.

Blair and Aidan were quickly up to speed, the boy putting his shoulder to the door alongside Hilde as the man bent to pick up the dislodged beam. Hilde was about to warn him it was too heavy, but then watched in wide-eyed wonder as the shipwright took the strain, heaving the wooden post into the air and lowering it back into its bracket with a resounding clatter. Fists pounded against the doors within the longhouse, accompanied by the panicked screams of Jarl Gudrun's warriors. Hilde staggered clear of the building, squinting through the drizzle as clouds of ugly black smoke began to belch from the roof of the jarlshof. The falling rain was lit from below as the fire within the hall illuminated the stormy sky above, the flames unquenched by the downpour.

"Is that all of them?" said Blair, gulping ragged breaths into his heaving chest.

The thunder rumbled in the dark heavens above whilst the jarlshof burnt and its trapped inhabitants screamed.

"What are the odds that *she* was in there?" asked Aidan, squinting at the flames that were now devouring the chieftain's hall.

He didn't need to name her. They were all thinking of her.

Blair took his sack and Frostmark's bucket from Hilde and gave her a perfunctory nod.

"Smart work back there, lassie. You saved our bacon."

Then he was on his way towards the harbour, sack over his shoulder again, bucket swinging at his hip as he descended the muddy road. Aidan handed Hilde's shield back to her. He was about to follow Blair but paused for the briefest moment, chewing his lip, his bruised face fixed in a crumpled frown.

"Thanks."

That was all he said, before turning away and following the shipwright down the hill.

A mad old hermit and a fool of a butcher's boy. Neither were Hilde's choice of travelling companion, but she was stuck with them for the foreseeable. And as she followed them towards Scatness town, her scax held tight in a scuffed-knuckle grip, it came as quite the revelation to her that she was grateful beyond the telling of it that she was with them this night.

CHAPTER TWENTY-THREE
FRIDA

She had been born aboard a boat. Like Frida, her mother was a shieldmaiden before her, and hadn't let the inconvenience of a bairn in her belly slow down her exploits. That woman had fought in the shield wall, had raided and pillaged, battled armies and burnt villages, sailed countless seas in search of plunder. Frida had entered that world of fire and blood beneath the clapping sail of a longship. It should have felt like home. Instead, it felt like hell.

Hell.

A Christian idea, that place where the damned were sent. Frida's people had their own name for such a place. *Náströnd:* the Corpse Shore where the great serpent, Níðhöggr, devours the dead souls of the dishonoured. Endlessly. Say that for the Norse gods; they knew a thing or two about punishing those who blasphemed them. And the Harrowed Men were fated to taste that purgatory one day, each and every one of them.

"She's mine, isn't she?"

Frida didn't need to look up, would know that voice anywhere. Nor did she bother replying.

"Your fisherman's girl, back in that hovel you called a jarlshof," said Hydyr the Hungry, craning his head beneath the deck canopy. "She's mine."

"She's not yours," replied Frida quietly.

"She's mine."

"She's probably dead," she lied, knowing full well that Hilde lived, or at least had been alive when Cormac last saw her. Anything to put him off her scent.

"She's probably alive! A father like me and a mother like you; she'll have that same survivor's instinct. A refusal to go quietly."

"That may be, but she's not yours."

His laughter was a real belly rattler, like it was the funniest thing he had heard.

"Frida, my love; you and I fought side by side, and we lay side by side. The child is mine."

She gave him a sideways glare.

"You never struck me as the kind of man who would pine for fatherhood."

"Oh, you wouldn't *believe* what I pine for, Frida Blackheart. But a daughter? Oh, such a thing is perfect. When she comes after you—"

"She *won't* come after me."

"You gibber like a drooling fool." He laughed. "Of course she'll come after you! She's a Blackheart! It's in her blood, and mine too, for that matter. She will seek us out . . ." He smiled knowingly, dreamily. "I sense her coming already . . ."

It was Frida's turn to laugh; a rare thing for the woman. And it was all she could do to try and put Hydyr off the scent, because Frida *knew* her daughter, knew that Hilde would not rest until she was reunited with her mother, or at the very least had wrought vengeance upon those who had killed her friends and neighbours. Of course she would be coming. She was, after all, a Blackheart.

Frida snorted. "You sense she's coming?" She nodded theatrically. "Sure you do."

That burst the Viking's moment of reverie. "You look like death, by the way."

"Damnation will do that to a soul."

Hydyr the Hungry sat down opposite her, grinning with youthful exuberance. And so he might. Here was a man who was at peace with his fate, hadn't just accepted the fact that he could no longer die – or rather, was difficult to kill – but had embraced it.

Frida looked along the length of the *Sea Wolf* in the direction of the prow. It would be dawn soon enough, the ship now sailing into calmer seas, the great storm that had savaged the Hjaltland Isles now behind them, rumbling at their backs. Norðvegr lay directly ahead. She cast her eyes over the prisoners, only a handful now remaining from those who had been stolen away from Unst. The Harrowed Men had been hungry. And Hydyr had been thirsty. She would be amazed if any of them survived by the time they reached her homeland.

"Why do you run away from your destiny, Frida?" asked Hydyr the Hungry, his voice annoyingly light and cheery. "Life would be so much easier if you simply accepted it."

"Life?" she snorted. "This isn't life. We are already in purgatory, you and I. The real death still awaits us. Not in the blessed hall of Valhalla, feasting with our brothers and sisters, but on the Corpse Shore."

A smiling Hydyr ran a hand through his thick black hair,

tousling it like the handsome wolf he'd always been. Frida looked away. She knew his games. If there was ever a vainer man in Midgard, she had never met him.

"You've spent the last fifteen winters trying to run away from your past—"

"I haven't run away from anything. I walked away from that, left that life behind me, my place in this battle-crew. I wanted nothing to do with the Harrowed Men. They're yours now, remember? Every cursed one of them. Every shred of blood, flesh and bone."

Hydyr sniffed his objections, thumbing his nose.

"Looked an awful lot like running away from where I was standing."

Frida levelled her gaze at Hydyr.

"What is the point of this?"

"Of what?"

She pointed at him, and then herself, and then whirled her finger in the air in all directions.

"This. What purpose does this service? You have destroyed my home, killed just about everyone I care about, and dragged me back to a world that I no longer belong to. I will not fight for you, Hydyr. I will not serve you. I am not that shieldmaiden any more.'

"I think you lie," said Hydyr, his face suddenly sober and serious, as if a cloud had appeared over his head. "The shieldmaiden is still in there, waiting to break out. That fire that raged inside of you cannot have been quenched. There was no more terrifyingly beautiful sight than Frida Blackheart charging into battle, breaking shield walls single-handedly, cutting down any champion who dared stand in her way. We just need to shatter those shackles. Unleash the beast. One final, glorious act of that would befit an ending to your saga."

She stared at him coldly. "The beast is dead."

Frida winced, another hunger pang coursing through her ruined body. It wasn't missed by her host. He nodded at her.

"I see you, Frida Blackheart. You're hungry, aren't you?"

She didn't answer, as he craned forwards, shuffling closer to her, almost coming within touching distance. He looked left and right, as if checking nobody was watching, and then whispered conspiratorially.

"Have a little drink, my love. What harm could it do?"

Frida said nothing. She folded her arms, gripped them about her belly, clutching her ribs. She felt the stitches catch and pull, where Cormac had fixed her wounds, that strange sensation of her undead flesh moving. She should have felt pain from those injuries, only she didn't. It was as if she were disconnected from the sensation. The only place she knew pain was in her mind, and her throat, and her marrow.

Because Frida Blackheart needed to feed. Needed to drink. She could smell it, all over that cursed longship, the entire drakkar coated in the stuff, its black timbers soaked in it. Old blood from decades of battle, from where Harrowed Men had fallen before they'd ever been damned. And fresh blood from the kills, from the sacrifices that very night, of those poor men and women from Unst who had been butchered to fill the bloated bellies and endless appetites of the Vikings.

"You're thinking about it, right now, aren't you?" said Hydyr, his voice warm and seductive. "The taste. It's succour. The magic that happens."

Frida shivered, closed her eyes. Only she couldn't shut her ears.

"Drink, Frida," said her old friend. "Drink and be well. You've earnt it, you more than anyone. This gift that the Harrowed Men had bestowed upon them, that was thanks to you. We brothers are immortal, Frida. We are as powerful as any of those fat fools who crowd Asgard. We do not fear the Gods. We *are* gods."

He snapped his fingers. "Erskine. Bring a bottle."

Frida squirmed, gritted her teeth. She heard the butcher shamble forwards from where he had been slumped in the stern of the longship. She could also smell the contents of the bottle he was reverently carrying, bringing it carefully and obediently to his new master.

"Good lad," said Hydyr, patting the Pict's gore-stained back before sending him back into the shadows beneath the tarpaulin.

The Viking popped the cork on the bottle. The smell of the fresh blood was overwhelming, hitting Frida like a punch to the face, assailing her every sense. The sound of it sloshing about within the container. The smell of it, sharp as the bouquet of the finest wine or mead. The taste of it, so close, that coppery, metallic tang on the air, promising satisfaction, guaranteeing delirium, and mending every rotten festering wound that covered her ruined body.

She turned her face away.

"Really?" asked Hydyr, unable to hide the disappointment in his voice, the allure broken. "You would deny yourself the chance to heal?"

"It's a trick," replied Frida. "You can't heal from these wounds. Not truly. It's an illusion. We are broken, irreparable, pretending to be living, breathing men and women."

She heard him move suddenly, felt his hand snatch at her face, bringing her roughly around so they were eye to eye. His face was darker now, as if his flesh were absorbing the very night that surrounded them. His eyes, ordinarily so very brown as to appear black, had changed somehow. The pupils had swollen, bleeding into and swamping the whites, and flecks of silver danced in them like tiny bright lights. They were mesmerising, and Frida couldn't look away.

"That's where you're wrong, shieldmaiden. I do not pretend to be a man any more."

"Draugr, then," she spat, her lip trembling.

Was this fear? She no longer felt fear, hadn't suffered that emotion in forever. So why did Hydyr the Hungry now scare her? He couldn't hurt her.

"You're a monster, a ghost, a ghoul that haunts the lands of Midgard, stealing all the love and life from every soul you meet."

Then he smiled.

Frida tried to recoil, but he had her held fast in his grasp.

Those teeth. Had they always been so sharp?

"The draugr are kindred to me," said Hydyr, his voice a throaty growl, "but I am no longer one of them."

Frida managed to shake her head, even in the grip of

Hydyr's cold, dark fingers.

"You lie," she said. "You and I, the Harrowed Men; we are all the same. Cursed to drink blood if we wish to *'live'*. But it's all an act. We're as dead as the corpses you burnt back on Unst. Until somebody puts a blade through our skulls and shatters our minds, we just don't know it. I *know* how the curse works, Hydyr. I was *there* when you brought your madness down upon the priests of Uppsala."

Hydyr's chuckle was that of a man who knew something Frida didn't. Secretive. Arrogant.

"I have ascended, my love. I am something *more* now."

"And what's that, exactly?" she managed to mouth, a strange and alien fear still inexplicably gripping her cold, dead heart.

For a fleeting moment, Frida heard a strange noise. At first, she thought it was on the wind, carried across the drakkar, but then realised it was a voice – Hydyr's voice – and it was a seductive whisper in her head. Just the one word:

Strigoi.

Hydyr loosened his grip on her, stroked her cheek, brushed her lip with his thumb. His face began to lighten suddenly, the whites returning to his eyes as a benign smile now graced his handsome face.

"You can join me, Frida. Together, we'll be more powerful than anyone or anything the Nine Worlds have ever known. We can rule together in His name, King and Queen over all races."

"Whose name?"

Softer though his face now was, there was a wildness in Hydyr's eyes.

"Hastur," he purred. "The Golden Jarl."

"Should I recognise his name?"

"Soon the Nine Worlds shall, and all will tremble."

"And how exactly do you differ from the draugr, Herald of Hastur?" she said mockingly.

Hydyr's face lit up at that. "*Herald of Hastur?* Oh, I like that!"

"You look like the rest of the wretched souls to me, decaying from within and without."

He opened the palm of his left hand before Frida and, with the sharp black thumbnail of his right, drew it down across the dirty skin. The wound parted, and a crimson line appeared, yawning open within that necrotic flesh. If the smell of Erskine's bottle of blood had left her dizzied, the scent of Hydyr's essence drove her to the point of delirium? She seized his hand by the wrist, brought her mouth closer in feverish anticipation. Hydyr's eyes widened with excitement.

"Good," said the jarl of the *Sea Wolf*. "Drink, my love. Be my bride once more. We can still be a family. Together we shall deliver our daughter to Him."

The motion of Hydyr's hand towards Frida's hungry mouth came to a juddering halt. She gasped, as if waking from a nightmare, still overwhelmed by the blood's strange hold over her. However, there was enough of the old Frida still in there, the bond that tied her to Hilde stronger than any dark magic at Hydyr's disposal. She threw his hand back in his face.

"A shame," said Hydyr. "You'll come round, though. I know you, Frida Blackheart."

She watched on in disbelief as the deep gash in the Viking's palm closed itself, as easy as an eyelid might shut. The hand appeared as good as new, no blood, no trace of the cut. Hydyr stood tall over Frida, who was struggling to understand what had just happened.

"It's almost dawn," said Hydyr. "It has been a busy night, and many of the Harrowed Men will need to rest – you know how they dislike the sunlight. And I shall need my sleep. Use this time wisely, Frida. Consider my very generous offer and the future you can enjoy by my side."

He raised a long, elegant finger into the air, as if remembering something.

"Oh, and one more thing, my love. That thing you stole from me in Uppsala. You know the one. I want it back."

"I don't know what you're talking about."

He smiled at the lie. "Fight me all you like, but I shall break that iron will of yours, Frida Blackheart. You'll tell me what has become of the World Ender before our saga is through. And we shall use it together, in Hastur's glorious name."

Hydyr turned his face towards the distant horizon in the east, where the night's sky was already beginning to brighten. He stood upon the deck of the *Sea Wolf*, hands out to either side. The Harrowed Men dropped their heads respectfully, and the slaves looked away fearfully. For a moment, Frida found herself thinking of the Christ-god that Brother Benedict preached of, arms cruciform, a figure of divinity.

And that word still echoed in the back of her mind: *strigoi.*

Then a fog appeared, rising from the surrounding waters like some dread monster, drawn from the cold depths of the *Nordsær* by dark, otherworldly powers that were at Hydyr's fingertips. The jarl headed towards the stern and the enormous battle chest that Einar the Small stood watch over, the mist building all around him. Einar reached down with his one good hand, grabbed the lid of the great chest and swung it open. Frida watched on, bewildered, as Hydyr stepped into it, the fog closing around him. The *Sea Wolf* had been hidden by it when Unst was raided, shrouded by it throughout the following day. Now it came again, a blanket of gloom that the sun could not penetrate. Falling over the black drakkar like a dead man's shroud.

CHAPTER TWENTY-FOUR
AIDAN

Scatness was indeed a ghost town. Aidan had hoped to see signs of life when they passed back through it on their way to the harbour, but every home and hovel they passed remained without light or life. He peered through windows and open doorways, spied uneaten food on tables, saw beds and cots still made, whatever meagre and humble items that passed for keepsakes and treasures left in their place. Nothing appeared to have been stolen. There were no signs of violence. It was as if every inhabitant had simply got up and departed, leaving all behind, running away from whatever horrors Hydyr the Hungry had visited upon the town.

The wailing cries they had heard earlier from atop the hill had now ceased, but Aidan got a distinct sense that something terrible still lurked out there in the night. It had to be Jarl Gudrun. If any of her warriors had escaped the jarlshof's inferno, they would no doubt seek out their mistress, but it appeared unlikely. Aidan imagined the jarl was alone now and in despair after what they had done to her home. She would seek revenge; no doubt about it. They would be lucky to live through what was left of this terrible night.

He glanced at Blair, whose steely gaze scoured the darkness, seeking out any threat. He was a couple of steps ahead of him and Hilde, his desire to keep them safe evident in all that he did. The shipwright remained a mystery, but he was a good mystery to have on their side. Aidan glanced to the girl by his side. Hilde had her shield on her left arm, her silver seax in her right hand, and was clearly ready for anything. She was a born warrior. And what did Aidan have? In his arms he carried the wheel of cheese he'd grabbed in the jarl's larder. Fat lot of good he was going to be in a fight.

A shape darted across the road ahead, causing Aidan to gasp out loud. It was a dog, a scrawny wee ratter, and it whimpered as it ran, abandoned by its human masters as they had fled. Aidan only hoped the people of Scatness had escaped the Harrowed Men, scattering across the island to settlements that were untouched by the draugr, or indeed crossing the water to neighbouring isles among the Hjaltlands. It was now clear to Aidan that Hydyr's ambitions were far more wide-reaching than he could have imagined.

"You see that?" said Blair, pointing ahead. "That's our way off this rock."

The knarr of Mistress Zaleska remained moored to the long jetty that extended out into the crescent-shaped bay. It was the only vessel in Scatness harbour, and a pair of lanterns swung from the prow and the stern respectively. It was different to a drakkar, the longship favoured by Viking raiders. This was a trader's ship, meant for commerce, not war. Its hull was wider and deeper than that of a drakkar, and this boat even appeared to have a hold, judging by the bulk at its centre.

"A question," whispered Aidan as they descended ever deeper into the heart of Scatness town. "How in the world do we three crew that boat?"

Blair grumbled. "We'll cross that sea when we come to it, lad."

The worst of the storm appeared to have passed them by now, its lightning flashes brightening the skies to the south, approaching the Orkneyar Isles. The moon was now visible, having broken clear of the brooding clouds, casting welcome beams over the town below, illuminating the way ahead. Aidan glanced up at the milk-white globe and got a face full of rain for his troubles. It was constant, a miserable drizzle that not even the approaching dawn could scare away. The ground remained treacherous underfoot, streams of mud running down the road and turning each of Aidan's steps into a game of chance. Somehow, he kept his feet as they arrived in Scatness harbour.

Blair stopped at the base of the jetty, where a clutch of fisherman's tools remained stacked inside an open barrel. He removed a long wooden pole with a wicked-looking metal hook on its end. Checking its weight, he gave the gaff a brief whirl in the air, appraising it like a grandmaster.

Aidan peered into the barrel, fished around for something he could use too. His hand closed around a wooden handle, and he withdrew a rusted old cleaver. Probably used for chopping up bait, and not a patch on the kind Rab Erskine had used back on Unst. But it was something. Aidan looked at Hilde, hoping for a nod of approval as she saw him stepping up, but he got nothing from the girl. She was probably anxious. *Who can blame her?*

The shipwright turned to his two companions, his eyes alight with a fierce fire.

"Whatever we find aboard that boat, you let me deal with it, right?"

Hilde jutted her jaw at him, threw him her grimmest glare.

"I'm a shieldmaiden. I could—"

"I would really like it if you could just stay alive, lassie. It would make me the happiest man in all Christendom. Stay behind me, Hilde. Please."

Aidan was looking at her earnestly, cheese in one hand, rusted cleaver in the other. He desperately wanted to say something profoundly heroic, let them both know that they weren't alone, that he had their back, was tough and reliable. Aidan could swing a cleaver, rusted or otherwise – it was one good thing Rab Erskine had taught him – and the lad was convinced that when it came down to it, when it *really* mattered, he could be there for his companions. He could fight by their side.

That was what Aidan wanted to say. What came out was something markedly less gallant.

"He talks a lot of sense," said the butcher's boy.

Hilde shrugged, resigned to Blair's plan, and presented her seax to him.

"You should use this, though."

He shook his head. "Keep it. You may yet need it before the night is through. Look after yourself and your pal here."

Aidan sensed Hilde look his way, but he wouldn't meet her gaze. Not even the weak moonlight could hide the blushes on his cheeks. The shame he felt was overwhelming; an old man and a girl left to look after him. It was like his pa had always said: Aidan was a *feartie,* a timorous, wee coward.

"Let's go," said the shipwright, and stepped onto the first plank of the wooden walkway.

No sooner did his foot land on the jetty, it felt to Aidan like a cold breath was exhaled from Scatness town, rolling out from the surrounding buildings and washing over the trio from Unst. He shivered, felt like he'd just passed over from this life into the next, and slowly turned full circle, as did his companions.

Maybe a dozen buildings faced the harbour front, each of them single storey with thatched or turfed rooftops. Not one of them had appeared occupied when the three had passed along the harbour road, each abandoned like every other miserable hovel in Scatness. Only the trio had been wrong. Figures moved within and around, between and on top of the cottages and huts. Just as the carls had materialised out of the darkness of the jarlshof loft, so these strangers appeared from the shadows, taking hideous solid form, black on black. Eyes twinkled in the gloom of the approaching dawn, oily black but shining with a sickly silver light, unblinking and unliving.

"Sweet Mother of God," gasped Blair. "It cannot be!"

The people of Scatness had not found a way to safety, by foot or by boat, by hook or by crook. The people of Scatness had not fled the town, had not escaped the dread touch of the draugr. It was like Jarl Gudrun had said earlier that night; her flock had not gone anywhere. Scatness was very much still their home.

Men and women, young and old, bairns and the bent-backed; they all stalked forwards from their resting places.

Some sunk like cats, slipping from one shadowy doorway to the next, in and out of cover, as they drew ever closer to the jetty. Others walked slowly, confident and carefree, safe in the knowledge that they had nothing to fear from the three mortal souls before them. A couple dropped on all fours, running like beasts, tearing up the ground as they ran across the harbour, hungry to reach their prey. Hungry to taste their blood.

But Aidan and his fellow survivors were already running, and it was the shieldmaiden who was first to the knarr. She swung the seax once, twice, and severed the mooring rope that held the ship in place. Hilde gave it a shove and a kick, and Blair joined her, adding his might to hers. Aidan had passed them by, his feet pounding the boards as he ran further along the jetty. As the boat began to push off, away from the timber pier, Aidan leapt over the widening gap of surging tide, landing in a tumble within the prow.

He struggled to his feet, wincing at the shooting pain he felt in his left ankle where he'd taken the brunt of the fall. There was his cheese, a bit battered and scuffed but still intact. He picked it up, heard the shouts and cries from the stern of the boat. He hobbled over to the side of the knarr, saw the white spumes on the tide as the waves rushed between ship and jetty. Aidan looked along the length of the vessel, where he saw Blair and Hilde battling with the hoard of draugr, of undead, of . . . whatever the hell they were. Hilde slashed at the creatures, chopping at hands and fingers, wildly lashing out, aimless with her seax. Blair was more measured, jabbing with the fishing gaff, stabbing and shoving, picking out his foes as they tried to board the boat.

Aidan took a step in the direction of his companions. Then stopped. His guts were in knots. Felt like he might soil himself at any moment. If he'd eaten anything in the last couple of days, they'd likely be seeing it around now, but he still remained hungry in a way he'd never known. Aidan knew what he should have done. He knew that those two people, the hermit and the jarl's daughter, needed help back there. But surely, he would just get in the way, right? Plus, he'd done his ankle in, and was about as much use as a trapdoor in a coracle. Better he stay out of the way, he'd only get himself hurt.

Aidan took a step away from the melee, leaving the others to defend the boat. He saw the undead townsfolk spilling off the jetty, landing in the surging tide, crushed beneath the hull of the knarr. He watched Blair and Hilde fight in desperation, trying to keep the monsters from clambering aboard. And Aidan continued to step away.

He heard a noise behind him, a jangle of chains. There was the smell of something rotten and brackish, like something dead and decaying had floated in on the tide. Then Aidan heard a discordant song, a melody so strange and unsettling, that for a moment he felt his heart had stopped, frozen in his chest. He turned slowly, reluctantly, dropping to one knee, his twisted ankle twisting that bit further beneath his trembling, terrified body.

The creature that stood over Aidan had shambled out of his nightmares, summoned into the world of the living. It was stooped, hunchbacked, a shroud of lichen and seaweed draped over its crooked frame. The skin beneath was grey and mottled, covered in bumps and contusions that resembled barnacles and blisters. It wore a collar of iron around its distended throat, the chain to which it was attached swinging before it, the rusted links catching against a pair of leathery breasts. Large, webbed hands reached towards Aidan, horribly long fingers flexing and twitching with feverish excitement. Tangled locks of lank, black hair hung like a curtain over a grotesque face, mostly lost in shadow but for a pair of pale, sightless eyes and a maw of daggerlike teeth that belonged to a beast from the depths of the darkest, most terrible ocean.

It was like his pa had always said: Aidan was a *feartie,* a timorous, wee coward. But one of these days, Aidan would prove Rab Erskine wrong.

The rusted cleaver clattered to the deck as the ball of cheese rolled away.

This wasn't one of those days.

CHAPTER TWENTY-FIVE
HILDE

There was no rhythm, rhyme or reason to her actions, no precision or finesse. She was wild and uncontrolled, an instrument of death, lashing and slashing, cutting and cleaving, striking out against anything that came her way. Jet-black eyes flashed and terrible teeth gnashed, but there was no distinction between where one monster ended and the next began. Her seax was a blur of white-hot fury, her rage-fuelled blood hot and hungry as it coursed through her veins, powering her on.

In that moment, Hilde felt removed, as if she were outside of herself, her conscience looking in through a window at someone she barely recognised. That piece of Hilde that still existed was weak and insubstantial. It was the merest shadow of who she was, the barest trace of the girl from Unst. She had no power over the warrior who fought in her skin, who revelled in the carnage of battle, who had given in to the bloodlust. She was a passenger, with no say over what her physical form might do next. She was lost. And it was both glorious and terrifying.

"Enough!"

She heard the voice, sensed her next foe coming at her from her flank. Her shield came up, beating her enemy back, and then the seax tore through the air, seeking out tender flesh that it could tear apart. Only it bounced off something hard – a staff? – and sent her staggering back. It was momentary though. Hilde was leaping again, her shield held before her, bashing her foe hard. She sensed the combatant go down, didn't wait, the initiative hers. Her seax rose, ready to descend, ready to spill more blood, only she felt her legs go out from beneath her.

"I said *enough!*"

The world turned as the girl was swept. She hit the timbers hard, stunned by the impact, the shield near breaking her arm as the seax span from her hand across the gore-slick deck. Hilde looked up, the world shifting in and out of focus, a great pounding sounding in her head and throbbing through her body. Her heart and lungs, beating and pumping as one, the girl returning, the berserker retreating to the dark, at least for now. She squinted, saw Blair standing over her, leaning on the wooden gaff as a cripple might rest against his crutch. He shook his head as he looked down upon her, his expression a mixture of fear and wonder.

"Hell's teeth, lassie, but you're a wild one."

Blair inspected the fishing pole, his thumb running along a deep ridge that had been carved into it.

"You did that," said the old man. "A moment slower parrying your sword, and you'd have opened my throat. And how would that have made you feel?"

"Bad?" replied the girl where she lay on the deck of the knarr.

Blair furrowed his bushy brow. "Can't lie; your answer doesn't sound entirely convincing."

He reached out and hauled her to her feet. She stood there unsteady for a moment, weak as a newborn lamb. Whatever had just occurred during the heat of battle, it had been spectacular and incendiary, taking her to dizzying heights she'd never known before. But now Hilde was coming down the other side of that experience, and her entire body felt burnt and spent. Her limbs were weary, and it was taking all her strength to stay upright. Fortunately, the old man sensed this. Blair reached an arm out, placed it around her shoulder, drawing her close. It was comforting, and the closest thing she'd felt to love in a long time. And that included those rare moments alone in her mother's company.

The pair of them looked over the side of the ship, back towards the jetty, the Norse vessel having already put some distance between itself and the wooden pier. The creatures that once lived, breathed, and inhabited Scatness were no longer on the walkway, having retreated to the deserted, dead buildings they'd earlier vacated. The first light of dawn reached its long fingers out over the harbour, chasing the demons back to the dark. The tide between the ship and the shore churned in and out, dismembered bodies riding the waves, bobbing up and down. Many of them still twitched and shuddered, thrashing about, without limbs but not without purpose. As the feeble rays of sunlight touched them, flames burst from their hair and flesh, engulfing them, gorging upon them. The fact they were submerged in the rolling tide made little difference to the fires, the water bubbling and smoking around the monsters as they were transformed into blackened, crumbling husks. Somewhere within the retreating town of Scatness, Hilde heard an agonised scream. She was in no doubt as to who it belonged to.

"The children of Jarl Gudrun," said Hilde, as much to herself as to Blair, and more dramatically than she'd intended. "She ain't happy."

"Which in turn makes them the offspring of Hydyr the Hungry," said the shipwright, no less dramatic but infinitely more troubled. "It's like Frostmark said: these are different to the draugr. The Harrowed Men shy away from daylight. Hurts 'em, but it don't kill 'em. As for these fiends . . . well . . ."

He watched the oily black smoke as it drifted upon the water. "It's worth us remembering, they ain't got no love for the sun."

"Nor silver," said Hilde. "I took the arm off one of them in the jarlshof and it burnt like a brand against its flesh."

The old man nodded, turned his nose up at the stench in the air, the severed parts of the creatures burning away to nothing across the deck of the knarr.

He scratched the thinning hair on his head. "Where this Hastur fella fits into all this is the most curious part."

"You heard what they said, Finn Frostmark *and* Agnes. The Unspeakable One, they called him. The Golden Jarl. He's their god."

Blair tugged his beard, flicking lumps of greying, rotting flesh from it.

"I'm not one for theology, bairn. I know my God, and

His son is the one who died on the cross for us. And you've got yours, a whole pantheon of 'em in your Norse tales. As I say, I ain't no priest, but I reckon there's already enough gods and monsters in this world without us having an actual God *of* Monsters."

Hilde nodded, though it was clear the shipwright was in denial about who, or what, Hastur was. She was about to call out Aidan's name when another voice sounded behind them, this one deep and gruff and belonging to a man.

"Well, well, well."

Blair and Hilde turned together, looking back along the knarr to its centre. The door to the hold was open, and two of its occupants had stepped out of the belly of the ship. Hilde recognised both of the men of Alba, the bodyguards who served Mistress Zaleska.

"Well, well, well indeed," agreed Blair, his chest puffing out as he manoeuvred Hilde behind him. "If it isn't my favourite pair of traitorous curs, as I live and breathe. The two rotten turds who would shackle their own kin and sell them to a monster."

Blair unhitched his shield from his back, still bound in wrappings, and stepped forwards, preparing for battle. Hilde didn't like this one bit. These two men looked younger, leaner, were certainly battle-hardened. They also had all the gear. The bodyguards continued their approach, fanning out. They each drew their swords from their sheaths, which prompted Blair to point his fishing gaff at the one on the right.

"See you've got something of mine," he said.

The bodyguard raised his weapon. Hilde recognised Blair's bone-handled blade with its distinct bronze pommel and cross-guard.

"This?" said the warrior and glanced at his sword-brother on the other side of the deck. "We did wonder. See, I've seen these swords before, old man. And they weren't in the keeping of some scruffy old, turd-stinking turnip. They belonged to the King's Guard."

Hilde tried to gulp, found her throat had seized up. *King's Guard?*

"Saw that loot you had, too," said the second bodyguard. "A king's ransom in that sack you carry, I reckon. Or maybe a queen's?"

The two warriors exchanged furtive looks, moving either side of Blair, as Hilde looked at the sack that lay on the deck.

"You're him, aren't you?" said the first bodyguard. "The one that stole the bairn."

Blair grunted, shook his head, but Hilde noticed his weatherbeaten knuckles were white and stark where he gripped the fishing gaff.

"You've got me confused with someone else," said the shipwright. "Maybe he was handsome, just like me." He gave them a toothless smile, his wild grey whiskers bristling.

"Where did you get this sword?" asked the first warrior.

"Bought it off a man in Orkneyar, twelve years back. He needed coin to get himself to Norðvegr. Maybe that's the man you're on about?"

The bodyguards glanced at one another, uncertain now, but still awfully dangerous. Blair pushed on. Wherever the truth was here, and Hilde had no clue, he was beginning to sound very convincing. Turned out the old man was hellish persuasive when he wanted to be.

"I'm just a simple fisherman from Unst, lads. We came to Scatness seeking vengeance against them what slaughtered our neighbours and kin; the Harrowed Men. And the pair of you, men of Alba; how far you have fallen. You work for some foreign slaver, selling your own folk to the highest bidder, even if they're monsters like Jarl Gudrun. Pictish blood flows through your veins! How can you betray your brethren?"

"Mistress Zaleska pays us well," said the second bodyguard, but Hilde detected a hint of something in his voice. *Doubt?*

"Those young men and women were Picts," said Blair. "They're dead now, or worse, if you can imagine that? It's not too late for you, boys."

The bodyguards dropped their heads, one of them finding his voice.

"I fear it is," said the warrior.

"No!" said Blair, now animated. "You have *one chance* at redemption. I beg you; do the right thing, sons of Alba. Get us far from Scatness and let us be on our way. Christ willing, we shall put an end to the horrors of the Harrowed Men, and perhaps the pair of you can return to the grace and light of God the Father."

The shipwright made the sign of the cross before him with the fishing gaff, adding further punch to his words. Hilde watched on with no small degree of wonder as both the bodyguards appeared to change their stance. They pulled back from their approach, once more sharing concerned looks with one another, their weapons lowered, the tension dissipating on the salty breeze.

Only it did not last.

A slow handclap from the hold's open door preceded the arrival of Mistress Zaleska. She smiled as she walked onto the deck of the knarr, her palms coming together in laboured and ironic fashion, her golden smile queer and quite frightening. Instantly, her men had their weapons raised once more, their focus returned as their paymaster strode into dawn's early light.

"A marvellous tale you tell, Master Blair. Truly imaginative. If your career as a fisherman fails to pan out, you could turn your hand to being a children's storyteller."

"I don't know what you think you know—" began the shipwright.

Zaleska raised a hand. Her green eyes shone bright and bewitching for a moment, like a pair of precious stones.

"*Silencium.*"

Blair ceased speaking.

With that single word, a cold dread washed over the deck of the knarr, chilling Hilde to her bones. The word reminded Hilde of the language Brother Benedict used. It was Latin, all right, but corrupted somehow, and behind the word it sounded like another voice was moving, something awful and ancient and utterly unholy.

Try as he might, Blair couldn't talk. He choked, spluttered, attempted to mouth his words, but he was struck dumb.

Worst of all, he could not take his eyes off the woman. He was utterly captivated by the slaver.

Zaleska stepped up to the bodyguard who held Blair's sword and held out a hand, and the man duly handed it over. The woman opened her mouth, lips peeled back, revealing those shining, precious teeth of gold. Then she ran her tongue the length of the blade, her eyelids fluttering with exquisite delight as she did so.

"Every weapon tells its tale. Its history is engrained upon it in blood, as a monk might illuminate a text with ink. This sword has drunk heartily down the years, cutting down men and women, young and old, and all by your hand. Do not think to deny your own handiwork. I know the truth, as do you."

She handed the sword back to her man, who wouldn't dare look her in the eyes, his gaze fixed upon Blair.

"No more lies, Uuen of Forteviot. You speak to Baba Zaleska, Daughter of Hecate, and no living man or woman may deny my command. I will only hear the truth from your lips."

Her terrible emerald eyes flashed once more.

"*Loquere.*"

To Hilde's keen ear, it sounded like another language was hiding behind and beneath the Latin. Piggybacking that ancient tongue, riding it like a parasite, a tick upon the belly of a beast. Only the spell was not directed at Hilde.

Blair spoke.

"My name is Uuen of Forteviot, son of Talorc, and I served as protector to Donald the Second, King of Alba."

Hilde was physically staggered and struggled to remain standing. The way Blair spoke, the hardness to his words were gone, and there was a gentle lilt to his accent that had been missing in the brief time she'd known him.

"Go on," said Zaleska with a triumphant smile.

"I was a faithful and loyal vassal to my king until..."

Blair looked in pain, sweat beading upon his filthy brow as he tried to keep the words in. He locked his jaw, grimacing with unimaginable pain, tears streaming down his sunken cheeks and into the nest of grey whiskers.

Zaleska stepped forwards, her face grave, the smile gone.

"*Perge.*"

"My only daughter, Alpia, served as lady-in-waiting to Queen Margaret, wife to King Donald. The queen was feared by all, not only for her temper, but also the company she kept, especially after dark. Furthermore, it was no secret that the queen was unable to deliver an heir to the king, which only drove the woman to deeper pits of despair."

Blair took a deep breath, the tears still staining his grubby face.

"I served King Donald well until he took kindly to Alpia. My daughter was left with child, which she bore outside of wedlock and without the blessing of the church. Knowing the queen's fury if the truth were to be revealed, Alpia came to me, demanding I take her child far away from the queen's vengeful reach. And so I did. Knowing my beloved daughter was doomed, I fled the court, I abandoned my king, I turned my back upon my sworn service, and I spirited my infant grandson away across Alba. I crossed seas to escape the reach of Queen Margaret, only stopping when I reached the Hjaltland Isles. I gave that boy to the blacksmith, let the man raise him as his own, and I had to watch on from a distance, unable to admit to him the truth of his birth. Unable to cradle my own grandson in my arms, for fear of revealing him to our enemies."

Blair ceased speaking. His head dropped, shoulders sagging, every fibre of strength having been drained through his terrible admission. Hilde stared at him, unable to believe, let alone understand, what she'd just heard.

She reached her fingers out and brushed his forearm tenderly, felt the sobs trembling through his body. Then she stepped past him, taking his place as protector. Hilde took courage from everything the old man had done and said, decided this was where she would make her stand, and to hell with the consequences.

"I know the boy Blair speaks of. He was my friend. What do you care about some young'un who lived at the world's end? This don't sound like your fight. Sounds like the fight of this vengeful queen to me. The fate of Cormac Erskine is none of your business."

Zaleska's smile was almost benign as she tipped her head to one side, regarding Hilde.

"You're a fascinating young lady. How very confident and cocksure you are. So much to say, and so much of it irrelevant. When one Daughter of Hecate is slighted, we are all slighted. Even now, my sister Margaret is aware that this boy lives; she feels it, she knows the bloodline of Donald "The Madman", dead King of Alba. The Daughters of Hecate shall find this boy and mete out justice in our sister's name."

Hilde turned her nose up at the woman, gave Blair's hand a subtle but sharp squeeze.

"You're a delusional old bag, aren't you? What are you, some kind of witch?"

Zaleska's laugh was rich and throaty. "I am exactly that, child, as are all the Daughters. Margaret has a child now, an infant son, Malcolm. He stands to inherit the throne of Alba once Donald's cousin Constantine passes, and that shall happen right soon."

"So," said Hilde, trying to appear the confident and cocksure young lady Zaleska had called out. "As long as Cormac lives, your wee mite Malcolm's claim to the throne is on shaky ground. Good old Mac, he always was a fly in the ointment of life. Anyway, that's good to know. When I find him, I guess I'll have to work my arse off to keep him alive. Because I promise you, here and now, that if you and your sisters come after my pal, it's me you'll answer to."

Hilde puffed up her chest, felt her strength returning. It was a bold statement, and a hollow threat, but she had to say something. She squeezed Blair's hand once again, hoping the old warrior had returned, because a scrap was coming right soon.

"Brave words, little shieldmaiden," said Zaleska, as her bodyguards watched on from either side of her.

Hilde picked up her silver seax from the deck.

"Yeah? Well, here are some more brave words, witch. How about you taste *my* blade?"

Hilde was about to pounce when Zaleska clicked her fingers, eyes shining bright as she beckoned the girl.

"Veni."

The young shieldmaiden stumbled forwards, leaving a shellshocked Blair swaying at her back. She took small steps, eyes wide, her jaw slack. Hilde came to a juddering halt in front of the witch, who looked down upon her with victorious contempt.

"I would know more about you, child. I would know your secrets, and your connection to my friends and enemies. I believe you have a great role to play in Hastur's new world order. You speak to Baba Zaleska, Daughter of Hecate, and no living man or woman may deny my command. I will only hear the truth from your lips."

Hilde looked into those deep green eyes, her own unblinking, as Zaleska uttered her spell of command.

"Loquere."

The girl from Unst took a deep breath, calmed her shaking nerves, and spoke.

"As I said, how about you taste my blade?"

In that moment, a number of remarkable events occurred in unison.

Hilde brought her seax back and was about to drive it through the witch's belly. Zaleska looked perplexed and horrified that she held no power over the shieldmaiden. Her two bodyguards stirred into action, only far too slow to protect their mistress. And if that weren't enough, a monster leapt out of the darkness, bounding from the prow of the knarr, hurdling the ship's hold as it landed on the slaver's back. A shawl of bladderwrack and kelp trailed from the grotesque creature's misshapen torso, and with all the hunger of a starving shark, it sank its jaws into the witch's shoulder.

Zaleska's scream would've awoken the dead.

CHAPTER TWENTY-SIX
AIDAN

He lay motionless on the deck of the knarr, his face fixed in a rictus snarl of terror. In his right hand, Aidan still held the rusted old cleaver, its blade now broken, a jagged ruin. Fragments from the makeshift weapon along with pieces of a shattered iron collar were scattered all about, littering the wooden boards around him. And the monster, around whose throat that ring of metal had moments ago been fixed, sat astride the helpless lad. Lank hair, seaweed and sagging skin hung over him as the creature brought its face ever closer.

Aidan had once seen a face such as this, though not on a human. A fisherman, long thought lost at sea, had finally returned to Unst, with all kinds of strange fish in his unusual catch. One such beast, dredged up from the bottom of the ocean, shared similarities with this monster; pale, apparently sightless eyes, long needle-sharp teeth, and flesh as ugly and discoloured as the darkest, angriest bruise.

For a moment, the boy considered driving the broken cleaver into the ribs of the beast but then had instant second thoughts. If it wanted him dead, Aidan would've already been missing his throat, and besides, wasn't this what he'd wanted? Had he not intended to break the thrall collar that kept the monster chained to the deck of the knarr? Or was that, perhaps, simply a fortuitous by-product, as he had swung the cleaver in a blind panic, lashing out at the fiend? Aidan tried to convince himself it was the former, but he feared it was the latter.

The horror's thin lips twitched, so close to touching Aidan's, its breath as rancid as week-old fish guts that had been left in the sun. Then it moved its mouth around the boy's face, to his ear, and whispered two words, the voice clearly female.

"Thank you."

Before Aidan could respond, the creature bounded away like some monstrous frog, leaping through the drizzle and onto the hold roof. It jumped once more, and wherever it landed there was an ungodly scream that shattered the dawn.

Aidan rolled onto his belly, panting, not quite believing that he had somehow survived his encounter with . . . *What was that creature?* There he lay for a moment, hugging the deck, his face flush to the timber surface, breathing great sighs of relief. The ship rose and crashed down, riding a wave, sending his head bouncing off the boards of the deck. Aidan scrambled to his feet, the ship pitching on the tide as it drifted away from Scatness and towards the rocks that thrust up around the island. Hit that reef, and the belly of the knarr would be ripped out, and he, Hilde and Blair would likely be drowned like rats.

Aidan jumped up onto the roof of the hold cabin, ruined cleaver in hand, and slipped and slid his way towards the stern of the ship – where a full-blooded battle was underway.

Hilde was engaged in a game of cat-and-mouse with one of Mistress Zaleska's bodyguards. The warrior was relentless, chasing her around the deck, swinging his sword but finding only air. Hilde was nimble, always had been. It was the reason she often bested Aidan in the scraps they'd had down the years, bar the times when he'd managed to grab the little scruff. Then it had been a different story, the strength of the butcher's boy typically getting the better of the jail's daughter. For now, Hilde was winning her fight, dodging her enemy's attacks, keeping out of his reach, but it couldn't last forever. She had her seax in hand, but it was no match for the man's larger, more brutal-looking blade.

Blair and the other bodyguard were trading fierce blows at the very rear of the knarr's stern. The old man's fishing gaff had been splintered by the other's sword – *Blair's* sword, Aidan quickly realised – and had resorted to using the two broken lengths of pole as a pair of clubs. He was fighting valiantly, but against a much younger man, and it was steel against kindling. Seemed likely to Aidan there was only going to be one winner of that duel.

As for the last fight, this was the most brutal of all. Zaleska was caught in a struggle with the beast Aidan had freed moments ago, the monster driven beyond a point of madness. The slaver's shoulder was bloodied, where the hideous creature had clearly bitten her, leaving the woman's left arm hanging limp by her side. In her right she held a long, curved knife that looked much like a sickle, and was frantically slashing at her assailant, gibbering curses in the process. Zaleska struck out at it with a booted foot, sending the fiend flying. Its head struck the ship's mast, hard, before it collapsed into a crumpled and confused heap upon the deck.

The witch shot a withering look at Aidan, her eyes bursting with green fire as she pointed at the stunned creature. The boy didn't need to understand the following command, didn't need to know that language – he knew fine well he was being commanded to kill.

"Bestia occidere!"

Zaleska had perhaps got halfway through saying the second of those words – at which point in time Aidan felt like the woman had climbed inside his belly and was pulling his innards apart – when Hilde barged straight into him, the two of them taking a tumble and landing in an ungainly embrace. Aidan felt nauseous, sick to the pit of that tortured stomach, thought he might vomit.

Hilde slapped him in the face. Hard.

"Don't listen to her, Aidan! And for Odin's sake, don't look her in the eye!"

She might have said more, only the bodyguard was charging towards them, sword raised, and Aidan had to think fast. He held Hilde tight to his chest and, before she could object, he rolled her over. The two of them disappeared under a rowing bench, and another, as the warrior was left hacking at the deck.

The two youths came up a short distance away, facing off against the man. Hilde gave Aidan a look, a fierce look. Right there and then, he was wholeheartedly convinced that she believed in him. That was new for Aidan. Nobody had ever had any faith in the butcher's boy, and that was enough to put a little steel into his spine where before there had only been shivers. The bodyguard came in hard and fast, probably thinking he could cut the pair of them down with one savage blow, or split them apart, but they bravely stood their ground. Hilde raised the seax, somehow managing to parry the blow aside, and it was enough for Aidan to dart in with his broken blade and score a line through the man's breastplate. Blood welled where the cleaver cut flesh. Aidan shared a look with Hilde of astonished triumph that was sadly short-lived. The bodyguard's arm came back the other way, his elbow striking the boy in the jaw, loosening a few teeth and sending him careening across the knarr. He lurched against the rail, almost disappearing over the side, his head in bits and guts churned up. Then he turned back to the melee.

All that followed happened so quickly, it felt to Aidan he was caught in a crashing wave and snared by the riptide.

Blair was on the deck, crawling away from his foe, the bodyguard advancing upon the old man. The shipwright struggled past his sack of swag and seized the lidded bucket, flipping it open. As Zaleska's man raised the bone-handled sword, looking every inch the executioner, Blair reached into the tub and whipped out Finn Frostmark's head, the rag falling from the Viking's gnashing mouth. He tossed the draugr directly at the bodyguard, Frostmark's battle cry met by the warrior's screams of panic. The man of Alba raised an arm to try and bat the head away, but Frostmark's teeth snapped around the flesh of his forearm. And Blair was moving. He leapt up from the floor, burying the remaining piece of splintered fishing gaff in the man's throat. As the bodyguard staggered away burbling, the Viking gnawing on his arm, he dropped his stolen sword on the deck.

Zaleska was busy slashing at the creature that lay limp on the deck, her curved blade finding the monster's dark leathery flesh time and again. She was screeching curses, hacking with abandon, out of her mind in a furious rage.

"I gave you *everything,* you miserable hag!"

"Zaleska!" shouted Blair, his own sword back in his hand.

The witch turned, her eyes glowing as she saw the old man, about to compel him with her words of magic, but they never left her lips. One long, distended arm shot up from the deck, the creature not as dead as it had appeared. Those gnarled, bony fingers, like the limbs of some demented crab, gripped the top of Zaleska's skull, shredding her headscarf in the process. The creature yanked the woman's head back leaving a wailing Zaleska staring skyward, just in time to see a dark shape descend from above. Siv swooped in, black talons finding the witch's eyes, digging deep and tearing the offending organs out of their sorcerous sockets.

Aidan's cheer was one of sheer, unbridled relief. However, his joy was cut short by the final bodyguard, who lurched forwards, finding his foe at last. The warrior's sword came in, stabbing straight for Aidan's chest. There was a sudden, confusing movement, as a figure leapt in front of him, putting their own body in the way of the man's deadly blow.

The wet rip, the puncture of lungs and the cracking of ribs. Aidan heard, felt, and saw the sword come out of the torso of the person before him, passing straight through, the steel cutting his own chest but stopping short of meeting his ribs. Then the blade was ripped free, leaving the brave soul dying in the arms of the lad from Unst.

"Find our friend, Aidan," said Hilde, coughing up blood as the light and life vanished from her eyes. "Save Cormac."

CHAPTER TWENTY-SEVEN
CORMAC

From his seat beside the black drakkar's mast, Cormac looked across at his former neighbours, guilt weighing heavy upon his shoulders. There were five villagers left, including Brother Benedict, the monk doing his best to lift their spirits and keep their hope alive. Prayer, that was the key. The one thing the men and women of Unst still clung to was the belief that all of this, all the horrors they were being put through, was for some kind of divine purpose. Lead a good life, have faith, believe in God the Father, and all will be well, if not in this life but in Heaven as reward.

Cormac looked at the backs of his hands, flipped them over to examine his palms. He clenched his fists, rubbed his wrists, relieved to be free of the bindings that had kept him trussed like a pig for the slaughter. Then he returned his gaze to his fellow Picts. Every one of those poor souls remained bound by ropes, their hands lashed in hemp cords. Cormac had been one of them, but not any more. Freed by Hydyr the Hungry, he was favoured by the Vikings, at least so long as he proved useful.

As if in answer to the boy's thoughts, Rab Erskine stomped along the deck of the *Sea Wolf*, a blood-drenched bucket under his arm. He walked as if in some kind of trance, reduced to a shambling, mindless puppet of a man, the bad-tempered butcher a fading memory. Just as the previous day, a handful of Norsemen worked the deck while the remainder rested or slumbered. It was to these warriors that Erskine headed, pausing obediently as they fished dubious chunks of meat from the wooden tub. Cormac shuddered as he watched the Vikings tear hungrily through their meals, shoving the foul food into their mouths, gulping the flesh down without chewing. The boy tried not to imagine what they were gorging on, tried to think of it as pork, or beef, but it was no use. He glanced at the prisoners once more – fleeting and filled with a damned and dreadful shame. Cormac knew right enough what was in that bloody bucket.

"You should eat, Cormac the Cunning."

Cormac almost slid off his bench, and looked up to see the brutish figure of Einar the Small towering over him, peering over his belly at the boy. Hydyr's second in command, so far as Cormac could tell, the big man ran the longship when the jarl was resting. Sleeping. Whatever it was he did. The blacksmith's boy knew what he was dealing with now: *the draugr*. The way Hydyr acted, though, suggested he was a different beast. What exactly that was, the boy with the bright eyes and even brighter mind had yet to decide or discover. And whatever Hydyr was, Cormac knew one thing for sure: the monster needed to die.

"I'm not hungry," Cormac lied.

Einar sat down opposite him, the strange mist that shrouded the ship billowing like smoke all about them. The bench groaned under his weight as he glared at the boy.

"You need to keep your strength up. A dead scholar ain't much use to Jarl Hydyr."

"Call me weird, but I'm not keen on what passes for food aboard the *Sea Wolf*."

"You were happy enough to eat the herring the other day, boy."

Cormac felt sick at the memory, knowing what the diet of the Harrowed Men consisted of, knowing what Erskine had done to his old friends in order to win Hydyr's favour. For a while, when he had been filling his face with those pickled silver fish, he had been able to push that awful truth from his mind. But that was a truth he could never hide from again.

"Reckon I'm done eating meat and fish."

Einar's one good hand worked its way under his bloated stomach, dipping into a pouch that was previously hidden by that enormous gut. He pulled out a knackered-looking oat-cake and tossed it to Cormac. He then took out a second, this one equally crushed and crumbling, and placed it onto the bench beside the boy.

Cormac sniffed the baked bun, got a whiff of honey.

"Where'd you get these?"

He caught the quick glance of Einar towards the enslaved villagers.

"Let's just say I took 'em off someone who had no need for them any more, eh?"

Guilt. It was a terrible thing, but Cormac was learning to live with it real quick. He took a bite out of the oat-cake, the taste exploding in his mouth. He savoured it, chewing it slowly, letting the sweet, sugary goodness register on his tongue.

"Fankoo," he managed to say, his mouth dry with sticky crumbs.

Einar shrugged. "Weren't much use to me." He winked. "Reckon I'm done eating buns."

Cormac almost found himself laughing at Einar's attempt at humour, only for good sense and decency to stop him dead. Einar the Small might have looked like a man, albeit a giant one, but it was just a mask, a disguise. He was one of the Harrowed Men. Einar was a monster.

"How long . . . till we make land?" asked Cormac, struggling down a mouthful of oat-cake.

The big man stared dead ahead at the mist and the waves.

"By nightfall, Hastur willing. Then the real work begins."

"What real work is that?"

Einar looked the lad up and down. "The chief wasn't kidding when he said you were inquisitive. Perhaps the less you know, the better for you."

Cormac bristled.

"Perhaps the more I know, the better I can help you?"

"Cocky wee pup, aren't you?" chuckled Einar. "How do you figure that?"

Cormac picked the crumbs off his cheek, careful not to miss any of them.

"Hydyr has freed me and kept me alive for a purpose. If he wants to use me, he should use me. Otherwise, I might as well be back bound to those poor souls."

He glanced at his fellow survivors in their miserable

huddle, surrounding Brother Benedict.

"If I'm useful, I'd like to know how."

"He wants you for that tongue of yours, your way with languages, that's obvious. I'm sure he has something else in mind for you too. You'll have a part to play in what's to come."

Cormac flinched. *What in the hell did that mean?*

"Be flattered, Cormac the Cunning. Not everybody receives the favour of Hydyr the Hungry. You're a special one, not like the rest of the sheep. Your name shall feature in the saga, when the true Ragnarok brings all to an end. You have a new jarl now, as do we all; the Golden Jarl, Hastur."

The boy looked back along the longship to where Jarl Frida sheltered beneath the tarpaulin. *She* was Cormac's jarl.

"This Hastur you serve. He's a God, right? Least that's what I'm figuring. How on earth do a bunch of Norsemen suddenly start worshipping another God? What would Odin say about that?"

"Odin be damned!" snarled Einar. "Him and all his kin. They cursed my sword-brothers, shield-sisters and I when we sacked Uppsala so long ago. I'd no more give prayer to Odin than bow down before the Christ-god. And there's plenty of my Norse brothers and sisters who've switched allegiance to that pathetic deity in recent times."

A glob of bloody spit flew from Einar's mouth, dribbling down his vast belly.

"No, Hydyr has revealed the One True God to us, and he isn't some old man in Asgard or a martyr on a cross. We are the children of Hastur, Cormac. We no longer walk in the light, but in the darkness, and the Unspeakable One shall watch over us. We have his protection, we have his blessing, and in Hydyr we have our king. Hydyr will show us the way, and we Harrowed Men shall ascend, just as he has."

"You say Hydyr has ascended, but he doesn't look so different to the rest of you. Certainly seems to share your diet!"

Einar stared wistfully into the mists that swirled about the *Sea Wolf*, lost in some lustful reverie.

"The Harrowed Men are merely draugr. We are cursed to walk Midgard, undead and undying, as bit by bit we fall and crumble. We eat the flesh of the living, which sustains us, halts the rot, but time will eventually wear my sword-brothers and shield-sisters down. Hydyr suffers no such handicap."

Cormac grunted. "I dunno. Cowering away from sunlight might cramp a fellow's style."

"A small price to pay for Hastur's blessing. These mists that surround us; they are the strigoi's doing, summoned by him, controlled by him. The speed of an elf, the strength of a giant, the ability to beguile and bewitch another with mere words, mere thoughts." Einar tapped his temple to emphasis the point. "The gifts of the strigoi are many. And this hewn and hacked flesh I wear? It will be but a memory."

"A memory?" asked Cormac.

"I shall be reborn and returned to the best version of myself, just as Hydyr was before me. Young. Handsome. Unblemished."

Cormac looked the other up and down, the big man's eyes sparkling deliriously. He could imagine Einar as being young, once upon a time, but handsome and unblemished was a stretch.

"The time for that ascension comes real soon; we shall know the strigoi's kiss. The Unspeakable One shall rise again, and Midgard, this world of men, will cower before a new race."

Cormac winced as he heard the man speak. Einar was undeniably passionate, but he was coming across like a lunatic presently.

"You sound possessed," said the boy, finding his nerve in the face of such madness. "It's like you're speaking in tongues. All this talk of unspeakable things and Hastur; you babble and gibber like a fool!"

"The Golden Jarl, lad," said Einar, giving him a sly and sinister wink. "He is your everything now; your father, your Jarl, your God."

Cormac couldn't help but feel sorry for Jarl Frida. She may have been cursed like the rest of the Harrowed Men, but the woman, the *jarl,* he knew did not deserve any of this, whatever crimes she had been party to in her past. Cormac might not have been Norse, but Jarl Frida was the closest thing to a chieftain he had ever known.

"And what fate awaits Jarl Frida?"

Einar sniffed. "Blackheart? That's up to her, ain't it? The longer she goes without feeding – and I mean *proper* feeding – the more she withers away. She shall end up meeting Níðhöggr right soon and be devoured for an eternity on the Corpse Shore. She's a stubborn one, but the chief sees something in her."

"You sailed all the way to Unst just to fetch Jarl Frida and return her to your crew. Why? Surely there are other warriors out there. Why is she so important to Hydyr?"

Einar clutched his hand to his breast. "Love can make a man do ridiculous things."

Cormac pulled a face. "Love? What do any of the Harrowed Men know about love?"

The brute looked wounded. "I knew love, lad. Love for my fellow man. I lost my brother in the sacking of Unst. Hastur only knows what became of him, but I fear Finn Frostmark has finally arrived on the Corpse Shore. Hope that damned serpent chokes on him."

Einar spat, muttering a few choice curses in Norse. It struck Cormac as tragic that Einar had such heartfelt words to share about the Viking. Cormac had met Frostmark atop the cliffs on Unst, fought him, fallen with him, watched Blair the Shipwright take that rotten head from his shoulders. Cormac didn't have the heart to tell Einar he was there when Frostmark died. Not presently, at least. Perhaps that gory little story could wait until a later date, when the revelation could have the maximum impact on the draugr's state of mind.

"I suppose I'm sorry for your loss," said Cormac, trying his best to look sympathetic to the killer's tragic tale. "Your fondness for your brother aside, I'm not so sure about the rest of the Harrowed Men. And Hydyr don't much look like a man who knows what love is."

"Hydyr always loved Frida Blackheart, lad, even in the greatest moments of chaos. Don't think he ever stopped loving that woman, in the fifteen winters they've been apart. He's been looking for her all that time, wants her to sit by his side as his equal when the Age of Hastur begins. Doubt he's thought about much else."

The blacksmith's boy shook his head. "That don't sound like love to me. That sounds like obsession."

Einar scratched at his rump.

"Oh, the chief knows all about obsession. Blackheart took something from Jarl Hydyr, something precious that he needs. Something Hastur needs. Hydyr wants that back."

"What *something*?" asked Cormac.

"A weapon, one that in the right hands could prove devastating. Been a long time since Blackheart led the Harrowed Men, and there were none fiercer than that shieldmaiden back in the day, when the red mist descended. Clearly Hydyr thinks she's still in there. Guess we'll find out soon enough. Reckon she's the one who can wield the World Ender."

Cormac looked up, the thick fog boiling in the air around the *Sea Wolf*, diffusing the light of the sun. He couldn't hide his smile.

"What's so funny?" asked Einar.

"The sun," said Cormac. "I see how you all shrink from it, how you fear it, how Hydyr cannot bear it. I know he channels a dark magic to conjure a mist from the sea, but that trick can only get you so far. You can't win, Einar the Small. Whatever Hydyr's plan is, it's doomed, so long as the sun is your enemy."

It was the big man's turn to smile, and the boy wasn't

sure whether he'd ever seen such a joyless and sinister expression.

"You just worry about where your next meal is coming from, Cormac the Cunning, and pray that our next meal isn't you. Let the Harrowed Men worry about the sun."

CHAPTER TWENTY-EIGHT
AIDAN

A maelstrom of chaos swirled about him, a tornado of blood and blade and breaking bone, but Aidan was removed from it all. Blair roared like a feral beast as he ran his sword through the belly of the remaining bodyguard and pitched him overboard, but the sound never reached Aidan's ears. Zaleska wailed and thrashed as she fell to the deck, face streaming in red ruin, hands flapping in vain to hold back Siv's savage attacks, but Aidan never noticed. He was in the eye of the storm, and all he saw before him was Hilde's body.

He laid her on the deck, his back turned to the violence, the boy from Unst utterly defenceless should some stray steel or beak coming flying his way. Hilde had already gone pale, the red stain that grew across her leather breastplate turning it dark and glistening, directly over the girl's lifeless heart.

It was all so unreal. A sick joke. A tiny part of his mind, now fractured, wanted to laugh out loud at the nonsense of it all, spurring him to wake up from the stupid, bloody dream. Only he wasn't asleep. This wasn't some nightmare that he could rise from and escape.

No. It was horribly, very real.

"Be still, witch, or so help me I'll tear your wretched arms off and beat you with them!"

Aidan stepped unsteadily back from Hilde's body,

the girl's head lolling gently from side to side as the knarr rolled on the waves. How was this the same girl who'd beaten him senseless a couple of days back? How was the fierce, wild-eyed young shieldmaiden now reduced to a pale and corpse? Two days they had spent together, this pair of vying, bitching, snapping and snarling, hating-one-another fools. And Aidan had begun to see another side to the jarl's daughter, a glimpse of who she really was, but that all counted for nought now.

"Boy!" shouted Blair, stirring Aidan from his state of hollow confusion. The shipwright had the witch in his embrace, as she thrashed and spat, biting and butting him. He kicked a length of rope Aidan's way.

"Bind her! And be quick about it!"

Aidan blinked, still unable to process what was happening, every inch of his flesh tingling as if charged with lightning. Numb and useless. He shuffled towards the rope, but saw a slender, gnarled, moss-coloured hand crawl across the deck and take hold of it.

The creature that had been chained to the prow crawled forwards from where it had been felled. It took hold of one of Zaleska's hands and pulled it so viciously that Aidan thought it might tear free from her wrist. The witch shrieked out loud, her screams reaching a new pitch, as the strange, weed-riddled humanoid lashed the rope about Zaleska's arms, good and tight. Blair grabbed the witch roughly and, holding her against the mast, threw another length of hemp around her, securing her in place.

As Siv wheeled overhead, the old man turned to the creature.

It still lay beaten and battered upon the deck, its flesh hacked and slashed by the demented Zaleska in a fit of fury. Blair held his hand out to the monster, that peered up at him through a curtain of greasy, grey hair. Its pale eyes blinked once as it looked at the man's hand with uncertainty and suspicion.

"Friend," said Blair with a grim nod of reassurance.

"Friend," said the creature, taking his hand and allowing him to haul it to its feet. Then it placed a hand across one of its butchered and bloodied breasts. "Magghurgah the sea-trow, at your service."

Blair cocked an eyebrow, his mouth working as if he were trying to get his head around the name's pronunciation. He clicked his fingers and pointed at her.

"Gonna call you Mag, if it's all the same?"

Mag nodded.

Sea-trows. Aidan had heard of the legend of the sea-trows – it was hard to not know about them, growing up on the islands. A race of beings that, story told, could calm the waves and bring about storms with their songs.

Blair looked Mag over, his weatherbeaten face wrinkling at the sight of her wounds, dealt to her by Zalenka's fancy curved dagger.

"It is fine," said Mag, second-guessing his thoughts correctly. "So long as I am near the water, I am a fast healer. Tis a talent of my kind."

"What do we do with her?" asked Aidan, startling Blair. The boy's voice was low, his attention focused on Hilde's body.

Blair joined the lad, bracing himself on the tilting deck.

Aidan heard the old man take a sharp intake of breath, like he was going to say something, but only a choked exhalation emerged, Blair's chest trembling with emotion.

"Poor lassie was a Norseman, had more stones on her than many I've faced in battle. They burn their dead, right? Or bury them in barrows. I don't much fancy setting a bonfire aboard this boat, and there ain't much chance of us digging a grave until we reach dry land either."

"Wrap her in her wolfskin cloak."

The old man and the lad turned to where Siv sat on the knarr's handrail. Aidan had known the raven all his life, never paid her much attention, dismissing her as a sorcerous thing that the pagan Norsemen had brought to Unst. But here now, after a brief time in Siv's company, she seemed almost human, so great was the sorrow in her rough and throaty voice.

"It was her mother's," added the bird. "We wait until we make land, give her the send-off she deserves."

Blair nodded, crouching to pick Hilde up. He cradled her body gently, reverently, and headed to the cabin, its door still creaking on its hinges as the knarr swayed from one side to the other. He disappeared belowdecks, leaving the strange group in silence but for the gurgling chuckle of Zaleska.

"So," said the witch. "The girl is dead, eh? Look where your meddling has got you. You should have taken death when it was first offered you, back on Unst, saved the delicious heartache you now feel. I can *taste* it," she said, licking her thin lips. "It. Is. *Delicious*."

"Shut your trap, you miserable hag," said Finn Frostmark.

Aidan turned to the Viking head with a healthy dose of surprise, his allegiance to the group more than a little unexpected. The severed head lay on its side on the deck, a lump of forearm flesh caught in his gnashing teeth, torn from one of the bodyguards.

Zaleska recoiled against the mast, her bloody face crumpling as Frostmark's voice registered.

"One of the Harrowed Men, in league with mortal fools? Hydyr will be displeased. What kind of draugr are you?"

"The kind who is without a jarl. Hydyr the Hungry abandoned me fast enough. Sword-brother, he called me, so long as I was of use to him. Well, what good is Finn Frostmark, without a body to swing axe or sword? I am done with him, and his quest to bring about an Age of Hastur. When the time comes, you'll find me on the Corpse Shore. I'll take the jaws of the great serpent, Níðhöggr, for eternity, over one more moment of loyalty to Hydyr the Hungry."

Frostmark blinked, almost looked like he was astonished now he had said it out loud. His face, hanging loose and sick over that decapitated skull, softened as he regarded Aidan.

"Reckon I've found myself a new battle-crew now."

The witch cackled. "Oath-breaker, I name you! Could a soul *be* more damned than yours, Finn Frostmark?"

The draugr didn't like that one bit.

"An oath goes two ways, witch. Hydyr and I swore that one would never leave the other behind. He broke our oath first."

"I'm sure a decapitated, decrepit, one-eyed Norseman is a *huge* loss to the Harrowed Men," Zaleska said with sarcastic glee.

"Still one more eye than you," said Frostmark, taking fresh delight from her seething, spitting response.

Aidan stepped up to Zaleska, considered giving her a poke with his finger to get her attention and then thought better of it. She was a witch, after all, and last thing he wanted was to be cursed or turned into a blooming toad or something. He picked up her sickle-shaped knife off the deck and gave her a hard tap with the flat of the blade. The feel of the fancy weapon in his hand gave him a little confidence. Not much, but enough to get cocky.

"You want to live, witch, you'd better start talking."

Zaleska sneered. "What is this? The inbred Pictish boy? Come to pretend to be a man? Are you happy now that she is dead? She was so much *better* than you, wasn't she? Smarter, stronger, faster. I sensed your hatred, your petty jealousy. How do you feel now, Aidan Erskine, butcher's boy, oafish, mutton-headed—"

It wasn't Aidan who punched the witch. It was Blair, having returned to the deck in time to hear her goading, gloating words. He shook life back into his hands, nursing his knuckles, as the witch's head lolled on her shoulders.

"You insult my wee pal, you insult me," said the old man.

Aidan felt a flush of something upon hearing Blair's words. Was this kinship? Could it actually be friendship? He watched the shipwright with something approaching admiration as Blair sneered at Zaleska.

"You going to talk to us, witch? Tell us all we need to know?"

Zaleska spat in the man's face. "I would sooner die than share a word of my business with you, Uuen of Forteviot. Former King's Guard! Pah! Another oath-breaker! You keep fine company with Finn Frostmark!"

Blair looked at the draugr on the floor, who rolled his one good eye. Blair nodded in acknowledgement and set about untying Zaleska.

"The Daughters of Hecate take their secrets with them to the grave. The Age of Hastur approaches, and . . . wait, what are you doing?"

Blair dragged Zaleska to the stern of the knarr, passing Aidan, Siv and Frostmark, the witch still bound by her wrists. He tied the trailing end of the rope to one of the rowing benches and then lifted her over his shoulder.

"Well, if you're done talking, ain't got much more use for you. Let's see if there's any big fishies out there that like the taste o' witch."

Before Zaleska could protest, he tossed her over the side. They heard the splash, and then her squawking, as she bobbed along behind the boat, bound to it by the taut length of hemp. Blair turned about and saw his companions all staring at him. Again, he gave one of his resigned matter-of-fact shrugs.

"She weren't talking," said the old warrior without a trace of humour.

"I know her plans."

The group looked up, saw that Mag had scaled the mast and was busy unhitching the knarr's great square sail from where it was bundled. She moved with strange ease, all gangly, amphibious limbs, sure-footed, without slip or stumble. With the last piece of rigging untied, Mag slid down the unfurled sail onto the deck, landing with an unexpected grace. A quick yank of a few ropes and the mast went taut, catching the wind and suddenly propelling the knarr at speed around the headland.

"And what of those plans?" asked Blair as Mag lurched past the strange group towards the stern of the ship, Zaleska's squawks burbling from the ship's wake.

"Do you conspire with the witch?" asked a suspicious Siv, hopping along the knarr's rail as Mag took up the tiller in those long-fingered hands.

"She's no friend to Zaleska," said Aidan, defensive of the sea-trow, surprising himself with the veracity of his words. "The witch had Mag shackled to the prow of the ship. Ain't no way they're pals."

The raven squawked her annoyance at Aidan. "I only say what we all suspect." The beady black eye was back on Mag. "If she's no witch, what in the name of Odin's beard is she?"

Blair gave the bird a brush with the back of his hand, sent Siv momentarily flapping in an outrage across the deck.

"You must excuse the rudeness of the night bird," said the old man to Mag. "She lacks the manners of the rest of us and clearly seems happy to leap to judgements based upon appearance. Easily done. After all, if I knew no better, I'd think ravens were just loud-mouthed, carrion-feeding, winged vermin."

Aidan tried to catch Mag's eye as the sea-trow kept her pale eyes focused on the shifting, tilting horizon. He saw muscles up and down those over-long, ghoulish arms, bunching as she kept their course steady, the knarr cutting over the waves like a skimmed stone upon the water.

"Speak, Mag," said the lad. "Tell us what you know."

Mag's eyes narrowed as if she was considering what harm it might do to share her knowledge with the strangers. Aidan managed to smile, his bruised face hurting with the effort, but it made the sea-trow's own visage soften.

She smacked her lips and spoke. "Zaleska is one of many in her order. The Daughters of Hecate can be found throughout Midgard, hiding in plain sight: a wise woman in a sleepy village, an innkeeper's wife in a bustling city, the mistress of a mighty king. They can commune with one another across land and sea, using magic gifted to them by Hecate, their mother and goddess. This sisterhood of witches is everywhere, and all of Midgard should tremble, for Hecate has aligned herself with Hastur. Zaleska is my keeper. I control the waters around her ship, keeping Zaleska and her cargo safe from harm. Zaleska worked for Jarl Hydyr, as did Jarl Gudrun, all to the same purpose."

"And was that your purpose?" asked Aidan. "Delivering live meals to Jarl Gudrun?"

He shuddered at the memory of the poor Pictish girl in the jarlshof, thought dead, only to come shambling back to life. Or un-life. Or whatever the hell it was she'd become.

Mag placed a free hand upon the rail of the knarr.

"This ship is a ferry. It brings folk, and it takes folk. Zaleska would bring folk from the Hjaltlands, Orkneyar and other islands. Jarl Gudrun and her kin would feed upon them, poisoning them, corrupting them. Changing them. Then Zaleska would ferry these creatures back to their homes."

The sea-trow raised a fist then unfurled those long, spidery fingers in a wide, splayed array, wiggling them, knuckles cracking.

"And from there, they spread the disease. Transforming more innocents into monsters. It's like a web, and it grows by the night, when they rise from their nests."

"Nests?" said Blair. "Like rats?"

"*Strigoi.*"

They all turned to Frostmark, who still rested on his side on the pitching deck, rocking back and forth. Blair collected the head, placed him upright where all could see him. Mag pointed a wavering, wand-like finger at the Viking, nodding her head, her throat making a strange clucking sound.

"What the hell is a *strigoi*?" asked Blair.

"You asked the same about the draugr not so long ago, Pict," said Frostmark, though his voice was joyless. "I tried telling you, back in the jarlshof. The draugr and the horrors that haunt Scatness are not the same. It's like comparing cats with dogs. The strigoi ain't like the Harrowed Men; they're so much more dangerous. And they're utterly, irrevocably devoted to the Golden Jarl. This was always part of Hydyr the Hungry's quest, to turn Hastur's dream into a reality."

Mag nodded sagely. "Humans are the key to all of this. The draugr need the blood, flesh and bone of the living to feed upon, but the strigoi need only their blood."

"The *baoban sith*," muttered a fearful Blair, making the sign of the cross before him.

"The what now?" asked Aidan, a cold dread seeping through him.

"The very same," said Mag. "It haunts every culture, that fiend that feeds on the blood of the living, shying away from daylight."

She raised two fingers of one hand, pressing her fingernails, thick as bark, to her throat.

"A bite to the neck, and the monster drinks deep. The baoban sith you may call it in Alba – the *"fairy hag"* – but it goes by many names. Strigoi. Vourdalak. Wampiri."

Mag's lips peeled back, revealing those needle teeth.

"Vampire."

Aidan clawed at his throat, hunching his shoulders, checking over them that no monster was creeping up behind him, about to strike. But there were no horrors, and the sun was shining in the bright morning sky. The storm had passed. For now.

Blair shook his head. "So, although the Harrowed Men are draugr, cursed to never die, that don't make 'em the same as the strigoi?"

"Not presently," said Frostmark, adding further grim colour to the conversation, "but that will change right soon. Hydyr the Hungry needed the Harrowed Men to carry him over the ocean. The *Sea Wolf* is his carriage, but he cannot drive it during the day. He has magicks of his own that can help him, such as calling mists from the sea that can shroud him, keeping the sun at bay. For the most part, he sleeps until nightfall. That is the way of the strigoi. It was always in Hydyr's best interests to keep the Harrowed Men as draugr for as long as possible, he needs us to move about in daylight. So, his sword-brothers and shield-sisters protect him, safe in the knowledge that they too will ascend when the time is right."

Aidan gulped. "Ascend?"

Frostmark bared his teeth, the rotten flesh of his neck squelching as his head shuddered in anticipation. "We were all in his thrall, all under Hydyr's spell. It's been that way since the beginning. We were promised that which Hydyr could give – we were promised a taste of Hydyr's blood, for that's where the magic is, lad. The gift of the vampire. The strigoi's kiss. And then we, too, would transform, as Hydyr has before us."

He grimaced sourly. "That's rather passed Finn Frostmark by, now, eh? But if I can help you boys stop Hydyr, I'll feel I've done some good in my final days before I head to the Corpse Shore. I may be cursed, but my vengeance against my brothers will be the stuff of legend."

Siv flapped her midnight wings, catching the collective eye of her companions.

"Sounds to me that the draugr and the strigoi and the witches are all in league with one another. They know one another's movements. How can they share knowledge over such great distances? They're stealing a living from me and my kin."

Mag shrugged, but Blair was already hauling on the trailing rope, dragging a spluttering Zaleska back onto the deck of the knarr. She collapsed, blind, half-drowned, but still cackling like a maniac.

"All is lost! You are doomed!" said the witch. "The Children of Hastur and Hecate shall inherit your world!"

Blair grabbed her by the scruff of her soaking coat and shook her, ramming her against the rail which almost splintered with the impact.

"What fate awaits my grandson?" roared Blair into the witch's face. "He travels with the Harrowed Men. He might already be dead. Or... worse?"

Aidan didn't need to ask what the old man meant by that. *Worse.* Might Cormac have been bitten by Hydyr, and even now was transformed into a strigoi?

"Rest easy, Uuen of Forteviot," giggled Zaleska. "The boy is not dead. Hydyr has taken something of a shine to him. He's a clever one, Cormac the Cunning. Yes, the boy still lives. At least for now."

Blair gasped, then whispered. "For now?"

Zaleska's ruined eye sockets appeared to open wider, more hideous than ever as she smiled. "Hydyr has tasted the child's blood. He already knows that the blood of a *king* flows through his veins. What a prize. What a treasure. What a *gift*. Could there be any greater offering Hydyr could place before the throne of Hastur, the God of Vampires, when the two eventually meet?"

Blair let go of the witch, stepped back, shaking his head in disbelief. Aidan moved closer, placing a comforting hand on the old man's trembling back.

"So you, your sisters and the strigoi have a way of

communicating with one another?"

"Aye," said Zaleska. "How else would I know that very pearl of wisdom I just shared with you? We speak through dreams, thoughts and visions. We are all connected, Uuen of Forteviot."

"Good," said the old man, unsheathing his bone handled sword. "If you can send messages to your sisters, then send them this."

One clean swing of the sword sent the witch's head spinning into the briny. Her headless corpse was quick to follow, disappearing beneath the waves that chased the knarr's wake.

CHAPTER TWENTY-NINE
CORMAC

It was the impact of the *Sea Wolf* upon the gravel shore that stirred Cormac awake. He raised his crumpled face from where he lay in the bow of the drakkar, as the Harrowed Men ran about him, leaping overboard and landing with a splash in the shallows. Cormac rubbed his bleary eyes, hauled himself to his feet and held onto the dragonhead. All about him, the Vikings waded and wallowed, crawling or striding onto the beach, in fine spirits and in full voice. Sword-brothers and shieldmaidens hugged one another, backs were clapped, heads were butted, and cheers were sounded. The fog bank that had followed them across the *Nordsær,* conjured by Hydyr the Hungry, was just dissipating, breaking up against the pebble shoreline, revealing their journey's end.

"Norðvegr," said the boy beneath his breath.

The landscape was like nothing he had ever seen before. Even by the fading light of day, the enormous mountains that rose in all directions were a thing of breathtaking, wonderous beauty. Rivers carved their way between the land masses, tumbling down gigantic cliffs in waterfalls, the height and like of which made Cormac's head hurt. Although it was dusk and the sun was but a sliver on the horizon at his back, an emerald glow seemed to radiate from the land, the sweeping fields and grassy hills more magnificent and verdant than anything one might find back home. This was Unst, only on an unbelievable, unimaginably huge scale.

"Grab your gear, Cormac the Cunning," said Dagfinn Bearclaw, the big Viking almost tripping over the rail as he hurdled the side of the ship and landed in the tide with an enormous splash.

His friend and sword-brother, Lief the Laggard, stood by his side in the shallows, beckoning Cormac like a gormless big brother. The boy had grown familiar with this pair, a ghoulish double-act, each of whom had spent the journey recovering from wounds dealt to them by Jarl Frida back in Unst. They'd livened up, if that was the correct turn of phrase for a pair of undead warriors, as they drew closer to home. Now, one would never have known they'd been skewered and near-decapitated by Jarl Frida a few days back. Time had been no healer; they had their diet to thank for their recovery, specifically the poor unfortunate souls of Unst that the pair had devoured.

"We are done with the *Sea Wolf* for now, lad," called Lief, his cheery face belying the demon within. "Come see the jarlshof of Hydyr the Hungry."

Cormac followed the draugr battle-crew as they made their way on foot towards the cliffs, where one of the waterfalls pounded the beach and made the ground rumble and quake. Just about all the Harrowed Men were present, in addition to the handful of prisoners who had survived the passage from the Hjaltlands to Norðvegr. Three. That's all that remained of the people of Unst. Two, in truth, for one of their number was the bedraggled Brother Benedict. Bound together, the trio drew all their strength from the monk, who continued to loudly pray, his words of Latin a sing-song accompaniment on their march of misery.

Whilst Lief the Laggard walked beside Cormac, his ever-present companion, Dagfinn Bearclaw, followed behind. The big brute carried Jarl Frida's body roughly over his broad shoulder, his thick left arm holding her in place behind the knees. To Cormac's eyes, he was looking at a corpse, her beautiful blonde hair as drained of colour as the pale skin of her body. Of Hydyr the Hungry, there was no sign. Cormac had to assume the leader of the Harrowed Men was still aboard the *Sea Wolf*, preparing himself for his grand return.

The procession made its way behind the curtain of the waterfall, the sound of the tumbling and crashing torrent deafening. Cormac was amazed to find the way ahead was lit by torches, and the further they moved through the cavernous cave network, the more he realised that this was no natural series of tunnels, forged by the pounding of the sea. He spied elaborate carvings, great runic symbols and characters that decorated the curved walls. Many of these were defaced and vandalized no doubt by the hands of the Harrowed Men, the art replaced by crude and indecent graffiti, their once-glorious splendour a thing of the past. Cormac had to wonder who was responsible for the carvings.

"The dwarves, lad," said Lief the Laggard, correctly

guessing Cormac's unspoken question. "You have entered Dvergatt, once-fabled city of the *duergar*."

Cormac gasped, unable to hide his amazement.

"The dwarves built all this?"

There was laughter from Bearclaw behind them. "Carved it out of the mountains, delving deep into the dark rock until they could call this place home. And now it's our home. And most of the dwarves are long gone or dead."

He spat at one of the carvings as they passed them by, a further insult to injury carried out by the draugr.

"Why do you hate the dwarves so?"

Lief sniffed. "Ain't just the duergar, the huldufólk too."

"The hidden people?" said Cormac. "What have the elves ever done to you? Do you hate *all* the vættir?"

"Oh aye. And the giants and trolls," added Bearclaw, suddenly animated as he shifted Jarl Frida's limp body on his shoulder. "Every one of them rotten vættir, from the smallest gnome to the tallest jötnar."

"See, all them faerie folk are of no use to Hastur," said Lief. "Their blood is corrupted, Cormac. It doesn't nourish. It *poisons*. It may taste bad to the draugr – and it surely does – but to the strigoi that can prove fatal. The only good vættir are dead vættir!"

Lief and Bearclaw brayed like the pair of idiots they were.

Cormac's question brought them back. "Strigoi?"

Bearclaw's chuckles died a death. "You'll find out soon enough, Cormac the Cunning."

The road (for that is what it appeared to be, so flat had the rocky passage been mined and fashioned) opened out into a huge cavern that seemed to disappear into the pitch black in all directions. Rooms and walkways, windows and doors had been hewn from the walls all around, connected to one another by bridges that spanned implausibly wide distances. Torches and lanterns cast their warm orange light around the vast space, twinkling in Dvergatt's gloomiest recesses and penetrating the total and utter darkness.

Up ahead, Cormac noticed that Brother Benedict had stopped walking, and ceased his prayers, his companions from Unst flanking him, the three bound in ropes. He craned his neck reverentially, looking up at the distant ceiling. He turned and looked at Cormac, a feverish light sparkling in his troubled, teary eyes.

"Tis a temple, Cormac," he said, joy as clear as crystal in his voice.

As he was pushed on his way by the Harrowed Men, Cormac couldn't help but grumble a reply.

"It's no temple, least not to any god you or I would worship."

The huge space in the centre of the cavern felt like a courtyard or market square, a strange sensation for Cormac considering this was effectively inside. At its centre, a long stone table, big enough to seat a hundred people, ran from the entrance to Dvergatt back towards a huge granite dais. At the head of this great, grey platform, sat high on a towering dais, was a throne of marble, all the colours of the night sky swirling through its white core. And the steps that led up to the chieftain's chair, the stone staircase that surrounded it, was littered with skulls and bones.

The dais wasn't the only place thus decorated. All around the monumental hall, Cormac spied clusters and collections of bone artefacts. Some were scattered, others were arranged decoratively, fixed to the stone walls and peppered with brightly burning candles. They put Cormac in mind of the gothi's hut, back on Unst, only infinitely more gruesome. These were human skulls and bones, or rather, humanoid. Judging by the size and shape of some, Cormac had to believe these had come from those very people that the Harrowed Men so despised: the faerie races, known collectively as vættir. And the larger ones – were they giant remains of the jötnar? Could they be trolls?

Whilst many took their seats along either side of the enormous granite slab, Cormac remained beside Lief the Laggard, who continued up to the head of the table. Dagfinn Bearclaw laid out Jarl Frida at this spot, her body draped in shadows at the base of the jarl's dais. Cormac watched her eyes fluttering, barely aware or conscious, but for a fleeting moment they locked with his. A look passed between them, and the blacksmith's boy didn't miss it.

Run.

But Cormac was no fool. This wasn't the time or the place to hare off away from the Harrowed Men. He had to pick his moment and do so carefully. If that meant keeping fools like Lief and Bearclaw onside, then so be it.

"Brothers and sisters!"

Einar the Small's voice boomed out from where he stood at the foot of the dais, looking every inch his nickname beside the monumental platform. He raised his one remaining hand and with a flourish gestured to the top of the structure.

"Our King, Jarl Hydyr! All hail, Herald of Hastur!"

And there he was, lounging upon his marble throne like he'd been there all along. Only he hadn't. Cormac looked around. How the hell had Hydyr got into Dvergatt, and reached the top of the dais, with nobody noticing?

As one, the draugr all struck their chests with their fists, or hammered their swords, axes and spears against their shields. This was adulation, and Hydyr was mopping it up, smiling that wolfish grin whilst he twirled his black beard, fiddling with his golden ring. He raised a hand high, and his sword-brothers and shield-sisters all took to seats at the table. Cormac took this opportunity to dash over to Jarl Frida and check in on his chieftain.

"Can you hear me, Jarl Frida?" he whispered as the Harrowed Men laughed and cheered around them. "I swear, when the chance comes, I'm going to end Hydyr for what he did to my pa and our friends on Unst."

Jarl Frida shook her head, feeble, every movement a pained struggle. Again, she simply mouthed the word: *run*. Then she raised a hand, tried to push him away, but there was no strength there. She may as well have been an infant, so weak had she become.

Hydyr clapped his hands, bringing the noise along the table down a notch until he had the attention of the Harrowed Men. All eyes remained on the jarl above, atop his throne.

"I promised you that once I found Frida Blackheart

and we returned to Norðvegr, I would share my gift with you. Never let it be said that Hydyr the Hungry is not a man of his word!"

A cheer went up. Cormac saw the eyes of the draugr, saw the hunger in them, feared what was to come. He looked down at the barely conscious Jarl Frida and made a snap decision. He bit his left palm, so hard, harder than he'd ever bitten down in his life. Hard enough to draw blood. Stifling a grunt of pain he pulled his teeth away, saw the teeth marks bloom red and wasted no time. He crawled over Jarl Frida's body and clamped his hand over her mouth.

Jarl Frida's eyes went wide, in reaction to the blood's warmth. Its smell. Its taste. She drank.

All the while, Hydyr continued his speech.

"My sword-brothers and sisters, you have served me well these fifteen winters since the fall of Uppsala. You have had my back, protected me, as formidable as any shield-wall this or any of the Nine Worlds have ever seen. When I have been weak, you have kept me safe. When I have been strong, you have fought beside me. When I have hungered, you have fed me. And when I searched for the answer, the cure for our curse, you were patient. You have watched on as I have enjoyed the blessing of Hastur for the last three winters, observed me bestow this gift upon our closest allies such as Jarl Gudrun, and other apostles who would spread His word and His seed. You have witnessed my change. My metamorphosis. My becoming."

More cheers from the Harrowed Men, reaching a point of delirium in the cavernous chamber, their hollering bouncing off the distant vaulted ceiling and sending waves of terror running through Cormac.

He felt dizzy. Nauseous. Saw silver lights shining in Frida's eyes. He tried to pull his hand away but one of hers flew up and seized his wrist, holding him in an iron grip.

Hydyr spoke on. "You have been patient, trusting me, awaiting your blessing. That time is now. I said you shall receive the strigoi's kiss, and that you shall. But first, I too need sustenance, if I am to share this gift with you."

His eyes searched the chamber, seeking out his prize. Then he grinned with delight and sprang from his throne.

Cormac heard him land a distance away, followed by a commotion and then a scream – one of the last survivors of Unst, accompanied by the other, no doubt witnessing the demise of their loved one. The boy tried to push the death cries from his thoughts, his own concerns fixed upon wrestling Jarl Frida free. With no other option left, he brought his hand back and struck her across the face.

She let go instantly, her head snapping back, feral and vicious as a wildcat. But as Cormac recoiled, retreating under the stone table, she relented. Jarl Frida shook her head, willing her old self back, struggling for dominion over the monster within.

Another scream, another cheer, the last survivor of Unst now taken by Hydyr the Hungry.

Jarl Frida wiped the blood from her lips, looking at the red stain upon her forearm. She looked back at the boy, the lad who was her daughter's best and dearest friend.

"Oh, Cormac," she whispered. "What have you done?"

"I've saved you."

She looked like she was going to say something, to argue the point, but thought better of it. Jarl Frida pulled back, crawling a way up the steps, to witness what played out amongst the Harrowed Men. Cormac did the same, then instantly wished he hadn't.

He had once visited a farm on Yell where they bred hunting dogs. Cormac had watched on in ghoulish wonder as the farmer fed a couple of live hens to his hounds, and they were torn to shreds in a fevered, bloody frenzy. This was similar.

The two villagers were dead and gone, what was left of them currently being thrown around the table as the Harrowed Men fought over their scraps. That was the flesh and bone, though Hydyr had already gorged on their blood. The jarl stood atop the table, Brother Benedict in his arms, the monk's hands reaching up, clawing feebly at Hydyr's face like a helpless infant. The lord of the draugr's mouth was clamped about Brother Benedict's neck, lips closed around the monk's pink skin. Cormac watched on in horror, Hydyr's throat blooming large as he took a few great and greedy gulps of blood out of the holy man in rapid time.

Then he pulled himself away, turning his face from the monk, blinking the madness from his dead, black, demon eyes. The Harrowed Men clamoured for the cleric, screamed for Hydyr to toss the man to them, but Hydyr was having none of it. He raised a hand to silence them, and when that wasn't enough he let loose a monstrous roar that quelled their agitation instantly, all the draugr scurrying clear.

"The priest will live!" shouted Hydyr the Hungry. "His Christ-god is dead. The Golden Jarl is Brother Benedict's new deity. He will be the first of his kind, a Head Priest in the Church of Hastur, a witness to our glory, promoting this new religion throughout Midgard."

Brother Benedict dropped to his knees at the feet of Hydyr, clinging to the jarl's boots, his throat ragged, the poor cleric driven beyond the point of human endurance. Cormac wanted to shout something, say anything, but knew the young monk was now lost.

Hydyr raised the forefinger of his right hand, let that sharp, dagger of a nail slice open the wrist of his left arm. Then he did the same to the other limb, as the Harrowed Men released a collective sigh of elation and electric expectation.

Cormac appeared all but forgot in the drama of the moment, as the draugr rushed past him, clamouring around the table where their lord and master stood. They climbed the stone table, clambered over one another, coiling and writhing around Hydyr's legs and torso, desperate to taste a few drops of that precious, magical blood.

Cormac couldn't watch. He turned away towards where Jarl Frida lay on the dais, surrounded by the bones of the dead, her own gaze fixed upon the boy from Unst. As a wolf may look upon a sheep.

Then Cormac heard the voice of Hydyr the Hungry echoing throughout the ancient, vaulted halls of Dvergatt.

"Come, Children of Hastur. Drink deep. Join me, my strigoi brothers and sisters."

And the Harrowed Men drank.

CHAPTER THIRTY
AIDAN

Kneeling beside Hilde's body, in the belly of the knarr, it felt like the perfect time to admit to one's sins. Aidan Erskine had been aware of Brother Benedict's ceremony back on Unst, performing his baptisms, knew there was a knack to washing away sins, but in all honesty the lad hadn't been paying too much attention. Aidan had been preoccupied flirting with Eithne and Erin, more intent on flexing his muscles than expanding his spirituality. He wondered what had become of the twins, but didn't dwell on it for long. The screams of the butchering still rang in his ears, kept him awake at night. He wondered if he would ever sleep again.

"I'm sorry, Hilde," he said quietly. "Sorry for being such an arseling. Sorry for being so insecure. Sorry for being an enemy when it would've been easier to be your friend."

Aidan patted the silver seax that was laid out on top of the wolfskin, the girl's body, hidden by the thick, grey pelt. He could discern the shape of her, Hilde's head and shoulders, chest and hips, legs and feet. Her right hand was the only part of her visible, poking out from under the fur, her pale fingers at rest upon the floor of the knarr's hold.

Steeling himself, he reached out and placed his hand over hers, the skin cold to the touch.

"I'm gonna find Cormac, Hilde. I swear, on my life, for

what it's worth. And if there's anyone left of our families, be it my pa or your ma, I'll find them too. I give you my word."

He gave the fingers a squeeze and shuffled away, back towards the door. Of course, he wasn't entirely sure what he'd do if he *did* find his father or Hilde's mother. Rab Erskine was the meanest man Aidan had ever known, and the lad doubted if Jarl Frida even knew who Aidan was. But still, hope remained, no matter how fragile, that he might do some good with what was left of his all-too-brief time on Earth.

Stepping out onto the deck, he saw that the sun was now down. He must have been in the hold for a good while, lost in his own thoughts with only Hilde's body for company. Aidan had had a lot of thinking to do, a lot of reevaluating about where he was headed in this world. If the strigoi *were* on their way, then the draugr were the least of his or mankind's worries.

"Will you teach me?"

From where he stood at the ship's prow, Blair turned to the voice, looked Aidan up and down.

"Teach you?"

"The sword," said the boy. "And the shield. I'm done being scared."

Blair gave Aidan a sad shake of the head. "You never quit being scared, laddie. The day you do, you get reckless. And that day is your last. I can teach you how to swing a sword and raise a shield, for sure. But I'll be damned if I teach you how to be fearless."

Aidan looked up and down the ship, taking in their strange company. Mag remained in the stern, one arm draped over the long wooden tiller, fingertips trailing in the water. The boat was travelling over the *Nordsær* at a rate Aidan had never before seen, racing fast as an arrow in flight. All the while, the sea-trow sang her eerie melody, communing with the ocean, calming the way ahead. It was a magical thing to watch and hear, and only confirmed to Aidan that he didn't have a clue about the world beyond the rock that was Unst. Mag had promised them she would get them to Norðvegr as fast as was humanly, or *inhumanly*, possible. And she was true to her word.

On the roof of the hold cabin, Finn Frostmark was wedged securely in place by a couple of wooden staves. The change in the draugr had been remarkable. It seemed that the longer, and further, he'd been away from Hydyr the Hungry, the less of a monster he had become. The cruel Viking who had caused such unrest and upset appeared to be a thing of the past, and Aidan was seeing another side to Frostmark. Softer side would be a bit of a reach, as presently Siv was busy feeding him morsels of dead bodyguard that she'd recovered from the deck. It was doing the trick, satisfying the undead warrior's appetite, though God only knew where the meat was going, considering Frostmark's entire being stopped just below his jawline.

"What's the matter, laddie?" asked Blair, noticing Aidan was frowning. "You look like you're trying to pass a pinecone."

"Just looking at our motley crew is all. Wondering how our rabble is supposed to take on Hydyr and his vampire god. We don't exactly strike fear into an enemy's heart, do we?"

Blair's grin was something to behold. "It's all about finding the weak spot. Every armour has a crack in it, a point that can be exploited, where the chain links don't meet or leather greaves don't match. That's where we strike. We just need to find the weakness in Hydyr's armour is all."

Frostmark piped up from the cabin roof. "His arrogance will be his downfall. Hydyr believes he's unstoppable, and that will come back and bite him on his arse. He's vainglorious, overconfident."

Siv tossed another spigot of flesh into the draugr's mouth. "He's every right to be confident. He's a strigoi. A vampire. That makes him more powerful than any and all of us thrown together."

Mag ceased her singing momentarily, which had an instant effect upon the vessel, the knarr's speed reducing but still going at a lick.

"Our numbers can yet grow," said the sea-trow. "There are others who we can beseech to join us, though they may prove difficult to find. The vættir."

Aidan's eyes lit up. "The elves, and the dwarves? The gnomes and the giants?"

Mag's voice was low and unmistakably sad.

"All kinfolk of mine, yet in hiding, and who can blame them? Their time in this world draws to a close. They are no longer welcomed by mankind, having faced persecution, their number dwindling. And now, with the coming of Hastur, they are actively hunted by the strigoi and the draugr. The vættir face genocide on an unimaginable scale."

Siv rapped her black beak on the cabin roof. "All the more reason they should join us now. This is everybody's fight."

Mag's laughter was a throaty burble. "When the time comes to speak with my cousins, you're going to have to be more persuasive than that, nightbird."

Aidan noticed that the injuries the sea-trow had suffered at Zaleska's hand were now all gone. Mag hadn't lied. Seemed her connection with the sea worked on many levels. Not only could she communicate with the water, but in return the *Nordsær* had healed her. A handy trick, and another example of the magic that was all around the naïve young butcher's boy.

"We start now," said Blair, clapping the boy on his shoulder and giving him a friendly squeeze.

"Huh?"

The old warrior unsheathed his bone-handled blade, which shone by the light of the moon and stars. He'd spent the best part of the day cleaning and polishing the weapon, having recovered it from the witch's bodyguards and killed them both in the process.

"Your training, lad. I'd start you with a wooden sword ordinarily, walk you through a fight nice and easy; footwork, cuts, thrusts and parries, all the usual stuff. Introduce you to it over time. Little late in the day for us to do that dance though, considering what awaits us. So, with that in mind, grab yerself a length of steel and we'll head straight into the screaming, the begging, the blood-letting, and the soiling your britches."

Aidan couldn't hide his smile from Blair. It was born out of admiration. Here was a man, an old one at that, whom he had only known for a couple of days, and already he was more of a father to him than his own flesh and blood.

Blair returned the smile.

Then he was suddenly launched forwards, knocking Aidan onto his rump, as something swooped across the deck, striking the bearded veteran hard in the back. Blair hit the knarr's boards, rolling like a rag doll. As he turned, Aidan glimpsed tears in his armour, great slashes that had been dealt him by whatever had attacked.

A shadowy figure with great bat-like wings flew back over the boat, briefly passing through the moonlight, before alighting upon the mast's long yard-arm. Aidan looked up from where he sat sprawled, his mouth hanging open, words failing him. He heard Frostmark's shouts, saw Siv take flight, watched as Mag lurched over the knarr to the aid of Blair. But the boy couldn't take his eyes off the creature.

She was a thing to behold, and utterly horrific. Born from shadows and cast in silhouette by the moon on high, leathery wings extended and fanned out from her back. Aidan recognised the demon right enough: Jarl Gudrun. The chieftain of Scatness was utterly transformed. Her monstrous, taloned feet clutched the yardarm, whilst her face was lost in darkness, but for that maw of awful, serrated, shining teeth, and her pale-grey eyes were now pools of black oil, darker than the space between the stars and utterly hypnotic.

That was the first time Aidan screamed this night.

Then he was running. The butcher's boy scrambled across the deck, felt his pants go warm with that familiar flush of fear. Terrified or not, he had to make a stand. Had to face the strigoi the only way he knew how. With a blade in hand.

He grabbed the door to the cabin, stumbled down into the hold. More cries went up on the deck. It was impossible to tell if they had come from old man, draugr, sea-trow or raven, but one thing Aidan was sure of: they were cries of terror. Hilde had said that the creatures had hissed and wailed at the touch of her silver seax. So be it, thought Aidan. He would use Jarl Frida's famous blade against their enemy. If he died trying, so be it. He would die like a warrior.

When he reached the corner of the hold where Hilde had been laid out, he found a discarded wolfskin cloak on the floor. His moment of confusion ratcheted up a notch when Hilde Blackheart stepped out of the darkness. The faint traces of moonbeams that found their way between the boards above their heads provided scant illumination, but it was enough. The hole was still there in the girl's breast, just as the bodyguard had left it, and her eyes shone with a pale, otherworldly light. In her hand she held her bright silver seax, and when she spoke it emerged as a growl.

"What's going on?"

That was the second time Aidan screamed this night. It wasn't to be the last.

CHAPTER THIRTY-ONE
CORMAC

He thought they would be distracted. He thought that the commotion around the table would hold their attention. He thought the darkness behind the dais was the perfect place to hide. He thought the favour of Hydyr the Hungry might afford him some protection. He thought if he stayed quiet, they would not know he was there. He thought if they had fed, they would not be interested in him.

He thought wrong.

Cormac was running. Not towards the great road that led into the dwarven city of Dvergatt, and out of it for that matter. That way was blocked by the Harrowed Men, the majority of whom remained gathered around the long table. Any semblance of decorum was now lost to the draugr, as they fell upon the enormous stone counter or writhed about upon the floor in a twitching, shuddering, orgiastic mass. They had all fed now, all tasted the blood of Hydyr the Hungry, and a seismic shift was taking place. The intermittent screams of the Vikings rose sharp and high from the moans and murmurs of their brethren, as their physiology went through a spectacular change.

The blacksmith's boy didn't look back over his shoulder as he ran into the depths of the city, but he heard them well enough, following him, hunting him. In one hand he held a torch, seized from a sconce beside the throne. In the other he carried a long, bleached white bone, one end of which was splintered to a jagged point. The femur of some poor unfortunate soul, be they man or vættir, who had run afoul of the Harrowed Men. It was the closest thing Cormac had to a weapon now, and he gripped it for dear life.

More screams echoed after him as he plunged onwards, signalling more of those final metamorphoses that the draugr were undergoing. Cormac had witnessed the wonders of nature back on Unst, in particular the life cycle of the butterfly. There was a magic to it, as the caterpillar fed to bloating and then transformed into a cocoon, reemerging as a thing of beauty and splendour. Only there was no beauty or splendour to be seen in the great hall of Dvergatt. It was a carnival of carnal, mind-bending horror.

The strigoi were born.

As Cormac ran blindly through the streets of the dwarven city, he was painfully aware of all the sounds around him. His feet hitting the ground, his panicked breathing, blood pounding through his ears, deafening and confusing him. The flames of the torch as it guttered and spluttered. The hungry growls of whatever was at his back.

A movement to his left. Cormac swung his torch, caught sight of a figure keeping pace; Lief the Laggard, a changed man. In that fleeting moment the firelight illuminated Lief's face; white as snow, throat dark with spewed blood, eyes black as night. The boy made to angle his run, peeling away from the monster and bearing right, only to see a larger shape bounding along that side of the street, running on all fours like a great hound. Dagfinn Bearclaw snapped his jaws as the torch swept his way, his serrated teeth catching flames as his slab of a head was showered in sparks.

The road was narrowing, the buildings here smaller. The edge of the dwarven city. No more turns. A dead end lay directly ahead, where the cavern wall remained simply that – a rock face, partially mined, sadly unfinished and apparently impassable. The granite cliff face, all boulder and fissure, loomed large before him. Cormac skidded to a stumbling and exhausted halt.

"You done running, lad?" said Lief the Laggard, his voice a rasp in the darkness.

Cormac swung his torch out behind him in a wild arc, trying to find the strigoi, but he was greeted by shadows.

"What does he taste like?" said Dagfinn Bearclaw, his growl a deep, hungry rumble.

Then the pair of them materialised, side by side, prowling towards the crackling firebrand.

"It's me, Cormac!" said the boy. "I'm no meal. I'm one of the Harrowed Men. I work for Hydyr the Hungry, remember?"

The strigoi paused their approach. It was a desperate ploy from Cormac, for he absolutely was not *one of them*. He may have enjoyed Hydyr's favour, but that appeared to count for nought now, in this dark and remote corner of Dvergatt, where he had been chased. Hunted. Cornered.

"Cormac . . . the Cunning," said Lief the Laggard, as if slowly remembering who the boy was, and his importance to Hydyr.

"That's right," said Cormac, nodding enthusiastically and

forcing a smile onto his terrified face. "Y'know, the kid who knew things. Languages and all that, yeah?"

He was backing up, felt the cliff face scrape his spine. He glanced left and right, just saw more rough rock wall in both directions. Cormac shivered as he felt a cool breeze brush the nape of his neck, having reached him from God only knew where.

"Cormac," agreed Dagfinn Bearclaw, struggling to say the name around his oversized, awful teeth. "Cormac... the Tasty!"

He ran a dark tongue over them, his cruel laughter joined by that of Lief. They prowled forwards once more. Cormac thrust his torch towards them, saw the strigoi briefly recoil, but they continued their advance. The boy shivered, his skin soaked in fresh and steaming sweat, the dread realisation that his race was run.

A figure suddenly barged between the two monsters, flinging them apart, before coming to stand protectively before Cormac.

"You leave the boy alone," said Jarl Frida, her strength clearly returned now, thanks to Cormac's earlier sacrifice. "He's mine."

The two strigoi leapt to their feet, hunkering low, swaying as they approached the jarl and the boy.

"Out of the way, draugr," spat Bearclaw. "This won't be as easy as the last time we danced, back on Unst."

"We are strigoi now," said Lief triumphantly. "You cannot—"

The length of bone was whipped from Cormac's hand

and launched by Jarl Frida with lightning speed. It struck the Laggard in his mouth, spearing him and sending him spluttering and choking to the ground. The torch was gone from Cormac's other hand too, and had landed with a mighty *whoomph* on Bearclaw, igniting his filthy animal pelt cloak. The strigoi stumbled clear, wailing, as the flames engulfed him.

"Thank you," the boy whispered to his jarl.

Frida's head spun about, as if noticing Cormac for the first time. Her face was both beautiful yet terrifying, her eyes flecked with that strange silver fire he had often seen in the gaze of the draugr. Only it burnt fierce now. Bright. As if fuelled by something remarkable, and Cormac instantly feared what that was: *his blood*.

She knelt on one knee before him, taking his warm hands in her own, which were corpse cold.

"When you fed me," she managed to say, struggling to get the words out, "you unlocked something. Uncaged something. And I fear... I fear I won't be able to control it."

She looked back along the road, as did Cormac. They saw shapes coming forwards, running towards the commotion. Many followed the path they had taken, while others leapt from roof to roof of the surrounding stone buildings, or bounded from wall to wall. And above them all, Cormac saw a winged thing, barely visible in the endless darkness of Dvergatt, but capturing the faint and distant fires from the great open hall.

Directly before them, Lief and Bearclaw burbled and burnt respectively, struggling with their hideous injuries.

Neither was dead – one choking on a spear of bone, the other batting at his cloak of fire – but they were incapacitated, at least for now. The question bloomed in Cormac's mind: *how do you kill a strigoi?*

Jarl Frida gave Cormac a shake, snapping his attention back to her.

"Let me be clear, Cormac; you are not safe. So long as you remain in the company of the Harrowed Men, your life is in danger. That's why you must leave. I shall distract them as best I can, bargain with them if I must, but you must be gone from this place, you hear me? Warn the world of what is coming. Somebody has to, and that somebody is you, Cormac Tulloch.'

He shook his head. "Hilde was my best friend. I won't leave you. I won't—"

Another shake from Jarl Frida. "You *will*. You're not safe with the strigoi. You're not safe with Hydyr the Hungry. And . . . you're not safe with me."

Cormac was confused. "You're my jarl, my chieftain. How can I not be safe with you?"

Jarl Frida let the tears roll free. "I have abstained from the draugr's diet of human and bone for fifteen years. I vowed I would never partake in such a foul and depraved act. But that vow is broken now, literally by your hand."

He glanced at the bitemarks in the palm of his hand, recalled the sensation of Jarl Frida gorging on the blood, siphoning it through his arm and into her hungry throat.

"I fear there is no escape for me, lad. I have a *taste* for it. I am set on a path from which there is no return. And if you remain close by ... it may happen again, only next time you won't be willing. And next time it will not end well for you."

Cormac's words came out accompanied by sobs. "Where will I go?"

"As far away from the Harrowed Men as you can go. And when you get there, go that bit further, you hear? Your blood is special to Hydyr, you're a prize worthy of gifting to the Golden Jarl. You must warn the world that the strigoi are on their way, prepare them for the Age of Hastur. The only way the dead are defeated is if the living are united. Let us both swear in the name of my beloved Hilde we won't let them win."

She held her hand out, and Cormac grabbed her forearm, the Viking way, and shook.

"I swear it."

They both turned back to the mob of strigoi who were now gathered before them, drawing ever closer. In their midst, he spied Rab Erskine and Brother Benedict, each of them shambling shadows of who they once were, broken by all they had witnessed and all that had been done to them. The monk's throat remained torn, his habit glistening, wet with his own blood. Einar the Small stood at the crowd's centre, hulking large over his sword-brothers and shieldmaiden sisters.

"You can't have him!" shouted Frida Blackheart, shepherding Cormac behind her back. "You hear me, Hydyr the Hungry? You shall not have the boy!"

With this fragile shield between Cormac and the strigoi, the boy could have been forgiven for holding on to a shred of hope, but that was ripped away as something seized him from above. The ground was left behind as he was dragged kicking and screaming up the cavern's cliff wall, leaving Jarl Frida below. She looked up to see who, or what, had seized him, as did Cormac.

Hydyr the Hungry clung to the jagged rocks like some monstrous winged lizard, his legs and one of his arms extended to the limit of their reach all around. His bare feet no longer resembled those of a human, ugly black talons on the end of long, reptilian toes that gripped the craggy granite like hooks of steel. With one hand adding extra purchase to the cliff, the other held Cormac in a rough scrag by the shoulder.

The boy felt Hydyr's dirty claws digging in, puncturing leather and flesh until they had grabbed hold of bone.

Two shiny black wings flexed behind Hydyr, where they arched out from his back, sending drafts of pungent, rotten air over Cormac, and the jarl's face – oh, but the jarl's face. It was so very changed.

The skin was drawn tight to his head, his flesh sunken, disappearing into the hollows of his cheekbones and the sockets of his eyes. His ears were elongated, their tips sharper, rising high and flush to the sides of his skull, while the black hair that covered the top of his head and that handsome jaw was all but withered away, only the golden ring remaining, hanging from a rat's tail of a beard. Hydyr's nose was no more, least to speak of, two narrow, cadaverous slits all that remained. And his thin lips were peeled back like the split rind of an over-ripe, desiccated fruit, revealing a portcullis of shining, jagged teeth that met in a grating, gnashing smile.

His eyes – those charming, mischievous eyes – were now otherworldly obsidian orbs that evoked utter, unspeakable dread in Cormac.

"I shall not have the boy, my love?" said Hydyr, jangling the lad like a plaything for effect. "I don't believe you're in any place to barter."

"Put him *down*, Hydyr," demanded Jarl Frida. "You want my cooperation, that comes at a price."

The lord of the strigoi hissed, his sinuous black tongue flickering like that of a snake. "You? Cooperate? Don't make me laugh! I have given you every opportunity to cooperate since I plucked you off that rock, and you have spurned me at every turn. You prevaricate and dodge my demands. You deny me the truth of my own daughter!"

He gave Cormac another rag, leaving the boy crying out in pain.

"You drink from this vessel? My precious gift to the Golden Jarl? I was protecting him, keeping him clean, untouched, unviolated. This child was a virgin offering to Hastur, the blood of kings rich in his veins, his skin untouched by the teeth and lips of draugr or strigoi, and now you have *fed* from him. He is soiled. He is nothing to me now, just regular blood, flesh and bone to feed my children."

The strigoi bayed with anticipation where they were gathered in the road.

"The boy is worthless," added Hydyr with a sneer of contempt.

Jarl Frida held her ground, overwhelmed but defiant. Cormac stared at her through pleading, teary eyes.

"Not to me, he isn't."

Hydyr's inhuman eyes narrowed, his thin nostrils flaring. "You are ready to make a deal?"

Jarl Frida shuddered as the shadowy throng of strigoi began to crawl closer. "Aye, I am. I shall tell you the whereabouts of that thing you seek, in return for the boy's life."

The Harrowed Men clucked and clicked, snickered and slathered. Cormac sensed their bellies growling at the prospect of devouring him. Hydyr held him out to his battle-crew once more, gave him a shake, ratcheting up the tension and expectation of the mob.

"You throw him to them, and you get nothing from me!" warned Jarl Frida.

Hydyr paused, considering the bargain.

The woman fixed her bright silver gaze upon the strigoi's oily black eyes. "We were lovers, once, you and I."

"We shall be again," replied the vampire, his tongue flickering once more between his terrible teeth. "I need you by my side, Frida Blackheart."

"And I need your word. You release Cormac, and the Harrowed Men leave him be."

"If he can find his way out of Dvergatt, the boy will have earnt his freedom."

"That's not enough. Your strigoi will drink him dry."

"Then I have one additional request, my love," said Hydyr, his voice a low, seductive purr at odds with his hideous visage. "Join me, drink my blood, and *you have my word* that my strigoi will leave the boy alone. My battle-crew will not attack Cormac the Cunning. I swear this to Hastur."

There were cries of dismay from the vampires, but a roar from Hydyr silenced them sharpish. Jarl Frida looked about, all too aware this was a dead end. Cormac saw how panicked she was, how tortuous she found Hydyr's proposal. He also noticed her hair flutter where, once more, a breeze came out of nowhere.

"Very well," said Jarl Frida.

"No!" shouted Cormac, only for Hydyr to swing him against the rock face, bashing him into submission.

"Don't hurt him!" cried Jarl Frida.

"Then tell me the whereabouts of the World Ender!"

"Ogvaldsnes," said the shieldmaiden, her shoulders sagging as she gave up her secret at last. "I delivered it to Ogvaldsnes, in return for the protection of King Harald Fairhair." She glared at Hydyr. "Protection from you."

The chief of the Harrowed Men laughed. "How did that work out for you?"

He let go of Cormac, who dropped limp, and unready, towards the rocks below. Jarl Frida caught him before he hit the ground, held him in her arms for a moment.

"Remember what I said, Cormac," she whispered hurriedly, as Hydyr leapt from the wall and landed behind her. "You run, you warn folk. The strigoi are coming. The Age of Hastur is upon us."

Then she was pulled away from the blacksmith's boy, releasing Cormac as Hydyr drew her into his embrace. The vampire chief drew a black clawed finger down his wrist, opening it up, a thick dark ichor welling from the wound.

"Open wide, darling," he said, as the strigoi massed around

Jarl Frida, seizing her and forcing her mouth open.

Cormac backed into the wall, watching on in horror as a thick blob of slimy black goo hung from Hydyr's wrist, almost gelatinous, like oily mucus, and then dropped into Jarl Frida's mouth.

"Good," crowed Hydyr the Hungry. "Good, my love. Drink it up now. Swallow it down."

The Harrowed Men released their hold on her. She dropped to the floor, landing on all fours, choking and spluttering, her back arching, body bucking and buckling as she screamed in pain. Cormac shook his head, sobbing, as Jarl Frida's feminine cries began to transform into a bestial roar. He could hear bones twisting, popping from sockets, breaking. Heard sinew stretching, tearing, reforming. Her head snapped around, her eyes no longer silver as they clapped onto Cormac.

The death-black eyes of the strigoi.

"You're still here?" said Hydyr in mock surprise as he saw the boy cowering at the base of the cliff. "You should have started running by now, Cormac the not-so-cunning. After all, I promised Frida Blackheart that you would be safe from my battle-crew, and I'm a man of my word."

His bony, clawed hand stroked Jarl Frida's hair as she continued to shudder and twitch at his feet, like a rabid dog. The shark's smile was back upon that ruined, demonic face.

"However, I made no promise that you would be safe from Frida Blackheart."

Cormac pressed even further back against the rock wall, shrinking away from the crowd of monsters. Once more the breeze was there against his neck. He reached a hand back, found a narrow crevice within the granite, a fissure that had been hidden by shadows. The boy crouched, twisted, squirmed, found a way into the recess, a space where he could retreat like a snail within its shell.

Directly ahead, Frida Blackheart began to advance, her hair having fallen in a lank curtain before her, all but obscuring her face. Cormac could hear her sniffing at the air, growling as she stalked up to the cliff. Her vampire brethren roared their approval from behind her, urging her on. Cormac couldn't help but let out a sob of horror, and the chief who he had once admired and respect lunged forwards, thrusting her head into the space where the boy hid. Strigoi jaws snapped together where Cormac had been a heartbeat earlier, as he dropped to the floor, kicked out and pushed himself further back, wedging himself into an ever-narrowing fix.

The boy from Unst felt her cold, dead hands grabbing at his ankles, claws scratching his calves. He kicked out, screamed, and before she could catch a hold of him, he felt hands seize his shoulders, drawing him away from Frida Blackheart and the Harrowed Men, dragging Cormac deeper into the darkest depths of Dvergatt.

The roars of the strigoi followed him all the way.

CHAPTER THIRTY-TWO
HILDE

Stepping over the prone figure of Aidan Erskine, Hilde stumbled through the belly of the knarr, the boat lurching and the world turning. She felt a tiredness like she'd never known, and an ache in her limbs that sent waves of pain coursing through her entire body. Furthermore, her head was in bits and pieces, her memory of recent events hazy and intangible, as if viewed through a fog. Hilde vaguely recalled their run-in with Jarl Gudrun's monsters in Scatness, the hoard of horrors that had swarmed the knarr, but after that it was all a blur. Felt like a nightmare that she'd just awoken from, and one that she was in no hurry to revisit. If she didn't know better, she imagined she might have been asleep for a week.

Hilde glanced back at Aidan where he lay collapsed in a semi-conscious heap. She wasn't entirely sure what had just happened to him, but she appeared to have given him such a surprise that he'd been damned near scared to death. His father, the miserable Rab Erskine, would often describe his son as a feartie, a timorous wee coward, but Hilde wasn't so sure any more. He was no longer that, least not in Hilde's eyes. However, the concerns for a stunned and gibbering butcher's boy would have to wait. The cries and screams above and outside were what drew her on now, as she kicked open the door to the deck.

The knarr was way out in the middle of the sea – a jarring notion to Hilde, as her last recollection was that they were still in Scatness harbour. The square sail was taut as a drum, propelling the ship over the waves at a pace, but there was nobody at the tiller, the wooden arm swinging back and forth as the vessel lurched about chaotically. The knarr crested a wave, sending Hilde staggering to her left. She grabbed a trailing mast rope as the ship dropped down to her right, striking the swell and sending a wave crashing over the girl and the deck. When the water sluiced away, she saw a shape directly ahead, slumped in the prow, unmoving.

Blair.

She was off running, skidding along the deck without caution as the knarr continued to ride the waves in a reckless fashion. Nothing about her movement was fluid or natural. Her arms and legs remained stiff and leaden, her hands numb and useless. Shooting pains continued to ricochet about her body, her nerve endings on fire, leaving her dazed, confused and deeply disoriented.

What the hell happened to me?

Hilde was perhaps halfway to reaching Blair's body when she heard a man cry out.

"Strigoi! Above!"

She recognised it as the voice of Finn Frostmark and went with his suggestion, raising her head to the star-scattered sky. A shape was descending from above, having leapt from the yardarm directly towards her. It fell with a strange grace, gliding through the night and the squall, and it was only in the last moment that she realised it was winged like a dragon.

Then the girl was flattened to the deck, the wind crushed from her chest as she was pinned to the brine-soaked boards by her wrists, her seax spinning across the floor.

"You!" screeched Jarl Gudrun, her voice caught between fury and delight. "You filthy little *hórbarn*! You ruined everything!"

The chieftain's face was transformed in hideous fashion. Whatever features Hilde had previously considered comely were now a faint echo, replaced by a monstrous mask. Gudrun's flesh remained pale and waxy, which only accentuated the cavernous darkness of her glassy black eyeballs. Her lips were peeled back in a rictus snarl, revealing an array of bright and deadly teeth, each as sharp and savage as an arrowhead and just as long. The spittle that flew from that awful mouth stank of death and decay as it spattered Hilde's face, making her gasp and gag.

The Gudrun-thing rose suddenly, like a snake about to bite, her mouth opening wide. Before she could strike, a rope noose was suddenly looped around her neck and pulled tight. Hilde watched on in shocked surprise as the monster was yanked off her, the length of rope getting hauled in by a dark figure that straddled the cabin roof. The figure was a shambling, terrible-looking wretch, its exposed flesh the colour of the ocean deep, a shawl of kelp flapping about its shoulders. There was something familiar about this creature, though Hilde couldn't place it. One thing was for sure though; this newcomer hated Gudrun just as much as Hilde, and that was no bad thing.

The girl still wasn't right, her body refusing to play

along and do what she willed of it. She rolled over, tried to drag herself towards Blair in the prow, whilst behind her the struggle continued.

Hand over hand, the sea horror winched the winged beast away from Hilde, knotted muscles bunching as their joint enemy was dragged wailing across the knarr. Then the Gudrun-thing squatted on the deck before suddenly leaping into the spray-showered sky, taking the rope and stranger with her. There was a brief skirmish above the deck of the ship, a gurgling scream, and then the rope landed on the deck in two pieces, accompanied by a shower of dark blood. Hilde heard the splash of something heavy hitting the waves nearby and looked fearfully over her shoulder. The Gudrun-thing swooped back towards her out of the night, an eagle diving in for the kill.

The monster struck the girl in her back, its taloned feet gripping her and lifting her into the air. The world turned, Hilde losing all sense of up and down, as the Gudrun-thing shrieked with wild delight. The young shieldmaiden saw the knarr flash by below her, then glanced up. The monstrous jarl was looking straight at Hilde, her face fixed in a grin of demonic glee.

But that smile was fleeting. Gudrun suddenly got a face full of ebony beak and midnight feathers as Siv chose her moment to strike. The raven raked at the monster, pecking at flesh, tearing at skin, Gudrun lashing out with claws of her own. Siv cried out, unable to match the might of the creature. The bird spiraled away, winged and wounded. Then the monster's black-eyed gaze returned to the helpless

Hilde. Her bat wings folded back, and the pair plummeted, the girl leaving her stomach behind as the knarr rushed to meet them.

The deck splintered with the impact as Hilde was driven into the timbers, boards buckling beneath the blow. Gudrun flipped her over, dropped onto her once again, snapping her jaws and belching bilious breath over her prey.

"Get off me, you filthy stinking cow!"

It was the best insult Hilde could come up with in the moment, and it was accompanied by a headbutt, straight to the bridge of Gudrun's nose. It crumpled under the impact, dark blood spraying across the monstrous jarl's face. Gudrun just grinned, a long tongue slithering out like a snake from between her saw-teeth and licking the gloop from her face. Hilde brought her knees up, but they met with stiff resistance, the hideous woman writhing atop of the girl, shifting her weight like a wrestler, keeping Hilde where she wanted her. Gudrun beat her wings with delight, providing further leverage in the fight, adding further pain.

"Struggle all you like, little bird. It will do you no good. You may have destroyed all my endeavours in Scatness, but you may yet serve a purpose. You can yet make a fine addition to the Children of Hastur. Like your mother was before you, you're strong, you have some fight, you have some fury in your beautiful blood. You are deserving of the strigoi's kiss. I am nothing if not persistent, and I serve Hydyr the Hungry and the Golden Jarl. He must not be disappointed. As they say, if at first you don't succeed..."

Gudrun gurgled, her jaws yawning open impossibly wide.

The stench of death rolled over Hilde, along with the drool and blood from the jarl's twitching lips and slathering tongue. Fast as a shark, her head came down, jaws clamping about Hilde's collarbone. Gudrun bit once, took a gulp. Hilde felt her lifeblood course from her body, rushing from her neck into the throat of the monster. She saw stars.

Then Gudrun leapt off her.

The hideous woman staggered back, clawing at her throat, her wings beating wildly as she went from one rail of the knarr to the other. As she lurched from side to side, her chest shuddered and trembled, her ribs bucking, torso shaking. Oily blood burst from her grotesque jaws, the sickly, slick projectile spraying the deck of the rudderless ship.

Hilde was scrambling across the knarr, retrieving her mother's blade and hauling herself to her feet, every sinew, muscle and tendon still aching. Something rolled past her feet, in danger of flying off the deck of the boat. She reached down, snatched it up, Frostmark's single eye staring at the girl out of his startled head.

"The strigoi!" shouted the draugr. "She fears your silver! Kill her! And be quick about it!"

Hilde still didn't know what the Viking meant by "strigoi", though she had a good idea she was now facing one. She saw Aidan emerge from the door to the hold, right beyond the shuddering, spasming Gudrun-thing.

"Stay there, Aidan!" she shouted, and though the butcher's boy screamed at the sight of the creature, he didn't need telling twice.

As Blair rolled over onto his back, struggling to come

round, Hilde threw Frostmark's head into the old man's lap. The two looked at one another in surprise as the young shieldmaiden turned to face the fiend.

Gudrun stood there, chest heaving, still retching, vomiting blood and ichor from her distended throat. Hilde got a good look at the monster now, for this was no longer a human she faced. Those shiny bat-like wings beat feebly where they emerged from her spine, whilst her legs ended in a pair of deformed, taloned feet, resembling those of a great and terrible hawk. Gudrun pointed a pale finger at the girl, bloody black tears streaming from her eyes.

"What . . . what are you?" she gasped, choking on the words, as Hilde strode up to her.

"I'm Hilde Blackheart, *strigoi*, and I am the end of you."

The silver seax barely made a sound as it took the wings from Gudrun's back. When the monster collapsed to her knees, imploring the girl for clemency, Hilde didn't hesitate. Her mother's precious blade disappeared into the creature's chest, piercing her dark and terrible heart. What happened next took all of them by surprise.

Gudrun's pale flesh blackened and blistered over every inch of her body, as if she were charred from within. The sound of her bones splintering and breaking made Hilde's skin crawl as the creature began to crumple in on itself, collapsing into a deformed heap upon the deck. The jarl's clothes fell away, as the muscle and meat of the strigoi was transformed into ash. Then only the bones remained, spread out in a splintered heap, rattling and rolling across the lurching knarr.

As Hilde stood there before the remains of Jarl Gudrun,

Aidan crept forwards coming to stand beside her. He placed a hand on her shoulder: whether to comfort Hilde or himself she couldn't know. But she accepted it, gripping it with her own free hand and squeezing tight. Blair staggered up to the young'uns, Frostmark's head tucked into the crook of his arm, whilst Siv limped out of the shadows, cawing in pain but thankfully still breathing.

Hilde suddenly snapped to attention. A shape moved in the darkness at the stern of the boat, dragging itself aboard from over the side. It was the creature that had fought with the strigoi, and seemingly lost. It looked every bit as monstrous as the strigoi Hilde had just dispatched. She shifted her grip on the silver seax and took a step in the direction of the sea-weed-covered figure, only for Aidan to grab her by her elbow, stopping her.

"She's a friend," said the butcher's boy, inexplicably.

Then they turned back to the ash-riddled, ruined remains of Jarl Gudrun, her severed wings splayed out behind her like enormous skeletal hands. Hilde's companions looked from the bones to the girl, their eyes settling on the shieldmaiden's heaving chest. Hilde looked down.

There was a neat hole through her breast, dark and deadly, leading to where her heart lived. The girl looked up at Blair, struggling to find the words, as Siv finally landed upon her shoulder.

The raven blinked at Hilde with her beady black eye.

"We need to talk, child."

ACKNOWLEDGEMENTS FROM THE AUTHOR

Huge thanks to the brilliant battle crew at Fox and Ink Books for helping summon the Vampire Empire. Hearty cheers to Jasmine Dove, Hazel Holmes, Charlotte Rothwell-Greenwood, Becky Mallett, Amy Cooper, Tilda Johnson, Antonia Wilkinson and Graeme Williams. To illustrator Gavin Reece, a clash of tankards for your stellar artwork that adorns the cover. I couldn't have asked for a better representation of Hilde, Cormac and Aidan. You've breathed life into my heroes and horror into my villains. And to my loving clan – Emma, AJ, Evie, Scarlett and Connie – thank you for always having my back. Skål!

I'll be the first to admit it (and it's probably my own fault), but this story doesn't behave itself like other stories do. It doesn't fit neatly into one specific genre. It's a fantasy, no doubt about it. But it's also a horror, with numerous horrific characters engaged in extremely horrific activities. However, it's also historical fiction (in parts), with places, people and events that I've plundered from a period of relentless research. With all of that in mind, it's only fair that I warn you, dear reader, that you're entering a world where myth and legend, fact and fiction, and history and horror all collide in a boiling, bloody soup.

The following glossary is my attempt at providing a little background to some of those words, terms, names and places that appear within this story. If you want to discover whether these have come from the history books, or from folklore, or from my own (admittedly corrupted) imagination, I strongly advise you engage in a spot of further reading. You won't be disappointed.

CJ, November 2025

GLOSSARY

baba An elderly woman or grandmother. Also, a title bestowed upon a witch.

baoban sith AKA "fairy hag", a vampiric female fairy from Scottish folklore that shares much in common with the succubus.

blót offering A Norse ritual offering involving the blood sacrifice – blót – of an animal or being in return for a blessing from the Gods. Often followed by feast and celebration.

carl A free man in Norse society.

drakkar A kind of Viking longship, characterised by its long, narrow and fast design. Its name is derived from the Old Norse word for dragon – dreki – due to the ornate dragon head and tail often featured on the bow and stern.

draugr A malevolent, reanimated corpse in Norse mythology. These revenants traditionally guard the treasure buried with them in their graves and burial mounds.

duergar The name given to the subterranean race of Dwarves in Norse mythology. Master craftsmen, they are skilled in working with metals to create magical and legendary artefacts for the gods.

gothi A Norse priest or holy man charged with carrying out religious ceremonies and rituals.

huldufólk AKA the "hidden people", a term broadly given to many of the fairy races, particularly the elves.

huscarl "Housecarl" – a soldier or bodyguard who lived in their lord's household.

jarl Old Norse word for earl. Any high ranking noble who held position just below a king.

jarlshof "Earl's mansion" – the home of a jarl. This would be a longhouse and feast hall, where the jarl could welcome his or her subjects or visitors.

knarr Norse cargo or merchant ship, crucial for trade, exploration and colonisation, and mentioned in the sagas. A more practical and utilitarian version of the Viking longship.

sea-trow   AKA "sea troll", found in the folklore of Shetland and Orkney. A mischievous, sometimes malevolent, spirit that haunts the waters surrounding the islands.

seax   A type of large knife or shortsword used by Norsemen and Germanic races.

strigoi   From Romanian folklore, another name for the vampire, a tormented spirit that rises from the grave. They are attributed with the abilities to transform into a beast, become invisible, and to gain vitality from the blood of their victims. It is related to the Romanian verb *a striga* – which means "to scream".

vættir   AKA "væsen". A term that loosely describes mythical beings and nature spirits in the Norse religion. These include the Alfar (elves), Duergar (dwarves), Jötnar (giants), and even gods, the Æsir and Vanir. Landvættir (land spirits) are guardians of specific grounds, whereas Sjövættir (sea spirits) are guardians of specific waters.

PEOPLE AND PLACES

Alba The Gaelic name for the Kingdom of Alba, founded in 843 AD and formed by the union of Scots and Picts. Their territory, ranging from modern Argyll and Bute to Caithness, across much of southern and central Scotland, was one of the few areas in the British Isles to withstand the invasions of the Vikings.

Dvergatt This ancient dwarven city was once the gateway to the underground realm of Svartalfheim. Built by the duergar, Dvergatt was left in ruins, abandoned by the builders as they removed themselves from Midgard and the world of men.

Føroyar Isles Old Norse name for the Faroe Islands.

Hastur God of Vampires, a Great Old One AKA The Unspeakable One, The Golden Jarl.

Hecate Greek goddess of magic, witchcraft, ghosts, the night, the moon, and crossroads.

Hel In Norse mythology, the Underworld.

Hjaltland Isles Old Norse name for the Shetland Isles.

Meginland	Old Norse name for Mainland, the principal island of the Hjaltlands.
Midgard	In Norse mythology, the Middle Earth, the abode of mankind, made from the body of the first created being, the giant Aurgelmir AKA Ymir.
Náströnd	AKA "corpse shore", a place in Hel where Níðhöggr dwells. It is the afterlife for those guilty of the most terrible crimes, including murder and oath-breaking.
Níðhöggr	A colossal, serpent-like dragon who resides on the corpse shore in Náströnd, endlessly devouring the souls of the dead and the dishonourable.
Nordsær	Old Norse name for the North Sea.
Norðvegr	Old Norse name for Norway.
Norsemen	The Norse were a group of people from Scandinavia who lived in modern-day Denmark, Sweden and Norway from the late 8th century to early 11th century. Only known as Vikings when they raided.
Ǫgvaldsnes	Best known as the seat of the first King of Norðvegr, Harald Fairhair.

However, kings and chieftains lived at Ǫgvaldsnes for thousands of years, all the way back to the early Bronze Age and throughout the Viking Age.

Orkneyar Isles   Old Norse name for the Orkney Isles.

Picts   Descendants of Iron Age people, the Picts lived in Scotland (300-900AD). *Picti* means "painted people", likely a Roman term.

Scatness   Old Norse capital of the Hjaltland Isles.

Unst   The northernmost island of the Hjaltlands.

Uppsala   The Temple at Uppsala was the most sacred centre of Old Norse religion, dedicated to the gods Thor, Odin and Freyr.

COMING SOON

THE VAMPIRE EMPIRE

BLACK HEART

2028

BY THE SAME AUTHOR:

WYRDWOOD

CURTIS JOBLING

Sticks and stones
will break your
bones . . .

GREENTEETH

The next instalment in the
Wrydwood series coming in 2027

HAVE YOU EVER WONDERED HOW BOOKS ARE MADE?

Fox & Ink Books is an award-winning independent publisher specialising in Children's and Young Adult books. Based at the University of Lancashire, this Preston-based publisher teaches MA Publishing students how to become industry professionals using the content and resources from its business; students are included at every stage of the publishing process and credited for the work that they contribute.

The business doesn't just help publishing students though. Fox & Ink Books has supported the employability and real-life work skills for the University's Illustration, Acting, Translation, Animation, Photography, Film & TV students and many more. This is the beauty of books and stories; they fuel many other creative industries! The MA Publishing students are able to get involved from day one with the business and they acquire a behind-the-scenes experience of what it is like to work for a such a reputable independent.

The MA course was awarded a Times Higher Award (2018) for Innovation in the Arts, and the business, Fox & Ink Books, was awarded Best Newcomer at the Independent Publishing Guild (2019) for the ethos of teaching publishing using a commercial publishing house. As the business continues to grow, so too does the student experience upon entering this dynamic master's course.

www.foxandinkbooks.com
www.foxandinkbooks.com/courses/
foxandink@lancashire.ac.uk